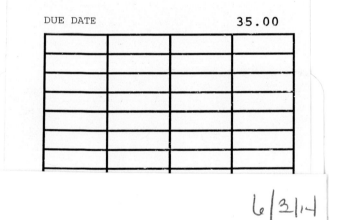

# The
# Book
# of
# Silverberg

# The
# Book
## of
# Silverberg

Stories in Honor of Robert Silverberg

Edited by
## GARDNER DOZOIS
and
## WILLIAM SCHAFER

SUBTERRANEAN PRESS 2014

This one's for Bob, of course.

# Table of Contents

# A Tribute

## by Greg Bear

---

In my distant youth—way back in the late sixties and early 70s, when Robert Silverberg appeared only slightly younger than he does now—I was tracking a number of writers whose works seemed to me to signal a new approach to storytelling and literary standards inside the science fiction community. I was looking for voices to teach me, to emulate—and Silverberg was at the top of that list. His prose was elegant, slightly cool to the reading eye. Wry and observant, Silverberg's acerbic approach to culture and science served up a refreshing sorbet between courses of my favorite hard sf authors. (Literature, like dining, is a process of moving from one fine dish to another, with palate cleansers in between. Silverberg could deliver both.) Along the way, we became acquainted through frequent convention conversations, and eventually, in 1976, Robert tapped me on the shoulder and bought a story for his *New Dimensions* anthology. I could not have been more proud.

To this day, it's always a pleasure to drop into Robert's fiction and see what new angle he's brought to the genre and to writing in general. The difference between his politics—McDuck conservative—and his writing persona could not be more profound. And sitting and listening to his stories about New York and publishing in the 1950s makes me wish I'd been born fifteen years earlier.

So much to envy! And more to come.

---

# An Appreciation

Barry Malzberg

H ere was the idea: write science fiction, yes, rigorous, well-plotted, logically extrapolated science fiction but bring to it the full range of modern literary technique. Write it as Nabokov or Phillip Roth, Malamud or Cheever would have written science fiction, as if Fred Pohl had come to them at a Milford Conference and had whispered, "I'll guarantee acceptance at our highest word rate, just do the best you can." As if Betty Ballantine or Lawrence Ashmead had sent an open appeal to the faculty at Iowa and Stanford Creative Writing Workshops. "I don't care how you write or what you write as long as I don't have to argue with the Editorial Board about it being science fiction." This was some time around 1960. "I just got bored with being a hack," Robert Silverberg told me a decade later, "I just wanted to try something different." So he tried something different. *Up The Line. Thorns.* "The Feast of St. Dionysius." "Born With The Dead." "Good News From The Vatican." Oh boy, those were different.

Well, okay. Alfred Bester, another Grand Master (1987), was trying the same thing in the 1970's. So was Theodore Sturgeon in that decade (no Grand Master for Sturgeon, he died in 1985, a few years too soon), and the Kuttners, Catherine and Henry, were lighting it up in the 1940's all the way through John Campbell's *Astounding.* (No Grand Master for the Kuttners either, Henry was dead in 1958 before the Science Fiction Writers of America were born and Catherine never published science fiction after his death.) Sturgeon, Bester, the Kuttners: fierce and in the fire long before our New Wave. But Silverberg's work in its grace, deliberativeness and great aggregation was not so much their successor as proof of a proposal. You really could do this stuff to the highest level of literary intent and it would be *better* science fiction because of that.

A revelation! Of course there were others who started at about that 1960 (whereas Silverberg had already had an sf career) who were doing this as well. Ballard, Aldiss, Gene Wolfe, Ursula K. LeGuin and maybe the merciless Raphael Aloysius Lafferty. But no one *this* prolific. The man was not only at the front of a movement, he was through fecundity virtually a movement himself.

So then and not a year too soon (a few years too late in fact), a celebration. Like Wallace Shawn's Designated Mourner I perch as Designated Celebrant. This had better cajole humility, for our newest Grand Master is indeed his own celebration. He needs no sounding brass, tinkling cymbal, not here anyway.

But let me, as Allan Tate said of Emily Dickinson's most famous poem, consider the situation.

An essay about our Grand Master, not about me, of course. But let me nonetheless note that I wrote a profile for the Special Issue (4/74) of Fantasy & Science Fiction dedicated to him and a year later the Introduction to the Pocket Books collection, *The Best Of Robert Silverberg*. Nice rounding effect, surely. In the magazine essay I proclaimed the author's height to be five feet seven inches and his condition as the best living writer in the language. Both judgments discombobulated their almost undiscombobulatable subject and so in the Introduction to the collection I had another go, estimating his height at a fraction under six feet (he has subsequently informed me that he is actually five feet ten inches tall) and adding less grandiloquently that he could be termed *one* of the ten best living writers in the language, thereby grouping him with the aforementioned Malamud, Roth, Nabokov, etc. This latter correction made him blush only a shade less brightly but I have nonetheless always regretted the correction. My first judgment would stand. Nabokov published *Transparent Things* that year and Malamud's *Dubin's Lives* lay ahead of him but neither was worth a Mass. "Born With The Dead" is worth a Mass. (Roth did become indisputably great but that took another fifteen years and *The Counterlife*.)

And another personal note: in 1984 our Grand Master introduced me in Brooklyn to his mother, Helen. She was—like my own mother, two years dead then—a retired schoolteacher who over a period of at least twenty years had lived less than a mile from my own dear Mom. I said to Helen in the most bemused fashion, "Your son has always been ahead of me. He is in fact the Stations of my Cross. I am a science fiction writer from Brooklyn, he is *the* science fiction writer from Brooklyn. (I wasn't ignoring Isaac Asimov, just striving to make a point in the broadest terms.) My first science fiction story was a 1200 word squib in the 8/67 *Galaxy*, your son had the lead novella ("Hawksbill Station") in that issue. I through luck and circumstance sell a couple of novels to Random House, he sells Random House *Born With The Dead And Other Stories*. I sell a 1000 word story to the gorgeous new *Omni* and two months later he sells them a novelette and then another and then another and then another. I publish a few okay science fiction novels, he publishes twenty masterpieces. I take my mother into a backdate magazine store on

Nostrand Avenue in 1980 and she says to the proprietor 'My son writes science fiction' and the proprietor says 'The mother of another science fiction writer comes in here for magazines with his stories all the time. She is so proud of him.' (My mother was not proud of me.) I might say that this was kind of humiliating except that he gives me honor by being my friend. He is not only ahead of me, he is ahead of us all."

Certainly true in 1984 and had already been so for almost twenty years. The accomplishment is so astonishing that the Grand Master conveyed is *obiter dicta*. Had he not gotten his right soon, right quick, the award would have been an embarrassment to any other recipient.

The acclaimed masterpieces—*Dying Inside*, *The Book of Skulls*, *Tower of Glass*—are indisputable of course but—ah, Fast Eddie Felsen, patron saint of the circumstantially challenged!—my deepest caritas is for the Silverberg novels at least as good which, because of his sheer prolificacy, never attracted the attention they deserved. *The Second Trip* (Bester's *Demolished Man* turned another way and ignited), *The Stochastic Man*, probably the best of all science fiction novels of politics, and the fierce and riotous *Up the Line*—the time travel novel about the man who pursued, won and bedded his remote ancestoratrice—is as stylistically poised, rococo, savagely baroque as anything by Bester and also over-the-top funny, a comic novel to stand with Voltaire's or those of Peter de Vries. Grand Masters get their due but not necessarily all their works.

Silverberg himself has dated the true beginnng of his more intense and literary work to 1962 with the short story "To See the Invisible Man," a riff out of Borges which was the first story written for Fred Pohl's magazine under an unusual contractual arrangement which gave Silverberg story-by-story utter creative freedom. (The arrangement: Pohl was compelled to buy the story submitted although he could then terminate the agreement. Silverberg found this to be utterly liberating, he could write to stylistic or subjectual limits, absolved of rejection.) "To See the Invisible Man," a narrative of social cruelty and alienation unusual for its elegance and restraint in the penumbra of a brutal theme, was more than commendable but its skill and force are in fact well foreshadowed in some of the earlier work. What Silverberg called "Birds of a Feather" (carnival time in the spaceways), "Warm Man" (more alienation), "The Iron Chancellor" (a house which could have been wired by Gallegher and locked by Kuttner) are considerable. Yard goods there were also, assigned space-filler for the Ziff-Davis magazines, but the early Ace Doubles show real craft and are better than most of the work surrounding them. (In an introduction written in 1978 for a reissue of those Ace Doubles Silverberg noted without inflection how many readers there were who felt that these were his best work, work before he had gone into the valleys of pretension, and he dedicated one of these reissues to such readers.)

Conventional wisdom, an oxymoron if one ever existed, gives us an "early" (pre-1967) Silverberg, a transcendent "middle" (1967-1976) and somewhat lesser "late" (to the present), but conventional wisdom is like payback. Conventional wisdom with its glass eye, cane and small, blurry features stumbles through the servants' entrance and falls down the stairs. From that "late" period came the novellas "In Another Country."

"The Secret Sharer," "Sailing to Byzantium," came "Hot Sky At Midnight," came "Blindsight" which was one of the brilliant dozen stories done for *Playboy* and these are not only to the level of "middle" Silverberg but in some cases ("In Another Country" in the 3/89 and published by Tor perhaps the truest culprit) perhaps beyond. Unlike so many of us, our Grand Master got larger, ever larger in forward motion.

An early (1974) collection of mine is dedicated to "Robert Silverberg, the best one." He's the best two and three, as well. All the dozens, all the variegate colors, all of the fire. I wrote when he was writing. I published contemporaneously in many of the places he published. These my greatest accomplishments by proxy.

# In Old Pidruid

## Kage Baker

One of the most prolific new writers to appear in the late '90s, the late Kage Baker made her first sale in 1997, to *Asimov's Science Fiction*, and quickly became one of that magazines most frequent and popular contributors with her sly and compelling stories of the adventures and misadventures of the time-traveling agents of the Company; later in her career, she started another linked sequences of stories there as well, the *Anvil of the World* series, set in as lush and eccentric a High Fantasy milieu as any we've ever seen. Her stories also appeared in *Realms of Fantasy*, *Sci Fiction*, *Amazing*, and elsewhere. Her first Company novel, *In the Garden of Iden*, was also published in 1997 and immediately became one of the most acclaimed and widely reviewed first novels of the year. More Company novels quickly followed, including *Sky Coyote*, *Mendoza in Hollywood*, *The Graveyard Game*, *The Life of the World to Come*, *The Machine's Child*, and *Sons of Heaven*, as well as the fantasy novel, *The Anvil of the World*. Her many stories were collected in *Black Projects, White Knights*; *Mother Aegypt and Other Stories*; *The Children of the Company*; *Dark Mondays*; and *Gods and Pawns*. Her most recent books include, *Or Else My Lady Keeps the Key*, about some of the real pirates of the Caribbean, fantasy novels *The House of the Stag* and *The Bird of the River*, science fiction novel *The Empress of Mars*, YA novel *The Hotel Under the Sand*, and the last Company novel, *Not Less Than Gods*. Her posthumously published *The Women of Nell Gwynne's* won a Nebula Award. Also posthumously published was *Nell Gwynne's Scarlet Spy*, *Nell Gwynne's On Land and At Sea*, with her sister, Kathleen

Bartholomew, and a big retrospective collection, *The Best of Kage Baker*. Baker died, tragically young, in 2010.

Before her death, in letters, Kage Baker said: "I have always loved the beginning of *Lord Valentine's Castle*, with the jugglers; I think I'd like to spin something off that." (Later, she added): "I'm 1500 words into it already, and having fun. Silverberg is so into botany, have you ever noticed? "

L ord Kinniken, sometime Coronal of Majipoor, had in his youth struggled with an addiction to pastry. As a consequence he had struggled with obesity as well. When it had become evident that he was shortlisted as a potential future Coronal, however, Kinniken had thrown himself into a rigorous program of diet and exercise. So effective was his personal fitness program that when Kinniken was measured for his green and gold Coronal's robe at last, the little Vroon tailor had clacked his beak approvingly and remarked that it wouldn't take half the costly eel-satin he had anticipated it would.

Although Lord Kinniken relapsed in his later years, especially after descending into the Labyrinth as Pontifex (when he became so fat that a special litter had to be built to get him from his bed to his throne), it remained his earnest wish that his subjects, at least, should keep in trim. Among his many decrees to that effect was the one instituting a Festival of Self-Propulsion in the great city of Pidruid.

The decree, as repeated each year since Kinniken's time by the Pidruid Festival Council, stated that, whereas it greatly concerned the Coronal that his beloved subjects relied on floaters and beasts to get about at the possible risk of causing their muscles to atrophy, an annual competition of decorated wagons was established in which all motive power was to be provided by humans (or Skandars, Hjorts, Vroons, Liimen, or Su-Suheris).

Kinniken was long dust and the ages had not been kind to his memory. By Lord Valentine's time, all that remained to show that Kinniken had ever existed was the handsome observatory he had built on Castle Mount and the aforementioned competition in Pidruid. The observatory was little used these days. The competition, however, was still being held…

———

"Those *bastards!*"

Flokkthan Canarkis's goggle eyes seemed to have swollen with rage, until they sat like bubbles on his warty face. Palmene winced and drew back, but the Hjort's wrath was not for her. "Those—those *provincials!* How *dare* they?"

"Relax! It won't give them any advantage," said Tribor, grinning. He was Palmene's older brother, one of a pair of identical twin humans, and nothing ever seemed to deflate his perpetual manic cheeriness.

"What'll they gain by telling everyone they're Pidruid's only all-human entry, anyway?" said Triren, the other twin, clapping Canarkis on the shoulder in a friendly way. "Everyone will think they're nasty bigots, won't they? And there are two Hjorts and a Skandar on the Judging Committee this year!"

"I suppose you're right," grumbled Canarkis, as his eyes receded somewhat. He cocked one of them at the twins. "I suppose someone might give some thought to spreading an effective rumor or two about such vicious enemies…?"

The *vicious enemies* to which he referred were the Falkynkip Gate District Players' Guild, rivals of some years' rancorous standing to Canarkis' own festival group, the Pidruid Harbor District Phantasists.

Palmene frowned, but her brothers looked at each other, their grins widening.

"Hmmm," said Tribor, and Palmene knew he and Triren were communicating somehow, in the unspoken way they had.

"Could always go to a few taverns and imply that actually they've hired on a few shape-shifters who only *look* human," said Triren, bright-eyed.

"Splendid idea!" Canarkis clasped his hands. "I knew I could rely on you."

"All we need now is a crown for expenses," said Tribor. Canarkis made a face, but dug in his purse.

"Well worth it," he said, handing Tribor a crown piece. "Go forth and blacken their names."

"Do you want to come along, Palmene?" Triren turned to her.

"No, thanks." Palmene shook her head, lips tight. She disapproved of such tactics.

"We won't be back too late," said Tribor, kissing her forehead, and Triren came and kissed her too. She watched as they walked away together, lean young men, already balding but with the gleeful faces of ten-year-olds who had found a way to break into a confectioner's shop. Which, in fact, they had done, at the age of ten; and stolen nothing, but left the shopkeeper a long list of ways in which he might improve his security arrangements. They had been orphaned when they were thirteen and Palmene was eight, and because they were geniuses they had been able to step into their father's place in the family business, which was making navigational instruments.

Neither compasses nor astrolabes were enough of a challenge for them, however, and so they had joined the Phantasists and devised the Entertainments.

Palmene turned and walked away across the campground. It was the traditional meeting place for festival entrants the night before the competition, a grove of vast fireshower palms at the edge of the sea. The sun was low in the west and threw long palm-shadows across the sand. The Phantasists' camp was pitched on a dune, a circle of tents arranged protectively around the Entertainments. The Skandars were already there in their open-sided pavilion, rolling out blankets for the night. Gortin Holt looked up as Palmene approached and nodded curtly to her. *He must be in a good mood,* thought Palmene. She lingered by the Entertainments, looking up at them.

On another world they might have been called parade floats, but here they did not float; they rolled, each on a single center-mounted wheel, and sawhorses propped them front and back when they were parked, as they were now. There were four, representing the four Powers of Majipoor. Each was cunningly articulated to perform wondrous tricks, but the motive power was supplied by the brawny Skandars, walking two to a side and pushing them.

Palmene walked around the float representing the Lady. It was ponderous, with the three tiers of the Isle of Sleep rising from it and a life-size effigy of the Lady herself at the top. When various concealed cranks were rotated, the Lady would raise and lower her hand in blessing, or open and close her eyes. More: when certain bellows were pumped, compartments within the Isle would dispense showers of paper-wrapped comfits, or flowers, or mists of perfumed water.

Slipping beneath, Palmene slid open the panel under the Isle of Sleep and scrambled up inside. Even at nineteen she was still lithe and skinny enough to fit within, and operate all the bellows and cranks. She turned a crank and heard the faint rattle and clacking she should have heard, the Lady's wooden hand rising to bless. *I wonder if you ever get tired of it all, Lady? I wonder if you ever wish your life would change?*

Palmene drew up her feet and sat crosslegged inside the Isle, luxuriating in self-pity. She had been sweeping floors and cooking dinner for her brothers for eleven years now, and, though she loved them dearly, she was nothing like them. She didn't *enjoy* the constant small explosions or flashes of light from their workshop, even on the occasions when shouts of triumphant laughter were the outcome, instead of sheepish requests for the burn salve. She hated coming down in the morning to discover some new untested device had been installed in her kitchen. Would it peel thlart-roots, or hurl them across the room in small bits? Would it neatly slice roast blave, or whack through the entire joint and the serving-platter too? Tribor and Triren were kind, uncomplaining, cheerful men, but they were also as mad as a couple of kassai in mating season.

*I just want a normal life,* Palmene said to herself, as she slid out of the float and closed the panel. Emerging, she came face to face with Howlimay Pilenthiso, the Vroon who had been her father's partner and now worked with her brothers. "Hello, Uncle Howlimay."

"Hello, child. Seeing that all is in readiness for tomorrow?"

"I was, yes."

"Favor me. Let us inspect the King of Dreams."

"Of course." Palmene followed the little Vroon around to the King's float. Here was a life-sized representation of Minax Barjazid, King of Dreams, lean and dark as a desert hawk, crowned in gold. His wooden arm was outflung in an accusatory gesture, and swiveled to point here and there when an interior crank was turned. Spiked and scaled desert creatures circled him, rigged to exhale dark smoke from reservoirs of chemical compounds within themselves. In the red cliff at his back a thundersheet was concealed, to sound the knell of doom to guilty dreamers.

Palmene watched as Howlimay examined the float, carefully picking his way around it to check the great wheel, extending a tentacle now and then to test the jaws of the smoke-beasts. She helped him open the panel underneath, and waited patiently as he scrambled inside and tested the gears and levers. "Are you afraid it'll break down during the parade?"

"I don't know, child. It's simply a feeling I have…"

"A what?" Canarkis came striding up to join them, regarding them with a fishy stare. "Have you a foreboding of treachery? No one would dare!"

"It's been known to happen," said Howlimay mildly, with a shrug of his tentacles. Canarkis glared across the campground at the Falkynkip Gate District Players' Guild, who were cooking their communal dinner over a campfire.

"No one would *dare*," he repeated. Palmene sighed and wandered off.

She made her way down the back of the dune to the beach. The green-bronze light of the sun seemed ancient, mellow, and a low salt mist rolled in above the combers. Beyond it lay the dome-topped wall of dense slate-colored fog, never far from Pidruid, ready to wash in like an etheric tide.

It was a perfect evening for being young and sad. Palmene walked along, watching the sun until it extinguished itself in the fog, and then trying to blink the red spots from her vision.

"Careful!" Someone caught her arm. Palmene looked down and danced backward a pace or two from the seabird carcass upon which she had been about to tread.

"Oh! Thank you." Palmene averted her eyes from the nasty sight and found herself looking into the eyes of a boy about her own age. He was tall and scrawny, with a shock of black hair and a handsome melancholy face. "I...I was just sort of drifting along. It's such a lovely evening and I..."

"Me too," said the boy, with a slow smile that flashed in Palmene's eyes like the afterimage of the sun. She felt her heartbeat speed up. Was he a fisherman's son, mending his nets on the beach? There was a popular song about a fisher-boy mending his nets and catching a girl's heart...

"So," said the boy. "Are you here for the competition tomorrow?"

Palmene nodded. She waved an arm in the direction of the campground. "I'm with—we're the ones with the floats."

"The Pidruid Harbor people? Right, I've seen the floats. I'm with the Falkynkip Gaters, myself."

"Oh, no!" Palmene threw up her hands in mock horror. "The enemy!" The boy grinned a little shamefacedly. Palmene, afraid she'd been too coquettish and the boy might misunderstand her, added in haste: "Our guildmaster's such an idiot, he takes it all so seriously! When it should be, you know... fun."

"I think so too." The boy looked over his shoulder at the campground. "Our guildmistress doesn't see it as a competition. More like a war."

"And that's so stupid, really," said Palmene. "Of both sides, I mean. So...what's your group doing this year? If it isn't a big secret?"

"Well, we have that stage on wheels, see," said the boy. "And we pull it along in the parade, and then when we stop in front of the judges' stand we put on a play."

"I remember from last year."

"Right, well, this year we're doing *Lord Valentine's Fall and Restoration.*"

"Oh, you probably shouldn't tell me," said Palmene, setting the back of her hand against her forehead and hoping the gesture came across as arch and clever. "We are rrrrrivals, after all. Are you playing Lord Valentine?"

The boy laughed out loud. His laughter was more dazzling than his smile; Palmene felt her heart fluttering again. "With *these* muscles?" he cried. "Not a chance! Here's what I do."

He snatched up a piece of flotsam from the beach, a slender length of wingwood, and crouched over it like a man bent with age. He took a few tottering steps up the beach and down, using the stick as a cane. In a cracked falsetto he recited:

"*Tyeveras am I, Pontifex royal!*
*Dweller in deepest Labyrinth!*
*Condemned to labor at incessant toil*
*And never once allowed down from my plinth!*"

"Ooh." Palmene seldom went to the theater, but even she could tell that was terrible.

"That's right. Ooh. Our guildmistress wrote it herself. To be fair, I guess it's hard to find a rhyme for *Labyrinth,*" said the boy, tossing away his stick.

"But, I mean, you were good. They've really got you playing the Pontifex?"

The boy nodded glumly. "With powdered gypsum in my hair and a white beard glued on. And greasepaint wrinkles. And baggy tights. And I operate some of the puppets."

"That's just unfair," said Palmene, setting her hand on the boy's shoulder and looking into his eyes. The boy shrugged.

"What do you do?"

Palmene imagined Flokkthan Canarkis's wrath if he could see her now, about to divulge information to a despised adversary. Her words fairly tumbled out of her mouth. "I'm in one of the parade floats. The one with the Lady of the Isle? I sit inside and work all the mechanisms that make things happen. Flowers and candy and all that? Next year my brothers want to see if they can't put in a sort of a panharmonium, which is—I don't know how it works, but it's a lot of musical instruments with bladders and bellows and things so they play themselves. My brothers would have had it built for this year, but they got distracted fixing the Coronal's float so he really juggles."

"He does?" The boy looked impressed. Afraid she had said too much at last, Palmene merely nodded. "See, your brothers are really clever. You people *deserve* to win. All we've got is that stupid stage and Rosamunda."

"Rosamunda? Oh, your guildmistress."

The boy shuddered and rolled his eyes. "That's right." As if on cue, a woman's voice cut through the evening mist, commanding and sharply audible even over the boom of the surf.

*"Disorn! We could use some assistance, dear!"*

"In a minute!" the boy said, half-turning to shout. "I'm sorry, I've got to go or she'll pitch a fit."

"Disorn? Is that your name?"

"Disorn Toulian. Listen—my father runs a teahouse over by Falkynkip Gate—if you'd ever like to come over for some tea or something—"

"I'm Palmene Falveras," she said breathlessly. "I'd love to stop by. We're Falveras & Pilenthiso Artificers, and I wish I could invite you over for something nice but all they make is springs and cogs and wooden gears—"

"It's called Toulian's—"

"*Disorn!*"

"The teahouse is, I mean. In a *minute* I said," cried Disorn, but he made no move to go.

"I have to go fix dinner, myself," said Palmene, withdrawing a step or two. "I suppose I'll see you tomorrow before the parade?"

"I guess so. Palmene, that's a beautiful name. Tomorrow, then," said Disorn, and turned and ran. Palmene watched him run, and marveled at the easy grace of his body.

———

Disorn stepped up his pace as he saw the campfires being lit in the gathering dusk; he'd been out longer than he'd thought. Rosamunda stood watching him atop the nearest dune. She was a slender woman in her late thirties, with flowing auburn hair. Bad temper glinted in her green eyes, but a certain amusement was there too as she asked: "Who was *she?*"

"Just some girl," said Disorn. "I thought you said we'd finished the rehearsals for today."

"We have. Your father requires a little help. I suppose I could always go explain you've been romancing someone," said Rosamunda, with a shrill giggle. Disorn didn't bother to answer as he ran past her, over the dune and into the circle of torchlight where the pageant wagon stood.

There was his father, seated on a keg as he peered at the wagon's rear axle. Mullum Toulian was a big amiable man with a prominent belly, and in his full costume as the Old King of Dreams he looked properly sinister and majestic. Unfortunately he was half out of costume at the moment, and the stickskin bald-pate piece sat askew above his mop of graying hair, like some absurd skullcap.

"Father, what's wrong?"

"Hm?" Mullum looked up vaguely. "Wrong? Nothing's wrong. Exactly. She wants this thing on here. I'm just trying to figure out the how of it all."

Disorn knew better than to ask him to clarify what he'd said. "You need more light," he said. He ducked into their tent and came out with a lantern full of sea-dragon oil. Lighting it from one of the torches with a palm twig, he came with it and squatted by his father. "Now, what are you trying to do?"

"Put this thing on so we tow it behind us in the parade," said Mullum, pointing to an upright wickerwork frame perhaps a meter square. It sat on four outsized wheels. Within the frame was a large gaily-painted sign: *ROSAMUNDA'S WOVEN CREATIONS!* In much smaller letters underneath was painted *at Falkynkip Gate, by Toulian's Teahouse.* Disorn, reading it, felt sullen anger welling up.

"Father, this is just advertising for *them!*" he said in a low voice, jerking his thumb at Rosamunda and her husband, Parl. "The teahouse should be on here, too!"

"Well, it is."

"In letters people can actually read!"

"I suppose, but everyone knows where we are," said his father, with a shrug. Disorn ground his teeth. After Disorn's mother had died, Rosamunda had made it her neighborly business to look after "that dear motherless boy and poor hapless Mullum," but in reality Disorn and his father looked after themselves and spent a lot of time obliging Rosamunda in a hundred little errands.

Mullum scratched his head, reaching under the bald-pate, and regarded the rear axle in mild bemusement. "See, it's supposed to trail behind us on this long thing? But if I tie one end to the axle it's just going to wrap round and round it as the wagon's pulled along, until it's yanked up *smack* to the axle."

Disorn scowled at the long rope of braided blave-hide. "I know what we need. I'll take care of it. You go get out of costume, Father, all right?"

"I'll do that." Mullum rose to his feet. "You need anything?"

"Bring me a couple of palm leaves," said Disorn, pulling out his knife. His father brought them and dropped them at his feet.

"Anything else, son?" Disorn shook his head, grabbing up one of the hard spiky leaves and setting to work slicing it into long fibrous strips. "Shall I make us some tea?"

"That's a good idea."

Pleased to be given a task nearer his heart, Mullum ambled off to the campfire and set to work brewing a pot of the fragrant and spicy tea that was his house specialty. Disorn worked quickly, cutting up the palm-leaf strips and braiding them into a stiff springy wand. When it was long enough he curved it around the rear axle of the pageant wagon and bent it into a figure-eight shape, closing the middle join with a few tight twists of fiber. He attached the rope to the other half of the coupling and gave it an experimental tug. It held. *And if it comes off during the parade and she loses her sign, that's just too bad,* thought Disorn to himself grumpily.

He sheathed his knife and blew out the lantern as he carried it back to the tent he shared with his father. Next to it was Rosamunda's and Parl's tent. They stood nearby in the gloom, just out of the circle of firelight, talking in low voices.

"Not a chance," Parl was saying. "The Hjort is over there lecturing everybody, and the girl's cooking them all dinner. It'll be hours yet."

"But you didn't see the brothers?"

"No. Speaking of dinner," said Parl, raising his voice, "Did I see your father's marinating tub in the back of your cart, Disorn? Is it possible he's going to honor us with his Grilled Fish Narabal Style?"

Disorn eyed him surlily. There had been no discussion of a communal meal that night, but he knew without asking that his father would have brought along enough to feed everyone. "I think so," he said. He disliked Parl, who was tall, handsome, and possessed of a bad back that made him unable to do any heavy lifting. Rosamunda cast up her hands now and made rapturous sounds, smacking her lips.

"Oh, delicious! You know, Disorn, I'm always telling your father, he could bottle that marinade and make a fortune."

"Maybe we'll do that," Disorn replied. Parl drew Rosamunda back into the shadows and they resumed their murmured conversation.

———

Palmene stirred the stew, looking up every now and then to see whether her brothers had returned. Howlimay Pilenthiso sat in silence, either praying or meditating. Canarkis the Hjort paced nervously. One of the Skandars, Angvar Klothis, approached her with his empty bowl.

"More, please," he stated, holding it out. "It's good. Considering your race."

Palmene, fully aware that he meant it as a compliment, merely said "Thank you," and ladled out another helping, leaving just enough for Tribor and Triren. *Perhaps they got something to eat at a tavern,* she thought. Just then the Vroon lifted his head, coiling in his tentacles.

"Here's trouble," he said. Palmene followed his gaze and saw another Hjort approaching them. In addition to brilliant magenta daubs of pigment on his whiskers, he wore brocade robes and a chain of office with the city insignia of Pidruid. Under his arm he carried a scroll. Thrust behind what might have been an ear or simply an especially convoluted wart he carried an ink-stylus. He drew his scroll out and consulted it a moment, glancing from it to the Entertainments with either eye.

"Entry Number Eleven?" he said. "Pidruid Harbor District Phantasists?"

"We are indeed," said Canarkis, clutching his lapels self-importantly and striding forward.

"I am Master of the Revels Travenhart. By the authority vested in me through the power of the Coronal and the Ruling Council of Pidruid, I will inspect your entries."

"Of course you shall," said Canarkis, rising slightly on his toes to try to seem a little taller than his fellow Hjort. He waved an arm at the entertainments. "They await your approval."

"Are you the Artificer?"

"Er—no, but—"

"Here we are!" Tribor and Triren came striding out of the darkness. Palmene uttered a silent prayer of thanks to the Lady for their timely arrival. Canarkis deflated slightly in his relief. They winked at him in unison, Tribor with the right eye, Triren with the left.

"And these are intended to represent the Powers?" Master Travenhart took down the stylus and opened the scroll. He walked slowly around the float representing Lord Valentine as a juggler. "Hmmm. This references the unfortunate events of the Great Treason. Is this quite a respectful subject, sirs?"

"Of course it is!" Canarkis inflated somewhat again. "It does not mock, but rather celebrates, our glorious Coronal's heroic achievement! Lord Valentine was unashamed to juggle on Castle Mount itself."

"And look at this!" said Tribor, as Triren slipped inside and operated the mechanisms. The wooden effigy of the Coronal, supported by the smaller figures of his Companions, began to whirl his cunningly articulated arms. Wooden balls spun through the air in a perfect circle, orbiting on an unseen wheel. The illusion was perfect and unsettling. Master Travenhart gaped at it, then cleared his throat so violently a collar stud popped.

"Suitable, I suppose. What are those pipes at the rear?"

"Mountings for fireworks," said Triren.

"Incendiary devices? Please submit them for inspection."

Triren obligingly fetched out the tub full of shaped charges, and the master of the revels picked through them to be certain that each and every one had the proper bureaucratic seal. He likewise demanded to see the bagful of silk flowers and comfits for the Lady's float, as well as the jugs of perfumed water, before he would check either of them off on his scroll. He watched, unsmiling, as the Pontifex's image rose slowly from a nest of rotating wooden spirals, stiffly made a sign of blessing, and sank back again, but he checked it off without comment. Canarkis followed him closely, nearly treading on the tail of his robe, as he walked around the King of Dreams.

"And what does this one do?"

Tribor scrambled inside and demonstrated. "And see these?" Triren tapped the little monsters at the King's feet. "See the open mouths? They exhale smoke."

"I see." Master Travenhart stuck his stylus behind his— ear? "More incendiary devices?"

"No, something better!" Beaming, Triren dove into a crate and hauled out an immense glass jug full of something black as ink. "A special formula! Our own invention. This goes into a reservoir under the float, you see, and as it interacts with the air it turns into black smoke! Comes rolling up pipes and out of their mouths. Gives old Minax his own rolling cloud of nightmares!"

"I *beg* your pardon?" Master Travenhart whipped out his stylus again and held it out accusatorily. "Am I to understand you are incorporating an *unapproved substance* in an entertainment for public display?"

"That's right," said the twins in unison, completely unruffled. Palmene clenched her fists. How many times had she reminded them to register their formula?

"A substance that has not been submitted to the Guild of Chemists for testing?"

"But it's perfectly safe!"

"Unacceptable!" Master Travenhart opened his scroll and began to scribble notes. "The rules clearly state—"

"We will be happy to submit a sample," said Canarkis.

"Pointless. The Guild offices closed this afternoon and will not reopen until after the festival."

"But it dissipates quickly," Canarkis said, a wheedling tone coming into his voice. "Harmlessly. I saw it tested myself. Surely, as one Hjort to another, you can extend me the courtesy of—"

"Inappropriate. I hereby confiscate that jar under the authority of the Pidruid Festival Council. And you needn't try bribing me, either," said the master of the revels coldly. In the silence that followed his remark, snickering could be heard coming from the camp of the Falkynkip Gate District Players' Guild.

It acted upon Flokkthan Canarkis's strained temper like a glimmer-screen flourished at a blave. He clenched his fists, his eyes swelled to moons, and a flush of turquoise appeared about his jowls. "How—how DARE you insult me thus! We, sir, have won the Grand Trophy in *three consecutive years* to overwhelming public acclaim!"

"Irrelevant," said the master of the revels, going turquoise himself. "You will not impede *my* office, sir!" He rolled an eye at the Skandars, who were getting to their feet and looming in what he took to be a threatening manner. He threw down his scroll, stepped forward and wrenched the jar from Triren's hands. It was heavier than he'd anticipated and slipped from his grasp, shattering against the stone campsite marker.

"Oh—" said Palmene in horror, before the world vanished in a cloud of inky chemical smoke. She saw nothing for several minutes but heard, quite clearly over the racking coughs and cries of alarm, the howls of laughter from the camp of the Falkynkip Gate District Players' Guild.

———

"That settles *them!*" Rosamunda cried gleefully. "That's got to be a deduction of fifty points!"

"If they aren't disbarred completely!" said Parl. "Thank you, new Master of the Revels!!"

"What happened?" Mullum looked up from the campfire, where he had arranged a grill and was cooking fish. "What's all that black smoke?"

"Only the doom of our disgusting rivals," said Rosamunda, doing a hip-bumping dance of triumph.

"They're just people like us," muttered Disorn, threading fish filets on a skewer.

"The untalented rabble of the harbor," said Parl. "Not artists. Rosamunda *deserves* to win that trophy. You know you do, my sweet."

"And you, at least, are supportive," said Rosamunda, stroking his unshaven jaw.

"Still, you know what they say." Mullum shook his head as he shoved a bit of driftwood in among the coals. "Don't laugh at the misfortune of others, because you never know when your own cup will spill."

Five minutes later he proved to be a prophet, as Master Travenhart came stumping over to their campsite. A black gloom still drifted about his garments, his eyes were watering, and his face was like thunder as he swept them with a glance and snapped open his scroll.

"Entry Number *Twelve*," he said. "Falkynkip Gate District Players' Guild. And I see you list yourselves as the only all-human entry in the competition? You are actually *proud* of that fact? There are no talented members of other races, is that what you're saying?"

"Well—we—" Rosamunda blinked in the firelight. "We held open auditions. We did. We just didn't get any applicants but humans."

Disorn hid a smile. Their Su-suheris neighbors who kept an antiques shop, the Skandars who lived on the other side of the shop and the Vroon who kept an augury parlor across the street all knew Rosamunda too well to want to join her troupe this year. Disorn and his father had only become actors at her tearful pleading.

"I *see*." The master of the revels's voice dripped disbelief.

"And, well, you see, when that happened—I'm a creative person and I said, 'Why, we'll just make it a strength! It will be a challenge!'" Rosamunda looked around in appeal, and Parl took her arm and nodded solemnly.

The master of the revels exhaled, sending a tiny puff of black smoke drifting across the camp. "If you say so. I will now inspect your entry."

Parl showed him around the pageant wagon, opening out the various painted canvas backdrops. Master Travenhart took notes, saying nothing, until he cocked an eye at Rosamunda and inquired: "And what is your theme this year?"

"*Lord Valentine, his Fall and Restoration.*"

Master Travenhart scowled. "Not the most original theme these days, is it?"

"But ours is the best," said Rosamunda swiftly. "My dear husband here plays the Coronal himself! In a yellow wig, of course. And I myself play the Lady. As well as the warrior-woman Lisamon."

The master of the revels cocked his other eye. "Indeed? Who, may I ask, portrays Lord Valentine's noble Companions?

The Vroon? The Hjort? The heroic and unlucky Skandars? Humans in costume, perhaps?"

"They're done with puppets, actually," said Parl. "Most of them. Disorn! Come show the worthy master."

Disorn got up and rummaged in the costume trunk for the straw wig he wore as Shanamir the Herd Boy. Clapping it on, he grabbed up the wide yoke from which the various puppets depended and put it across his shoulders. The tiny marionette representing Autifon Deliamber waggled its beak, and Disorn spoke for him:

> *"My Vroonish senses tell me true*
> *Lord Valentine is none but you!"*

"Show him the Hjort," insisted Rosamunda. "You'll like the Hjort, Master, he's really very cute."

Disorn swung round the bulging body of the puppet representing Vinorkis the Hjort Companion. Hastily he blew through a pipe, and the puppet's jowls and eyes expanded.

> *"I was a base and hireling spy*
> *Yet now reformed, most loyal I!"*

Disorn recited in a croaking voice. The master of the revels's whiskers quivered. His entire head turned turquoise.

"I have never seen anything so offensive in my life," he said. "This would cause rioting! You are hereby disqualified from the competition for gross racial insult."

Not all of Rosamunda's tears and protestations sufficed to change his mind. The result of five minutes of escalating appeals and refusals was that Master Travenhart went stalking away in one direction while Rosamunda ran sobbing away over the dunes with the avowed intention of drowning herself in the sea. Parl followed in hot pursuit.

"That's too bad," said Mullum, looking over his shoulder as Parl vanished into the night. "I'm sorry for her. Do you suppose we ought to go do something?"

Disorn shook his head. "He'll save her."

"Poor thing. Still, this time tomorrow we'll be back in the teahouse!" Mullum perked up distinctly. "No more fuss and bother. Something to be said for that, eh, son?"

Disorn nodded. They ate their dinner and turned in early. Disorn was awakened at some point in the night hearing Rosamunda's voice.

"What did you do with them?"

"Pitched them into the sea." That was Parl, speaking in a low voice.

"Good." Rosamunda still sounded hoarse with weeping. "*That* much at least I will not have to endure."

They said nothing else, and Disorn drifted off to sleep again.

———

Palmene had lit the breakfast fire and was frying oysters when her brothers emerged from their tent.

"*Good* morning!" they said in bright unison.

"What's so good about it?" said Palmene crossly. "After last night?"

"We figured out a way to make the King smoke after all!"

"It'll be easy. We just replace the reservoir chamber with an incense burner!"

"One of the big ones, like in the Lady shrines?"

"And rig it with a bellows to pump the smoke up the pipes and out through the lizard mouths!"

"But the final check is in two hours," said Palmene. "You can't get all that bought and built and installed before the final check!"

Tribor and Triren looked at each other, eyes gleaming.

"We can't?" said Tribor.

"Watch us!" said Triren. They sprang to their feet, paused only to grab a couple of oysters from the skillet, yelled "Ow! Hot!" as they stuffed them in their mouths, and sprinted away into the morning fog.

"Did I hear our Artificers announce a hopeful solution to our difficulties?" The flap of Canarkis's tent was raised and a goggling eye peered out.

"You heard correctly," said Palmene.

"Wonderful boys! I knew they would redeem themselves." Canarkis sniffed the air and emerged from his tent on hands and knees. "Vile, detestable Master Travenhart! And to think I dared hope a fellow Hjort would be a more agreeable master of the revels. Old Zurkin Fellfoyd was at least gracious about accepting bribes."

"Master Travenhart won't be on the panel of judges," said Palmene. "That's something, anyway. And he didn't actually disqualify *us*."

"How true." Canarkis glanced over his shoulder at the Falkynkip Gate camp and allowed himself a smile. "I knew their abominable boast would backfire."

"Do not rejoice at their woes." Howlimay Pilenthiso came hurrying up. He pointed a tentacle at the Lady's float. "We have fresh woes of our own."

"What's that?" Canarkis looked around sharply.

"It would appear we were robbed in the night."

"What? You can't be serious! What's missing?"

"The silk flowers and the comfits, as well as the scented water for the misting device," said Howlimay somberly. "It would appear they attempted to break into the tub with the fireworks, but those were beside my tent. I woke in the night with the distinct impression someone was out there, and went out and dragged the tub into my tent. By morning light it looks as though someone pried up one corner of the lid before they were obliged to flee."

Palmene almost smiled at the image of anyone fleeing from the little Vroon, but Canarkis bounded to his feet in rage. "Villains! Assassins! Monsters! Thieves—" He choked on his own spraying spittle and collapsed, clutching his hearts. The Skandars, roused by his shouting, had emerged from their pavilion by this time and stood staring down at him.

"He'll be all right. It's just spleen," said Gortin Holt.

"May—as well—return to our homes," croaked Canarkis. "What endless perfidy—"

Palmene, exasperated, slammed down the breakfast skillet. "Not after all my brothers' work! Here." She got up and wrenched Canarkis's purse from his belt, and drew out a few crowns. "Here! Holt, you go find a confectioner's and buy all the comfits you can with that." She grabbed one of his big hands and pressed a crown into it, and looked around at the other Skandars as he trudged away obligingly. "Klothis, you take this crown and go to a perfumers'. Get a pint of their cheapest flower essence."

Angvar Klothis drew himself up in offended male pride. "I'm not going anywhere to purchase *perfume!* I'd be a laughing-stock!"

"I will go for it," said the Vroon, reaching into her hand for the crown piece.

"Thank you, Uncle Howlimay." Palmene swung around to glare at the Skandars. "Since you're too manly to buy perfume, I suppose none of you would be willing to come help me pick flowers?" She pointed at the plumbialis bushes on the edge of the campground. They bore rather sticky blue flowers and were the sort of hardy unremarkable shrub planted in municipal gardens, easily plundered.

"It matters not whether *they* will assist," groaned Canarkis, getting to his knees. "I myself will lay aside my personal dignity and pick flowers. The more shame to them if they refuse."

———

Rosamunda, sipping hot tea, turned her head to watch when all the commotion broke out. She smiled evilly.

"Dear me, has someone sabotaged the Harbor District clowns? It sounds as though someone has. *They* won't win this year, at least, which is certainly a consolation."

Disorn, remembering the words he had overheard in the night, looked over at her in disgust.

"Everybody's having such a hard time this year," remarked Mullum, shaking his head as he stirred the breakfast porridge. "It just seems to me it's not worth doing if you don't have fun."

Rosamunda hummed a little tune, looking smug. Disorn leaned and peered across the campground, watching Palmene and Canarkis raiding the plumbialis bushes.

"I wonder if I oughtn't go alert the camp authorities about floral theft." Rosamunda had another sip of tea.

"Oh, give it a rest!" Disorn told her. She gave him a mischievous smile, narrow-eyed.

"Misery loves company, I suppose." Mullum presented her with a bowl of porridge. "There you go. You just eat that instead, eh? It's sweetened the way you like it, with droft-honey. That'll put you in a better mood."

She thanked him prettily and the three of them settled down to eat. Parl's snoring drifted from her tent. It was another half-hour before he woke with a snort and crawled out, shirtless and yawning.

"Want some porridge? It's still hot." Mullum handed him a cup of spiced tea.

"Thanks, that would be wonderful." Parl flexed his brawny shoulders and grinned at Rosamunda. "So! Have they discovered they've been robbed yet?"

Rosamunda made a face and shushing motions at him, but Mullum looked up from the porridge kettle. "What?"

"He went over there in the night and stole some of their supplies, and dumped them in the sea," said Disorn.

"Heh heh," said Parl, and gulped down his tea.

"You never!"

Rosamunda toyed with a lock of trailing hair. "All's fair in festivals and war, you know. Healthy competition and all that."

"But we weren't competing anymore. We'd been axed. And you really went over there and *stole* from them?" Mullum clenched his fists. Disorn couldn't ever remember his father making a fist.

"Not so loud," said Parl.

"I can't believe this! How could you do such a thing?" Mullum was quivering with indignation. They stared at him openmouthed, all three. None of them had ever seen Mullum Toulian angry about anything. He swung up his arm and pointed his finger at Parl—just exactly like the King of Dreams, and not the cackling old villain of Rosamunda's play but the *real* King. "You go straight over to them and confess and apologize, and you do it now, or I'll go tell them myself!"

"Wait, Father." Electrified by an idea, Disorn jumped to his feet. "There's something better we can do!"

———

A couple of the Skandars had finally come and helped pick flowers, sweeping them from the stems with basketlike hands. Palmene was just holding the sack open as Hurgan Kopinnik dumped in all the blossoms he'd gathered when she heard Canarkis' voice raised in protest.

"This is too much! What right have you to gloat over us?"

Palmene looked around and saw the entire Falkynkip Gate team venturing into the Harbor District team's campsite. In the lead was the dark boy, Disorn. Palmene dropped the sack and ran to meet him. He was holding up his hands in a placating gesture, looking earnest.

"We haven't come to gloat at all. We'd like to help. We have a proposition for you."

"A likely story!" said Canarkis, and one of the Skandars growled.

"No. Really. Listen. We've been disqualified—you know that, and you probably know why, if you can hear us as well as we heard you. At least you haven't been thrown out of the competition. We hate Master Travenhart. *You* hate Master Travenhart. We ought to work together to foil him. What if we join your team? We've both got the same theme this year, correct? What about a grand five-wagon entry? Nobody'd have anything like it. It'd be spectacular! And then, in front of the judges, we'd all put on Rosamunda's play."

"*We* as in you?" Canarkis looked shrewdly at Rosamunda, who pursed her lips.

"No," she said sullenly. "All of us. We need more actors."

"Wouldn't you like to play Noble Vinorkis?" Disorn asked Canarkis. "Who else could do the part justice, but you?"

"I don't know that I'd have time to learn the lines." Canarkis rolled his eyes diffidently.

"They're easy. Nobody has more than a few rhyming couplets," Disorn explained.

"I think it sounds like a good idea," said Palmene. "Especially if Tribor and Triren don't manage to get the smoke effect fixed. We're going to need every extra bit we can get, what with *things being stolen*." She looked hard at Rosamunda, who turned red and looked down.

"We'll help all we can," said Disorn, taking Palmene's hand.

At this moment the Vroon returned, snapping his tentacles in agitation. "Child, I have been to no less than five perfumer's shops. Every one of them is closed until after the parade today, when the streets clear. There was not so much as a drop of flower essence to be had."

"We can help there," said Mullum. "Rosamunda has a bottle of perfume in her cosmetics case. Haven't you?"

She looked around in alarm. "But—that's *A Night in the Gardens of Tolingar!* It costs a crown a bottle—"

"And our friends need it more than you do," said Mullum firmly. "If they're going to help us put on your play."

Emotions warred in Rosamunda's face, before she tossed back her hair. "I'll just go get the bottle, then," she said. "And the script."

"Good!" Mullum looked around at everyone and smiled. "Why don't I brew up some more tea for everyone? We've got a lot of work to do."

———

Master of the Revels Travenhart glared, monstrously affronted when he came around for the final check and found the two teams amicably wedded as one, but there was nothing he could do: there was nothing in the rules that specifically forbid such a last-minute alteration. The offensive puppets had manifestly been done away with. There was a real Vroon portraying Autifon Deliamber, the Heroic Skandars were played by real Skandars, and that buffoon Canarkis was himself smugly intoning the lines written for the Noble Vinorkis. When Master Travenhart insisted on another inspection of the float of the King of Dreams, he found Disorn underneath it busily removing the reservoir that was to have held the black smoke mixture. "We want to comply with your orders, after all," Palmene told him sweetly.

———

They were given their official entrant's ribbon, they were allowed to wheel the floats and the stage to the open sandy area from which the parade stepped off; and still there was no sign of Palmene's brothers. Gortin Holt at least returned after three hours' absence bearing an immense sack of lusavender-seed comfits, and though that obscure flavor was disliked by everyone other than Gortin Holt, no complaints were made; he had walked five miles to get them through sticky heat, after the morning fog had burned off, and returned in a foul mood even for a Skandar.

It still lacked a half-hour to noon when a Ghayrog official climbed to the top of a wooden platform and called out through an amplification sphere: "Attention! Will all parade participants please form up in the order of their entry numbers!"

"Pidruid Harbor District Phantasists!" Canarkis shouted. "Take your places, if you please!" The Skandars moved the floats into a line and, somewhat grudgingly, backed up to allow the pageant wagon to be rolled in ahead of them. Equally grudgingly, Rosamunda and Parl took their places at the pull-trace at the front of the wagon; only Canarkis would be permitted to strut at the front of the entry, bearing his Guildmaster's staff and banner.

"But where are my brothers?" Palmene fretted.

"I'm sure they're just delayed," said Disorn, patting gypsum into his hair and setting out the straw wig he would clap over it as Shanamir. "If it was that hard to buy perfume or comfits today, it must be really hard to find an incense burner for sale."

"I just hope they haven't been arrested again."

"Does that happen often?"

Palmene nodded sadly. "Crimes against public safety. They get what seems to be a wonderful idea and just charge ahead with it without ever thinking of the consequences. They blew the roof off a public lavatory once. You don't want to know how. I'd have a nice dowry by this time if we hadn't been fined so often."

"Dowries aren't important," said Disorn. He gave her a rakish grin as he donned the straw wig. "If I loved a girl, I'd marry her even if she had nothing."

Palmene dimpled. She looked down shyly. "Your father makes very good tea, by the way," she said.

"And he can cook. Makes the best fish stew in all of Pidruid."

"I can cook, too."

"Really?" Disorn thought about what he might say next. *Maybe the two of you could exchange some recipes* just sounded silly. All the other phrases he came up with he discarded hastily because he was sure they'd come out sounding suggestive of something improper. In the end he just said "That's nice. Not too nervous about playing Beautiful Carabella?"

Palmene laughed. "Not when she's only got one line! Rosamunda wrote all the good lines for herself, didn't she?"

"At least I'm spared having to play her." In a fluting soprano Disorn cried *"And I, my loving lord, faithfully will follow you!"*

Their laughter was interrupted by Canarkis storming along the parade line. "Where are the twins? The first of the entries has moved out!"

It was true: the Pidruid Gate of Dreams Marching Band had already raised their ghazanwood horns and blared out the fanfare that opened the city anthem.

"Here we are!" Palmene's brothers cried, shoving through the crowd. Tribor held an immense ceramic tea-urn, from one side of which a bellows protruded. Triren's arms were full of brackets and tools.

"What is that?" demanded Canarkis.

"Well, all the incense burners we borrowed wouldn't work," explained Triren, as Tribor dove under the King's float and set to work fitting the tea-urn-turned-smokepot where the reservoir had been. "Though we did borrow a week's worth of incense. Well, bought it, actually, because we won't be giving it back, so we left a crown for the hierarch to find—and then we found the urn in a trash dump, it's cracked but we're not making tea so who cares—and then we had to take it back to the shop and modify it with the bellows—and then we had to wait for the glue to dry—"

"I don't care!" Canarkis bounded up and down in his agitation. "We're about to step off and the *float's not ready*! In your places, the rest of you!"

Palmene started off toward the Lady's float. She turned back and kissed Disorn. "Good luck!" she cried, and fled. Disorn, feeling happiness expand inside himself like a flower opening, looked around and found Triren staring at him.

"Who're you?"

"We'll explain later!" Canarkis snatched the tools from his hands. "In your places, I said!"

Triren shrugged and ran off to climb inside the Coronal's float. Howlimay was already inside the float for the Pontifex, with a tentacle positioned on each of the seven different levers he must work. Disorn looked down at Tribor, who was hastily screwing in the brackets that held the smokepot in place.

"Can I help you?"

"Yes. Got a firepoint?"

Disorn fetched out his firepoint on the cord with which he wore it around his neck, and slipped it over his head. "Here you are."

*"Entry Number Eleven, Pidruid Harbor District Phantasists! Please proceed!"*

Canarkis dropped the tools and ran off, with a long despairing wail, to the front of the line. Disorn, having passed the firepoint to Tribor, scooped up the tools and secured them in his pockets. "I have to go!"

"Go ahead," said Tribor, his head vanishing in a cloud or fragrant smoke. A second later the rest of him vanished too, as he seemingly ascended into the cloud, his feet disappearing last into the float's interior. Disorn ran forward and joined his father at the rear of the pageant wagon. Looking over his shoulder, he saw smoke beginning to roil from the float, just as the King of Dreams rattled to mechanical life and swung his accusatory arm.

"And off we go," Mullum grunted, setting his shoulder to the wagon. Disorn pushed with him and the wagon started forward with a lurch. Ahead, they heard the cheering of the crowds lined up for the parade. Behind them, the Skandars shouted all together and the Entertainments began to roll.

———

And in the end they won the Grand Trophy again that year. There were, of course, several furious squabbles afterward concerning whether the trophy cup should be displayed in the front window of the Canarkis Investment Brokerage or Rosamunda's Woven Creations. The lawsuit dragged on for some years, by which time all but Canarkis and Rosamunda themselves had ceased to care. As old Mullum Toulian observed—dandling his twin granddaughters on the back steps of the teahouse, as they all watched the spiral of smoke that marked where the roof of Falveras & Pilenthiso Artificers had just been blown off again—there were more important things in life.

# Voyeuristic Tendencies

## Kristine Kathryn Rusch

Kristine Kathryn Rusch started out the decade of the '90s as one of the fastest-rising and most prolific young authors on the scene, took a few years out in mid-decade for a very successful turn as editor of *The Magazine of Fantasy and Science Fiction*, and, since stepping-down from that position, has returned to her old standards of production here in the 21st Century, publishing a slew of novels in more than seven genres, including writing fantasy, mystery, and romance novels under various pseudonyms as well as science fiction. She has published more than fifty novels under her own name, including *The White Mists of Power*, *Snipers*, *The Enemy Within*, and *Fantasy Life,* the seven-volume *Fey* series, and *Alien Influences*. Her most recent books (as Rusch, any-way) are two popular multi-volume series of SF novels, the "Retrieval Artist" series, which includes *The Disappeared*, *Extreme, Consequences, Buried Deep, Paloma, Recovery Man, Duplicate Effort, Anniversary Day, Blowback*, a collection of "Retrieval Artist" stories, *The Retrieval Artist and Other Stories*, and "Retrieval Artist" short novels such as *The Recovery Man's Bargin, The Possession of Paavo Deshin*, and *The Impossibles*, and the "Diving" series, which includes the novels *Diving into the Wreck, City of Ruins, Boneyards*, and the latest, *Skirmishes*, as well as the short novels *Becalmed, The Fleet of Lost Souls, Stealth, Becoming One With the Ghosts*, and *Strangers At the Room of Lost Souls*. WMG Publishing is in the process of releasing her entire backlist, including all of her copious short fiction, in e-book form, and has already published a dozen collections in print form. She has won many Readers Awards from the readership of

*Asimov's, Ellery Queen Mystery Magazine, Science Fiction Age*, and *Analog*. She's the only writer whose short fiction has appeared in all four Dell magazines (*Asimov's, EQMM, Alfred Hitchcock's Mystery Magazine*, and *Analog*) in the same year, a feat she has accomplished several years in a row. She continues to edit, having just finished the first year (seven volumes) of the anthology series, *Fiction River*. She acts as series editor with husband Dean Wesley Smith, and volume editor on three of the year's books. As a writer, she has been nominated for every major award in mystery and science fiction. She has won awards in each genre she's published in, from the Herodotus Award for Best Historical Mystery (for *A Dangerous Road*, written as Kris Nelscott) and the Romantic Times Reviewer's Choice Award (for *Utterly Charming*, written as Kristine Grayson); as Kristine Kathryn Rusch, she won the John W. Campbell Award, been a finalist for the Arthur C. Clarke Award, and took home a Hugo Award in 2000 for her story "Millennium Babies," making her one of the few people in genre history to win Hugos for both editing *and* writing.

Kristine Kathryn Rusch says: "I've loved Bob's stories since I first read them in the 1970s. Mostly, I read his short fiction then, and missed the important novels. So when the invitation to be a part of this came, I decided it was time to read *Dying Inside*. I would work off that. And no one had taken it! I was stunned. Then pleased. (My next choice would have been *Enter A Soldier, Later, Enter Another*.) I loved the book, as I knew I would, and enjoyed writing the story."

T he old man found me. I didn't know how. That was my first concern. How did he find me? How did he even know to look for me?

No one finds me. I am a ghost. I find other people. I *spy* on other people and they do not know it. I learn everything about them, and they never even see me.

No one sees me, except a few delivery guys. Various ages, various ethnicities. And only a few of them remember me, and only because they've been coming to the apartment for a very long time. To the rest, I'm the androgynous skinny kid in the unwashed t-shirt and ancient jeans, grabbing some crumpled twenties from my pocket, then snatching the greasy bag away as if I haven't eaten for a week.

I always eat. That's rule number one.

Rule number two? Sleep—at least eight hours.

Keep the mind fresh.

The old man tells me sleep doesn't matter. Food doesn't matter. All those exercises the "experts" recommend for keeping a sound mind well into your dotage—those don't matter either. Crossword puzzles, music lessons, one hour of exercise per day—none of it will matter.

I will lose my mind somewhere around forty.

When the old man says he lost his.

———

The old man found me in, of all places, the Carnegie Deli.

I love the Carnegie Deli. It's so big I can slide in after a show ends, listen to the theater traffic, pick up tidbits from the tourists excited to be in "The Big Apple."

Like we call it that. New Yorkers. To us, it's the City, a place the tourists visit and pollute with their Disneyfication and their gawky mawkishness at Ground Zero. They get coffee at Starbucks and eat at the MacDonald's on Times Square, spurning the real places, showing up at Sardi's and the Carnegie only because it's part of their theater package or because the concierge at their hotel recommended it for the real New York experience.

The Carnegie, it is *a* New York experience. A real deli, serving real corned beef and matzo ball soup and cheesecake made from real homemade cream cheese, so light and fluffy you wouldn't know it has more calories than a Big Mac with fries, not that I care. I can eat a gigantic slice of Carnegie cheesecake every week, along with some real New York pizza, one of Nathan's dogs, a bagel every morning and twice on Sundays and never gain weight.

That's one of my special talents—a real talent, considering I'm female and most females store fat for that day when their body fulfills its primary use and carries a child. Maybe mine knows it'll never carry a child, so it doesn't do the yeoman's work.

Or maybe the high metabolism is a result of my other special talent, the one that brings me to the Carnegie.

After all, the old man had that same talent, and the old man was never fat.

I know this because he's shown me pictures. He even had me read his journal, written in 1976, when he lost it all. *That* was an experience, let me tell you, reading some old man's secret thoughts. It's not like what I usually do. Usually I steal a moment, maybe troll for some secrets, and then I get the hell out.

This guy voluntarily wrote this crap down, about women and douching and muffdiving (he doesn't call it that) and taking LSD and sleeping around and all the good and the bad, mostly the bad, of his small little life.

We all have small little lives, but most of us aren't aware of that. Those lives seem important to us.

And I can speak in the Royal We because I know. I've been in other people's minds.

That's what I do. I peer. I slide in, steal what information I need and a lot that I don't, and move along. I am a one-way telepath. A stealth telepath, if you will.

I can reach in, explore, learn all about you, and you'll never even know I was there. But I can't talk to you. I can't fill your brain with my thoughts. I can't send over long distances. Hell, I can't send over short ones, not even if we were touching foreheads and concentrating.

I can only nab what's in your head—and it's not like reading.

It's like peering in, looking through a foggy window—at least at first—and then things become clearer and clearer and suddenly I'm inside. *Your thoughts to my thoughts* or *my thoughts to your thoughts*, whatever the hell Spock says in the Vulcan mindmeld.

Only *Star Trek* likens a mindmeld to rape at worst, a joining at best. As usual, the larger culture gets it wrong.

It's not a joining. It's more like a piggybacking, a parasitical adventure. You don't even know I'm there, unless I reveal myself—verbally, aloud, I make some kind of mistake, knowing something I shouldn't know.

And even then, who suspects telepathy? I've been accused of overhearing phone conversations, of peeping through keyholes, of reading private e-mails.

I do none of those things.

I don't have to.

I just have to dip into your mind, and I know it all.

Or at least, I know what you know. For that moment anyway.

And sometimes—often—that moment is enough.

———

So, the old man. The old man is David Selig, seventy-five, graduate of Columbia University, Class of 1956. Has an apartment he bought in the late 1970s with a down payment he borrowed from his sister. She took pity on him, because he had lost everything—her words, not his, although he thought that accurate at the time.

Lost everything and gained a comfortable life. Amazing, he thinks even now with a sense of disbelieving awe, amazing the benefits a normal life can bring.

I don't believe that. I don't want a normal life. I like mine. I'm thirty-two years old, live in an apartment I bought at the height of the real estate boom with money I earned because of my special talent. I don't regret the loss of equity these past few years. I don't regret paying too much. I like where I live. I like the stone building with the thick, old-fashioned walls, the solid floors. So many in Manhattan complain about the noise, but I don't hear much of it. I'm protected by masonry and windows two inches thick, a corner apartment overlooking a little-used courtyard, and one giant television set in the second bedroom (yes, I have a second bedroom) along with Bluetooth headphones that broadcast in stereo.

I can literally shut out the world, and I do on a regular basis. After reading the old man's journal, I think he didn't shut it out enough.

But I didn't tell him that.

I didn't tell him anything. I never tell anyone anything. Why should the old man be any different?

———

He scared me when he slid into my booth at the Carnegie a few weeks ago, smiled, and said, "Maggie," like he'd known me all my life. He even called me Maggie the Cat, which is what my dad called me from when I was little, not—like I used to think—because I padded through the house on little cat's feet (I was a great lover of Sandburg, even from an early age) but because of Tennessee Williams' *Cat on a Hot Tin Roof*, which I wasn't allowed to see or read until high school, and then I saw it on Broadway, and felt shocked that my dad—my prudent prissy dad—would nickname his daughter after such a woman.

But Maggie, they tell me, was my grandmother's nickname, although my father never would have called her Maggie the Cat, even if she had deserved it in later years. (Sometimes he would wonder how he could be so embarrassed by the woman who gave birth to him, and I would so want to volunteer to tell him, but I never could since he never expressed the thought out loud.)

But the old man, who didn't remind me of my father at all, said, "Maggie," as if he had known me, as if we'd met. We hadn't met. I would have remembered him.

He didn't look seventy-five. He was that nebulous age men get where they could be a distinguished fifty or a well preserved eighty. His back was straight, his hair so silver it looked like it could have come from a bottle. No wrinkles, except around his eyes, and those looked more sunkissed than anything. He was slender, and he had sharp features— high cheekbones, a pointed chin—which kept him from looking too old.

And those eyes. Clear, and filled with a deep intelligence.

"Do I know you?" I asked, even though I knew the answer. I'd had a sense of him as he came into the deli. Lifelong New Yorker, a bit of contempt for the tourist crowd, disliking the bright lights from the remodel up front, remembering an older, more distinguished deli that seemed—from his memory at least—a bit shabbier, but cozier, and the food homier.

Not that it could be homier for me. I was eating pastrami on rye, stacked so high that I couldn't bite it without mashing it down. String fries on a separate plate, and the best coleslaw in the city, bar none. I was eating slowly, trying not to fill up, because this was once-a-month-cheesecake day, even though I'd had a slice the previous week, celebrating a large success and an even larger check.

I had left his mind after that initial unpromising encounter, dipped into a few others, searching for a somewhat furtive tourist mind, one that held just a bit more guilt than usual and a touch of excitement as well.

I hadn't found one yet, but I would before the night was out. Then I'd search even harder, find the name of a spouse or someone who "couldn't know"—and dig until I found the address or a phone number. God bless cell phones. Seriously. People look at them, see the numbers and don't really see them at all.

But I do.

Then I tap them into my iPhone, and let technology do the walking. I got an illegal app downloaded from a floating site that gives me the power to find everything from a credit history to an email address with just a few taps on my clear little screen.

My iPhone is my own personal god. I use it to take pictures, capture information, and write my e-mails, all of which allow me to get a lot of money from unsuspecting people.

Or I should say, previously unsuspecting people.

I troll the Carnegie to get the out-of-towners. The ones whose spouses are on vacation—often with someone else's spouse—so excited over the illicitness of it all that their brains broadcast.

I get the illicitness, the secrecy, the guilt, and the arousal it all brings from their minds. I get the phone number by looking from their eyes at their own cell phone screens. I get names, e-mail addresses, and income verification from my lovely little app. Then I find out where they're staying with their paramour, along with their schedule. I show up at the hotel as they're checking out or if I'm really ambitious, for breakfast.

I take pictures in the deli first. Usually innocuous things on the surface—an intimate smile, a clasp of hands on the tabletop, a kiss promising more later.

Usually it's more than enough to show the cuckolded spouse the lovers in the deli in New York. The deli photos usually work because the cheating spouse isn't supposed to be in a deli or even in New York. The cheating spouses have lied, saying they're traveling somewhere else, working late in the office, any one of a dozen excuses. The excuses are even easier now, because of cell phones. (Gotta love 'em.) Now the cheating spouse can be in, say, Cancun, and the cuckolded spouse can just call the cell, and the cheating spouse can look at the weather channel and say, Jeez, you wouldn't believe the snow here in Denver, and the cuckolded spouse says, you should see it here at home and oh? How did the meeting go? And the cheating spouse makes up some lie or maybe it's not a lie like, *The meeting went beautifully.* Only the cuckolded and the cheating spouses would be talking about two different kinds of meetings.

That's the beauty of what I do, the meeting of my mind with the cheating spouse's. I not only get the images, the furtive guilt, and a few voyeuristic memories to tide me over on the lonely nights, I also get the excuses, full blown and clear. Often I get the excuses first, in fact, because the cheating spouses are always worried about how to spin the trip so that they don't get caught in a lie.

Except by little nosy parasites like me.

I take the pictures and make notes of the lies. I gather up a few clients on tourist nights, because those are the most lucrative. Experts say a cheating spouse spends upwards of 5K over the space of a year for an out-of-town affair, so that spouse comes from a household where 5K can be spent, spun, and not really missed.

Which means my fee looks cheap by comparison.

And that's what I say when I e-mail the poor cuckolded spouse. I use a high-end laptop for the e-mail. I bought the laptop for cash in Chicago, even though I use it in New York. That's the first sidestep, should anyone want to track me. The next is the e-mail addresses I use. I use seven different proxy sites, bouncing my e-mails through countries that don't cooperate with U.S. investigations very often.

I learned a lot from some pedophiles I found accidentally (those are minds you really don't want to troll). I gathered information on them too, and mailed it to the police. I do that occasionally, find people doing something illegal, and I get proof and I stop it. But from a distance. No one ever knows it's me, just like the cheating spouses never know I ratted them out. I spy, literally. Invisibly. I make good use of my voyeuristic tendencies.

At least, I like to think so.

In the case of the pedophiles, I learned a lot on my way to getting them arrested. I learned how many proxy servers it takes to keep a website hidden and how many e-mails you should send before you shut down the account and get a new one and how to scrub your computer (laptop) so that no one can find incriminating photos—and on and on and on.

Those guys were a wealth of information, which I feel was more than enough compensation for the crap memories they gave me, the ones I'll never be able to get out of my mind.

I gotta tell you, there are times this mind-surfing stuff is just plain disgusting. So disgusting you want to scrub your mind the way you'd scrub a gas station toilet before you ever sat down on the damn thing.

I use a lot of those computer skills in my cheating spouse business, which is where I make the bulk of my money. I send the anonymous e-mail, say I'm a friend they actually know—often, I pick convincing details from a variety of friends, courtesy of the cheating spouse's traitorous mind—and then I volunteer to hire someone who can spy and see if this is more than an innocent misunderstanding.

One in ten say no, they trust good old cheating spouse.

But those nine who say yes do so within a day, and then I contact them with a new e-mail address, pretending to be the private detective mentioned by me in a previous e-mail, a private detective who takes payment via Paypal, thank you very much. Five hundred dollar retainer, more if they want video, and I promise to have the entire thing resolved within a few days.

A week's work would pay my bills. But there are so many people out there, and so much trolling, and I get out a lot, this being New York, and I don't like having a lot of interaction—at least of the talking kind—so I usually have five to seven years expenses in the bank, not counting the investments—and me,

I never invested in securities or those risky derivatives or anything that wasn't pretty much a sure thing, just because I knew the financial guys weren't investing in the products they were peddling either. And if they're not going to put their money in their products, neither am I.

But I digress.

Because the old man bothers me.

He's bothered me since I met him.

He sat down, looked at me with those clear, intelligent eyes, and said, "Maggie the Cat," and then he waited.

In fact, he waited for me to say, "Do I know you?" because he knew I'd make a verbal gambit while I slid into his mind.

*Hello*, he thought. *I can almost feel you barging around in here.*

He replayed the thought twice, which let me know he couldn't feel me, but by then I was so startled, I almost backed out.

I'd met a few other stealth telepaths—that's creepy enough. They read me, I read them—it almost mimics real telepathy.

But the old man had no telepathy.

Now.

He'd had it and lost it, two years before I was born.

There's an empty spot in his mind, a burned out spot. I'd felt empty spots before, in Alzheimer's sufferers (please God don't ever let that happen to me), in people with traumatic brain injuries—that kind that impair their minds, and in people in comas (I tested that only a few times. Never again. Sometimes there's awake, trapped people in there, screaming but making no real sound).

But I'd only experienced the burned out empty spot a few other times before, mostly in recovering drug addicts. (You can't tell with current drug addicts. They're scary and I stay away from them, because otherwise, I might share their trip.) The recovering longtime addicts have a lot of empty spots in their brains. These folks are never quite right again, even if they're off the junk, and I know why.

It's like someone fried the circuits. Literally. There are normal connections, and then there are gaps. Big gaps. Empty spots. But more precisely, burned-out spots. Like a fire went through, but only destroyed selected parts of the building. The rest remains standing, but no one rebuilds the ruined parts.

The old man had a burned-out part. I checked. He only had one drug trip, and that one was accidental and odd, leaving no chemical reaction. It wasn't until I read his papers later that I realized he had vicariously shared an LSD trip, and it had destroyed his relationship with a woman he truly cared about.

I almost felt sad for him then. But I didn't entirely, because I wanted to know how he found me. Why he found me. What he wanted from me.

And those thoughts were carefully guarded in his mind.

Most people, when they guard, make the mistake of putting the guarded thoughts front and center. But the old man, he knew the best way to guard against a stealth telepath is to forget what you know. Put it away, far away, and don't think about it. Deny it. Don't remember it. Certainly don't concentrate on it.

My frustration must have shown on my face, because he smiled.

Then he stood. "I know you have questions," he said aloud. "I'll answer them tomorrow—at your usual Friday lunch place."

And he walked away. Quickly, almost at a jog.

He knew, the bastard. He knew how hard it was to probe over a distance, how much harder it was to go deep in a crowd. Other thoughts intrude, thoughts not his, not mine, random thoughts, other people's thoughts.

Guilty thoughts.

Damn. There were potential jobs in this deli.

That thought was enough to distract me, just for a moment, and I lost the thread of the old man's mind. David Selig's mind.

David Selig, Columbia graduate Class of 1956's mind.

I pulled out my iPhone and began tapping.

But for once, the damn program wasn't helping me. It was telling me things I already knew.

———

Five potential clients. Five. A better than average night.

I should've been elated.

Instead, it was everything I could do to get home, upload the pictures, and send the first e-mails. I had four hotels to hit in the next three days. (One couple was a twofer—she was guilty, he was guilty, they both worried about their spouses—and each other's spouses. [How civilized of them.])

I did my work, stared at my big screen, and thought about some mindless entertainment, but I knew it wouldn't help.

I needed more information on Selig.

I spent half the night trolling the web, and found out a bunch of random, somewhat useless things.

David Selig wrote for a living. Useful things, cheater kind of things, like English Literature for Dummies (which wasn't the exact title, since he wrote for a Dummies rip-off company, not the real Dummies company). He wrote teacher's guides on how to spot forged term papers. (I didn't realize the irony until later, when I learned he used to make his living writing term papers for lazy students.) He wrote all kinds of things, as well as freelanced edited, and freelanced copy-edited.

He even wrote one novel, badly received, on, of all things, telepathy. The dumb reviewers claimed that Selig didn't add anything new, that he seemed not to understand the phenomenon at all.

I was of half a mind to order the book, but I didn't. I wasn't sure how deep I wanted to get with this guy.

I had no idea then that we'd get deeper than I ever expected.

———

"How did you find me?" I asked.

We were in the Chinese restaurant around the corner from my apartment. I didn't know the name of the place because I'd never bothered to look. But it was old like the Carnegie Deli, but had never been remodeled. Ancient food smells caked the interior like the yellow paint.

I had ordered family style before he arrived, figuring if the old guy had been bluffing, I would have food for the next few days. A gigantic bowl of hot and sour soup steamed on the lazy Susan, along with an appetizer platter and a big plate of General Tsao's chicken. The old guy showed up and added a platter of stir-fry chicken with asparagus, a meal designed more for the health conscious than the things I'd ordered.

I'd ignored his food, concentrating on mine while I waited for him to answer. I wasn't asking how he found my regular Friday lunch spot, although I very well could have been. I was asking how he found me. Just me.

He ignored my question, at least at first, maybe waiting for me to probe his mind for it. I could, I suppose, but that empty spot in his brain bothered me. I deliberately didn't touch him mentally, listening instead to the random noise around me. Most of the thoughts were from the staff, and they weren't in English. They were in Mandarin or some other dialect, which I didn't speak. Sometimes you could get context from mood, but I wasn't trying. I let the unfamiliar sounds wash over me like a piece of music I hadn't heard before.

Finally, the old man used his chopsticks to remove a pot sticker from the appetizer platter.

"It bothers you that I found you," he said. "That's why you want to know."

He smiled at me. I dug into my General Tsao's chicken, keeping an eye on him, and trying to conceal my own expression.

He was irritating me already. People did that. In direct conversation, they often bothered me, just because their thoughts ran a half to a full step ahead of what they were going to say, and what they edited was a lot more interesting than what actually came out of their mouths.

But I wasn't monitoring his brain. I just didn't like his tone.

"You know what's fascinating," he said. "If you want to find someone nowadays, all you have to do is Google, and you get all kinds of information about a person."

He couldn't have Googled me and found me. I'd done it, which showed me just how little information there was on me. My name only appears a few times—in two separate alumni lists, one from high school and another from college—and in the blog of an old boyfriend who called me freaky and weird, which was a lot better than the terms he used for other old girlfriends, who were generally (according to him) slutty and stupid.

"All you need are a few contacts," the old man said, "and you can go beyond Google. You can, for example, find a driver's license or track a credit card or—"

"What do you want from me?" I snapped. I no longer cared if he knew that he was bothering me. He was trying to bother me, and he was succeeding.

He set the chopsticks down. He hadn't eaten the pot sticker. It sat in a pool of soy sauce, getting soggy and inedible.

"You're related to a man by the name of Tom Nyquist." All of the charm (what little there was of it) had left the old man's manner. He was deadly serious now.

I didn't know the name Tom Nyquist. I searched my memory, seeing if I'd ever run across it, and just as I was about to deny the connection, I remembered that there were Nyquists on my mother's side.

"I never met a Tom Nyquist," I said.

"I would be surprised if you had," the old man said. "He avoided family."

"No one ever mentioned him," I said.

"That's not a surprise either," the old man said. "He's a cousin five times removed or something like that. Your great-grandmother's cousin, I think. I don't remember exactly."

But he *did* remember exactly. I got the self-satisfaction of that thought without even trying. However, I didn't probe to find out the exact relationship.

Instead, I ate another bite of the General Tsao's then decided it was greasier than usual today. I grabbed a spring roll. "So? I might be related to some guy. So what?"

"So everything," the old man said. "There's a genetic component to your—what do you call it? Talent?"

That's what he used to call his. Along with a curse and a blessing and a special gift, and all those things you use when you're ambivalent about a part of yourself.

I shrugged. I wasn't going to tell him anything.

"That genetic component is rare. In my lifetime—or at least, in the lifetime of my gift—I'd only met a few people with the same ability. A few—"

And there he had a dim memory of a boy in school, a boy he hadn't liked. Somehow I was inside the old man's head even though I didn't want to be. That meant his personality was powerful.

As if I couldn't have figured that much out on my own.

"—didn't have much ability at all. Just a glimmer. But some had it strong. Just like I did. Just like you do."

"You think you know something about me," I said.

"I do know something about you," he said. "I know how you make your living. Smart, that. But sad, too. And dicey. It could get you in trouble."

"I don't do anything against the law." I sounded defensive, even to me.

He looked at me for a long moment, sizing me up. I almost dove deeper into his mind then, but I held back. Sometimes you really don't want to know what someone else is thinking.

"I suppose, technically, you're right," he said. "There are no laws against what you do because so few people can do it."

My cheeks warmed. I poured myself a cup of oolong tea just to cover my own discomfort.

"It wasn't your work that gave you away, though," he said. "It was your blog."

I started. No one was supposed to know about my blog. I signed up for it under a false name on a freebie site, and accessed it through my favorite proxy servers.

"Random Thoughts," he said. "Cute title. Enough to make people nervous, I bet, since the random thoughts aren't yours. They're theirs."

The real name of the blog was Random Thoughts Overheard Around New York. I did post random thoughts, the most interesting, the most unusual, the most bizarre. Sometimes I made comments—but usually only when I got mad.

I didn't get a lot of visitors, but those I did get returned often.

"Your proxy servers are good," the old man said, "but my guy's better. He found you. And you were on my list."

I didn't ask what list. I went into his brain this time. I was tired of the dance, tired of trying to stay out. He had something to tell me, and he was going to tell me the way most people did—avoiding the center of the topic, going at the edges, taking my damn time until I asked enough questions to show both interest and ignorance. Then he might—might— tell me what caused him to track me down.

The list was the beginning. His list was a long one. It had the names of all the biological relatives of himself and this Tom Nyquist. Selig never married. His family line ended with him; his sister was adopted. But he had cousins and second cousins and all kinds of peripheral relatives.

Nyquist had never married either, but he had accidentally fathered a few children. He also had a slew of nieces and nephews, whom I apparently descended from.

The list had actual highlights in Selig's mind. The highlights were in various reddish hues. It only took me a moment to figure out that he had highlighted anyone with a glimmer of telepathic ability. I found it amusing that he actually mentally saw the highlights in color.

If I hadn't already known the man was a perennial student, I would have realized it then. That highlighting of important information was trained, so ingrained in the older generations that they often thought in highlights—but usually in faded yellow highlights, covering black and white thoughts.

Selig's highlights were easy to track, not only because they were in color, but because he had memorized the names (and addresses) of the important ones. Out of several hundred relatives on both sides of both families that he found, there were about five names in red, four in pink (lesser talents, he dubbed them) and a few a pale rose.

My name was bright red and starred.

"So I'm related to these people. So what?" I said, mostly to keep him talking while I investigated the answers myself.

The deeper I went, the more emotion I found. Beneath it all, an anger, a sense of loss so profound that it almost unhinged me. Selig wanted his talent back. He wanted it back and he wanted—

"—to use it to communicate. I think we only got half of the talent," he said. It took me a moment to realize that the calm words he was speaking matched the charged emotions I found in his head. "If there's a genetic component, it has to be more than just a random mutation. The genes had to exist for a reason. And it stands to reason that there's another group out there, one that can insert thoughts."

I shuddered. Insert thoughts. Instead of passively receiving other people's thoughts, someone would be able to control what others actually thought.

I had tried doing that early on, particularly with good-looking boys back when I was in school. I wanted them to think I was attractive. I wanted them to see me as something other than the skinny toothpick of a girl whom they felt sorry for because she wasn't pretty or built or even very interesting.

Little did they know about how interesting I was.

And that was the problem. Little did they or anyone else know.

Except this Selig guy.

He knew—and it made me uncomfortable.

"You don't have any talent any more," I said as brutally as I could, mostly to shut him up.

It worked too. His mouth clamped closed, and anger flared at me—*stupid cunt, who the hell does she think she's talking to? Doesn't she know*—and then he clamped on the thoughts as well, getting up, leaving his napkin on the table, murmuring an excuse, and I thought—stupidly and inconsequentially— that he was leaving me with the bill, not that it mattered, I could afford it, but it was that kind of rudeness, that kind of thoughtlessness that made people undesirable to me, any interaction always left me feeling like I was stuck with the bill, the emotional bill mostly, the shadow of someone else's pain or the force of someone else's anger, the names he just called me in his head, the filth trailing away with him as he disappeared—not out the door, but in that narrow corridor that housed the men's room.

He was calming down.

I had to do the same.

I pulled the wadded twenties out of my front pocket. I never carry a purse because a purse would identify me as female. Nowadays I like being the androgynous scrawny kid, even though I'm really not a kid any more.

I had gotten most of the answers I wanted. He found me through a name, a relationship, a blog, and "a guy" who had hacked his way to me, just like I hacked my way to my clients.

And he wanted something from me, something that had to do with those burned out spots in his brain.

I had long ago stopped caring about people who wanted something from me. It turned out most human interactions were all about wanting. Wanting to ease loneliness. Wanting to get information. Wanting to get even the scrawny girl into bed because a little sex with an ugly person was better than none at all.

I waved the money at the waiter, who came over with some to-go boxes, bags, and the check. I put the twenties on top of the check and was packing up the food when Selig came back.

"Caught you. Good," he said. "Because otherwise I would have had to go to your apartment."

He said that to put me off balance, and it worked. Of course he knew where I lived. Of course. He had found my blog which was the hardest thing about me to track, so he had found everything else as well—the bank accounts, the investments, and the apartment with my address front and center and only around the damn corner.

He was still angry, but he had tamped it back, knowing that I could have found worse things, things that would have angered him more, and I hadn't.

I could look now, but I didn't want to.

I just wanted this lunch to end.

"Sit." he said.

I did, leaving the food half packed. I stared at him as the waiter brought back my change. I didn't touch that either.

Selig held out a giant cotton swab wrapped in plastic. "All I'm asking is that you rub this on the inside of your cheek. I'm going to send it to a lab for a DNA profile. It'll be anonymous."

I stared at him.

"We're doing a study," he said, his mouth a quarter step behind his thoughts. "You, the others I can find, to see if there's—"

I stopped listening to his words and concentrated on his thoughts. They were looking for a genetic marker for telepathy. This was actually legitimate research, with real funding, albeit from a private company out of California. The daughter of one of the red-highlighted names, who knew all about the telepathy and hated it, decided to see if she could find the marker so that she could abort any of her fetuses who had it.

Selig disapproved of that. He disapproved of a lot of the reasons behind the research, but he was willing to use her. Just like he was willing to use a few other interested parties, to see if they could find the corresponding gene, the one that allowed thoughts to transmit.

Privately, he wondered if some of the people called charismatic had that ability. The power to charm, to persuade, might simply be a mental push—

"Bullshit," I said. "There're no mental pushes. I would have found them in all the searching I did. No one ever convinces anyone else of anything, not just by thinking of it."

He looked startled. Apparently his thoughts were way ahead of his mouth or maybe he hadn't meant to say any of that.

I had probed deeper than I had planned.

"You just want this research to work so that you can get your power back," I said. "You feel so weak and ineffectual without it. You—"

"I felt weak and ineffectual *with* it," he said. "It doesn't change your life."

"You don't believe that," I said. Because he didn't. He missed it. He missed knowing what people thought. He really missed learning where he stood with other people, who they really believed him to be, what they wanted him to be.

He missed it now, in conversation with me.

"You should care about this research," he said. "Because you're going to lose your ability. Everyone does. I've studied that too. Somewhere around forty, forty-one, forty-two, it just fades away. And there's nothing you can do about it."

I felt stunned. I probed a bit more, saw the evidence he had seen—everyone he had known with the gift (from a glimmering to a full-blown power) had lost it in middle age.

My stomach clenched—and I knew that wasn't because of the greasy General Tsao's.

Another word floated through his head.

*Yet.* That was the word. *There's nothing you could do about it. Yet.*

Because behind the hocus-pocus and the dream of two-way telepathy, he hoped for gene therapy. Maybe some stem cell research, the ability to regrow that burned out portion of the brain.

His hope was so deep that it pained me.

I looked away.

Then I grabbed the stupid cotton swab. I opened the package, pulled out the swab and rubbed it on the inside of my cheek. Then I held the wet thing out to him.

"Now what?"

But he was already pulling out a plastic container.

"Thank you," he said. "I'll let you know the results."

"Please don't," I said.

He looked at me then, his face full of contempt. "You'll wonder."

"No, I won't," I said.

"When your abilities go," he said. "You'll wonder if I found the solution, if I could have helped you before the talent frizzed out. Because that's what mine did. It frizzed out. Like a radio signal, getting dimmer and dimmer, until you can't hear a damn thing. You're all alone in your head."

I wanted to be alone in my head. I've always wanted that. I live among crowds because it's safer than living with one other person. Crowds provide white noise. While only one other person's thoughts seep into mine, like his had done.

But I also live among crowds because I can't stand to be alone. Living in a house on some deserted island would drive me insane. I need interaction. I need to see varied faces. I need stimulation from new cuisines to new entertainments, and I wouldn't get any of that by being alone.

"Your scientists won't find anything," I said.

"Nonsense," he said. "We will. You know we will. We've already found a lot. We'll find more. And you'll want to know."

I could feel his desperation as if it were my own. Or maybe it *was* my own. He had tapped into something I thought buried. My fear and concern and love of my difference.

That ambivalence, the kind I accused him of. I have it too.

He had tapped into my ambivalence because he still had his. About himself, about his past, and about his present.

He had hated who he was then, and he hated who he was now.

I don't hate myself, not with the vehemence that he felt.

But I don't like myself much either.

I feel as trapped by my abilities as he had, maybe more so, because I use my abilities to make my living. He had resisted that, and when he tried, he had done it badly— deliberately, it seemed, because he worried about other people's privacy.

In the 21$^{st}$ century, privacy is an old-fashioned concept.

Even he had to know that.

"Fine," I said after a moment. "So tell me. But don't expect me to care."

"Oh, you will," he said. "Believe me you will."

———

I played that conversation over and over in my mind. Both of the conversations I had with him, replaying them like a CD stuck on repeat. For a while, I wondered what about the conversations so obsessed me, and then I realized what it was.

He knew me better than anyone else. Certainly better than anyone I knew now, and maybe better than anyone I had known before. I don't make friends easily, and I had never told anyone about my abilities. Not even my parents.

I hadn't even really told him. He had figured it out.

Because he had had the same abilities once.

And those old abilities meant he understood me, maybe better than I understood myself.

I did some research on my own, going over the names I'd seen on his list, reviewing, finding the few people he had known who had the same abilities. Tom Nyquist killed himself shortly after his fiftieth birthday—alone and unmourned. Selig was still alive, and so were those people with glimmers—although the glimmers, what they called their intuition, had indeed faded with age.

And that terrified me.

The thought of losing my ability—of having it burn out—terrified me.

I found myself studying professional athletes, wondering how they lived with their inevitable decline. Most of them became regular citizens, like Selig. Forgotten except for dusty images on old sports programs, except for names and stats in old record books.

I wouldn't be forgotten, because I was never known.

And that was how—that was why—I ended up spending more time with the old man. I didn't believe in his genetic pipedream. I figured there were a lot better uses for gene therapy than rebuilding some psychic's one-way communications equipment. And I met (and didn't trust) the lead scientist, a woman set on eradicating psychics with pseudoscience, the way that certain Christian sects wanted to eradicate homosexuality with prayer.

I'm a planner. Worse, I'm a planner with a pessimistic bent. I can't assume that science will save me. Nor can I hope that I'll avoid the old man's fate.

So I had to figure out how to survive that fate, just like star athletes survive retirement. I probed Selig's mind. I read the journal he kept as the talent faded. And I looked deeply at that burned out spot. It did seem like a reservoir that had emptied of water, and then imploded by trying to force itself to refill.

I could ease off the probes of other people, but then I might be wasting the last decade of my talent. I wouldn't panic like Selig had. But I knew I'd be at loose ends, like he was even forty years later.

I needed something to keep me occupied, and that something couldn't be the dream of a miracle gene therapy resuscitation.

It had to be something else.

And finally, the answer came from a completely unexpected place.

———

It started with six kids, six teenagers riding the 1 train down the island, trolling, as it turned out, for victims.

I caught edges of their thoughts in a crowded subway car. I wouldn't have noticed, except that the thoughts were loud and insistent and *excited*. The kids used to bum bash but had moved on to rich snobs—their term—which really was cover for beating poor middle-class wage earners just trying to survive the day.

The kids played it like a mugging, usually after dark, and they always recorded it. Then they'd upload it to a YouTube wannabe site, competing with other kids for prizes—like the best bruising, the worst beating without serious injury, the most cash recovered, and on and on.

I only figured out who belonged to the thoughts because everyone else on the car was moving away from them. Subtly moving, sliding just a bit to one side or turning their bodies away so their backs would be to the kids.

I couldn't tell if the movements were because the kids were big—and they were, football big—or because of the things the kids were saying.

I was having trouble differentiating what they were saying from what they were thinking; the thoughts were that loud.

I snuck out my own cell phone and recorded them, capturing audio and visual. If they said anything incriminating at all, I could use it, because I also had their names, their home addresses, and the name of the website along with the titles they'd given to the videos they were oh-so-proud of.

I didn't follow them—I figured I didn't need to (and didn't dare, since my skinny kid looks and my middle class bank balances put me in two of their target demographics). I got home, so furious that I could hardly think.

I logged onto my blog, wrote down their thoughts, wrote down my reaction—and, spent, paused.

I wondered if I'd be able to do this when the ability burned out. This vigilante shit both frightened and exhilarated me. It made me feel a bit like the Batman, fighting crime when no one knew exactly who I was. I'd lose this too, and I'd miss it a lot more than the income. I'd miss this most of all.

I ended the blog with a statement of disgust, then uploaded the video from my cell phone so that I could e-mail it to police.

And as I watched it, I realized that the kids had said enough to incriminate themselves. They spoke half of their thoughts aloud, which was why people moved away from them. They were trying to scare the folks on the train—and they succeeded.

But in the process, they also confessed, enough so that someone with my tech skills, even one who wasn't psychic, would be able to find their posted videos, enough that I could still contact the police—only without the names and addresses.

And, I would wager, I might have had enough to find out if the kids were in the system. I could illegally download face identification software.

There is no privacy in the 21st century.

That's what I realized, deep down, maybe for the first time. There is no privacy at all.

And somehow that relieves me. Even the worst case still allows me to spy on people. Sure, I can't find out what they thought of *me*, but that matters less to me than it had to Selig. I'm more disconnected than he was, and I want to remain that way.

But I want to spy more than he had ever wanted to. And I will still be able to do that, even without being able to read minds.

I will plan for the death of my talent. That's what I'm calling this potential event. Not some dramatic term like losing my mind. Selig may have lost his, but I'm going to keep mine—at least as much of it as I can.

I eat well.

I sleep every night.

I still do the crosswords and the language exercises. I use my talent, each and every day.

And hope that I'm going to be the lucky one, the one whose talent survives. Because if we're talking science—and the old man does all the time—we don't have a large enough statistical sample to know if everyone's talent flames out at forty or if only a few people's do. Or maybe, with practice and less angst, the damn talent will remain—like aging athletes in golf and cycling and baseball—tearing down records, doing what was once considered impossible.

The old man scares me, but he's also saved me.

He not only gave me hope for the future, but he gave me a future. A future I didn't even know I had to plan for, at least until I met him.

I repay him with an occasional swab of DNA, a bit more truth than I would give to other people, and some help in his search for more people like us.

I owe him that much.

I owe myself that much.

And we both know it.

# Bad News from the Vatican

## Mike Resnick

Mike Resnick is one of the best-selling authors in science fiction, and one of the most prolific. His many novels include *Santiago, The Dark Lady, Stalking The Unicorn, Birthright: The Book of Man, Paradise, Ivory, Soothsayer, Oracle, Lucifer Jones, Purgatory, Inferno, A Miracle of Rare Design, The Widowmaker, The Soul Eater, A Hunger in the Soul, The Return of Santiago, Starship: Mercenary, Starship: Rebel*, and *Stalking the Vampire*. His collections include *Will the Last Person to Leave the Planet Please Turn Off the Sun?, An Alien Land, Kirinyaga, A Safari of the Mind, Hunting the Snark and Other Short Novels*, and *The Other Teddy Roosevelt*. As editor, he's produced *Inside the Funhouse: 17 SF stories about SF, Whatdunits, More Whatdunits, Shaggy B.E.M Stories, New Voices in Science Fiction, These Are My Funniest*, a long string of anthologies co-edited with Martin H. Greenberg— *Alternate Presidents, Alternate Kennedys, Alternate Warriors, Aladdin: Master of the Lamp, Dinosaur Fantastic, By Any Other Fame, Alternate Outlaws*, and *Sherlock Holmes in Orbit*, among others—as well as two anthologies co-edited with Gardner Dozois, and *Stars: Stories Inspired by the Songs of Janis Ian*, edited with Janis Ian. He won the Hugo Award in 1989 for "Kirinyaga." He won another Hugo Award in 1991 for another story in the Kirinyaga series, "The Manumouki," and another Hugo and Nebula in 1995 for his novella "Seven Views of Olduvai Gorge." His most recent books are a number of new collections, *The Incarceration of Captain Nebula and Other Stories, Win Some, Lose Some: The Complete Hugo-Nominated Short Fiction of Mike Resnick*, and *Master of the Galaxy*, and two new novels, *The Doctor and the Rough Rider* and *The Doctor and the Dinosaurs*. He lives with his wife, Carol, in Cincinnati, Ohio.

Mike Resnick says: "Bob Silverberg was a giant—albeit a very young one—when I broke into the field in the 1960s. These days he's an Elder Giant, but the operative word remains. Just as John Campbell dragged science fiction, kicking and screaming, into the mid-20th Century, Bob and a small handful of other dragged it, screaming even louder, into the late 20th Century. I've always admired "Good News From the Vatican", Bob's 1971 Nebula winner about the first robot pope. When I was invited to contribute to this volume, there was no question concerning to which story I would write a sequel, because I think the ending of Bob's story implied numerous consequences, and I thought it would be interesting to examine some of them. I hope you—and Bob—agree."

I am Cardinal Richard Moore, and the task of telling you the true story of the reign of Pope Sisto Settimo has fallen upon my shoulders.

I was born in Chicago 77 years ago, in the northeastern area of the city known as Rogers Park. I grew up there, less than a mile from Loyola University, which of course I attended. In due course I became a priest, and over the years I rose in the hierarchy, becoming an archbishop at 50 and a cardinal a decade later. I had hoped to be assigned to the Chicago diocese, where my roots were, but instead I was invited to serve in the Vatican, an invitation that I of course accepted.

I was a member of the College of Cardinals when Pius XIII died, and I had no hesitation about casting my vote for Cardinal Mechanismo, which was his name before he became the first robot Pope in history. He was possessed of a brilliant mind, he was an expert in Catholic doctrine, and he clearly was better versed in his religion than any of the other candidates. He was not shaped quite like a man. He moved on treads, his torso was more rectangular than human in form—but his smile was contagious, his eyes missed nothing, and if he had a single quality in abundance other than his intellect it was his compassion.

We—the College, the Curia, the entire Vatican—anticipated some resistance, but there was much less than we had expected. After all, he did not come directly from a laboratory to the Papacy. He had served in some of the worst hellholes in the world, places we would never send a living priest. His work had been exemplary, he had never complained, and wherever he went he attracted people to the Church. When his successes could no longer be overlooked, he was brought to Rome for a decade. Then, at his own request—which was unheard of; no member of the Curia ever asks to be reassigned once he is in Rome—he was transferred once more, first to Tibet and then to the Central African Republic, where he ended the reigns of two genocidal maniacs, not by force of arms, but force of faith and force of reason.

By then the international media realized what a very special priest was among us, and after he negotiated the freedom of Father Rishad, who had been incarcerated in Pakistan for sixteen long years, it would have been all but impossible not to elevate him to the position of Cardinal—and indeed that is what John XXV did. By the time Pius XIII ascended to the papacy, Mechanismo had been a member of the Church for 93 years, and was recalled to the Vatican to serve almost as an animated history book.

Then there was what came to be known as the Brussels Incident. Pius, accompanied by Cardinals Carciofo and

Mechanismo, went to hold a Holy Mass in Brussels and speak to the clergy on matters of import to Western Europe. I didn't go, but of course I was in constant contact with all of them—well, all except Pius—throughout the conference. You all heard about it. A madman named Jean-Claude Breque led a small army of equally-deranged followers into the Cathedral, intent upon killing Pius.

They had him surrounded, at gunpoint, when Mechanismo stepped forward and said that if they must kill *someone* to take his life instead. Breque laughed and said that Mechanismo wasn't really alive. And with holographic cameras trained on the tense and potentially cataclysmic scene, Mechanismo argued with decisive logic that he and Breque were both God's children. He was prepared to stand on his record and face his God for judgment; was Breque?

Within a handful of minutes Breque was in tears and on his knees, and Mechanismo had stepped forward and laid his shining hands on Breque's head and was speaking to him so softly that even the most sensitive holocams and microphones couldn't pick it up.

When the police arrived a few moments later and went to arrest Breque, Mechanismo raised his hand and told them to stop, that Breque had repented of his actions and would be accompanying the Pope's party back to the Vatican. And Breque remains there to this day, serving as Mechanismo's (or as he's now known, Sisto's) personal valet.

It was the Brussels Incident that allowed some people to think the unthinkable: that maybe, just maybe, it was time for a robot Pope, as long as the robot was Mechanismo. When the press asked him his thoughts about it, he replied that he had been created without ambition—except to be the best child of God he could be—and that he had no desire to become Pope.

That seemed to end it. But then, the third or fourth time it came up, someone asked him if he would refuse the Papacy if it were offered.

"The Papacy is never *offered*," he explained patiently. "It is God's will, and what servant of God would oppose His will?"

That opened up the subject all over again.

Before long everyone was choosing sides. *Should* there be a robot Pope? Did it say anywhere in Church law that there shouldn't be? His knowledge was unchallenged; so was his empathy and his compassion. But did knowledge necessarily lead to wisdom? There were a lot of examples of it having done so, and more than a few examples to the contrary.

The debate continued unabated until a few days after Pius's death, not from any particular cause, but simply from the combined infirmities of old age. And then came the vote, and suddenly the debates and disagreements were over, for we had Sisto Settimo—Sixtus the Seventh—the very first robot Pope. His initial appearance as the new Pontiff, which saw him soaring above the Sistine Chapel via his hidden levitator jets to bless the entire city was absolutely magnificent. It made every newscast in the world, and was shown again and again. You couldn't ask for a more memorable debut.

The next two years were routine. (Well, as routine as a Pope's life gets.) He issued two minor encyclicals, made brief visits to Brazil, Slovakia, and New Zealand, and saw an endless line of visitors—politicians, actors, wealthy donors to local dioceses of the Church, even the President of Iraq.

His first major trip was to be to the United States. It was to last two weeks, and he would be speaking in major venues all across the country—baseball stadiums, football stadiums, even a racetrack.

I still remember when we began planning it. We decided he would appear nowhere that couldn't accommodate at least 75,000 people, and to borrow a theatrical term, we expected every place he spoke to be SRO. He would end the whirlwind tour on the final day, meeting in private with the President, and then, for the first time in history, a Pope would enter the Capital dome and address the Congress of the United States.

We actually had to hire a pair of top security companies from America to help us determine what we needed to assure his safety. A bullet couldn't injure him, of course—though if properly placed, it could require a new prismatic eye or possibly even a new audio transmitter (though of course Sixtus had back-up systems). But what about a hidden metallic plate that could be suddenly electrified when he stepped on it? What about super-powerful magnets, the same things that could wipe a computer's memory clean? Was there some powerful acid that could be hidden in something that could pass the electronic security devices, such as, say, a child's squirt gun?

Those were the threats *we* thought of, but we were a handful of Cardinals, Bishops and priests who, despite our world travels, had led truly sheltered lives when it came to things like this. The companies informed us of 53 methods that had been used against other robots in business and politics, and told us what measures they would take to prevent such attacks. They then laid out another dozen that the criminal element—and the fanatics—hadn't yet attempted, but for which they were prepared.

They requested access to Sixtus, explaining that of course not all robots were constructed alike, and they needed to examine him to determine any potential vulnerabilities he might have.

I was having dinner with Cardinals Asciuga and Carciofo, and I asked why we had to go to all this trouble and put the Pope through these personal indignities—or, if they *were* necessary, why we hadn't done so with his New Zealand and Brazilian and Slovakian trips.

"Because he only went to totally protected areas and every person who got within a mile of him had passed through thorough security checks," answered Asciuga, "and then he had flown in and out on our private plane. But in America, he'll be in a different hotel every night, a different city every day, and there will be days when one hundred thousand people are within weapon range of him."

"Surely he doesn't have to stay in hotels," I said. "After all, he never sleeps."

"He is not a man, so he feels he must do everything men do so that they will accept him," replied Asciuga. Suddenly a grim smile flashed briefly across his face. "I've already tried to talk him out of it."

"In fact," added Carciofo, "I suggested that he simply appear on holovision. His answer was that if he did that, why was he traveling to America? Why didn't he just record his sermons here and transmit them?" He sighed. "He is the Pope of the people, and he refuses to cloister himself in the Vatican any more than his predecessors did."

So preparations continued. Word reached us that six of the stadiums had already sold out, although "sold out" is a misnomer, because Sixtus refused to appear in any venue that charged people to see him. Still, they couldn't have millions showing up, as was possible in a dozen of the larger cities, so tickets were given out on a first-come first-served basis.

It was seventeen days before he was due to leave that Sixtus issued a new Papal encyclical, which made clear, beyond any shadow of a doubt, that the Church was still unalterably opposed to abortion under any circumstances, and that anyone who participated in an abortion—and it was clear that he meant mothers as well as medics—was guilty of the mortal sin of murder.

It was well-written and well-reasoned, totally in keeping with previous teachings and encyclicals. It should have been read by members of the hierarchy and the clergy, made the subject of a Sunday sermon or two, and not forgotten but filed away in the great library with all the other Papal encyclicals, to be read and referred to by Church scholars.

That's what its fate should have been. Instead it became the most important encyclical in history.

President Bradford Egan happened to hold a press conference two days later. Mostly he talked about the newly-established lunar colony, and the recent riots in Uruguay, and the economy. He was about to end it when one of the reporters asked him a question about the encyclical.

"I'm afraid I'm not aware of it," said the President.

"It claims that abortion is a mortal sin, without exception," was his answer.

"That's hardly anything new," answered Egan. "That's been the Church's position throughout history."

"Since America and Switzerland still allow abortion, it was anticipated—hoped, actually—that Pope Sixtus would moderate his position."

"Well, he didn't," said Egan, "and I can't say I'm surprised."

"What is your position as a Catholic, sir?"

"Catherine and I are a little long in the tooth to be considering any more children"—he smiled, and a number of the reporters chuckled since he and the First Lady were both in their mid-sixties—"but as a practicing Catholic, I would never have considered abortion, and I'm sure I speak for Catherine too."

"Even in the case of rape, or to save her life?"

"Stop splitting hairs," he said, and he sounded a little annoyed. "You asked, I answered. I'm opposed to abortion."

"But America has twenty million abortions a year," persisted the reporter.

"As the President I am sworn to uphold the Constitution," answered Egan, "and until it's changed or reinterpreted, the Constitution of the United States permits abortion."

"Don't you feel a moral conflict?"

"No more than I did this morning, before you told me about the encyclical. I was elected as the President, not as the Catholic President or the white President or the heterosexual President."

That actually brought a standing ovation from the forty or so journalists in the room, and it was the end of the press conference—and (we thought) of the issue.

But that evening Sixtus joined us for dinner, which he had never done before, since of course he did not eat food.

"Your Holiness!" said Carciofo, as we all rose to our feet. "To what do we owe the honor of this visit?"

"I wish to make a speech tonight," said the Pope.

"You mean a sermon?" I asked.

"I mean what I said," replied Sixtus. "The only audience I require will be the holo cameras." He turned to me. "Richard, you are an American."

"I *was*, Your Holiness," I said. "Now I am a citizen of the Vatican."

"But you grew up in America, and you understand better than the others how it works."

"Perhaps," I said hesitantly, because I couldn't see what he was driving at.

"Can the President change the Constitution by executive fiat?"

"No, Your Holiness."

"Can he disobey it?"

"I suppose Presidents disobey it on trivial matters all the time."

"And on something major?" he persisted.

"Never," I said adamantly.

"Never?" he repeated.

"Never successfully," I amended. "Actually, it's been done twice. One President resigned from office, and the other committed suicide."

"I was afraid that would be your answer," said Sixtus. "Thank you, Richard."

"I'm honored to have been of help, Your Holiness—*if* I have," I said.

"You have," he assured me.

"Might I ask what this is about?" interjected Bishop Mboka, who had recently arrived from Zambia.

"Come to the holo studio tonight at nine o'clock and all will be made clear," said Sixtus. He turned to Cardinal Asciuga. "Have the technicians there ten minutes before nine."

Asciuga bowed. "It shall be done, Your Holiness."

Then he was gone, and we spent the rest of the meal discussing what had just transpired and what it might portend. But none of us guessed the truth.

We all arrived by 8:30 PM and took seats some thirty feet away from the speaker's platform. The holo crew showed up a few minutes later and made sure everything was working. Then *he* appeared, clad in his silver and gold papal robes. He looked neither right nor left, but took his place and stood absolutely motionless, for all intents and purposes a deactivated machine, until one of the holo operators began giving him the countdown. When he reached "Five" he stopped speaking and just held up five fingers, then four, then three, and finally just a fist.

"Good evening," said Sixtus in perfect, unaccented English. "I come to you bearing unhappy tidings. As many of you know, I have been planning to visit your country in just two more weeks." A pause. "I am afraid I must cancel that trip."

There was a gasp of surprise among the assembled cardinals and bishops, but he paid us no attention.

"Not long ago I published my third encyclical, which is entitled *In Sanctimonia of Humanus Vita*. It explains in more detail than ever before, with more rigorous reasoning, why the Church is unalterably opposed to the practice of abortion. We believe that the human soul is created at the moment of conception, and the advances of medical science have actually confirmed this." He paused to let the statement register with his unseen audience. "There was a time when almost every premature baby died, and science—which claims to be rational but is all too often merely Godless—assured us that all of those millions upon millions of aborted babies were without souls, that if there was a soul it took the full term of the mother's pregnancy to appear. But over the centuries we have found ways to keep alive those babies who have been carried for first seven months, then six, then less than half the normal term. Each of you knows someone, a family member or a friend, who was born months early, and surely none can deny that they have souls. It is inevitable that we will soon be able to save human children, possessed of souls, two and three months into a mother's pregnancy, and one day we will save them even sooner. So medical science, which in the past has been the enemy of so many unwanted children of God, has now found ways to begin making amends for its past sins."

Another pause, and his mechanical eyes seemed to bore into the holocam.

"The practice of abortion, once widespread, has over the past century been outlawed in almost all civilized countries," he continued, with an emphasis on the word *civilized*. "Even China, once one of the worst offenders, has recently forbidden it. Only one major country maintains this barbaric practice." And we all knew which country that was.

"Your President, Bradford Egan, is a practicing Catholic. He believes abortion is a mortal sin. And yet he will not lift a finger to eradicate this evil practice in the country over which he presides. I cannot break bread with a Catholic who willfully allows this practice to continue, nor will I visit a country that gives legal cover to those who are serial"—a pregnant pause—"*or single*"—another pause—"practitioners of this singularly immoral act. I wish conditions were otherwise, and perhaps someday they will be, at which time your Shepherd will be proud to visit that portion of his flock which resides in the United States of America."

He fell silent, and when it was clear he was not going to say anything further the cameras stopped.

"Do you mean it, Your Holiness?" asked Cardinal Asciuga.

Sixtus merely stared at him, as if the question not worth the effort of answering.

"But all the arrangements have been made!" protested the Cardinal, who had spent weeks making those arrangements.

He looked directly at Asciuga, "Unmake them." Then he turned to the head of the holo crew. "Send a copy of that to every computer network, every American video and holo station, and bounce it off every satellite capable of transmitting it."

"Would you like to record it in Italian as well?" asked a crew member.

"If you will check your computer in another hour," replied Sixtus, "you will find translations in all the major languages of the globe."

"Do you want it sent to every holo station in the world?"

Sixtus shook his head. "This is between me and the people and President of America. The other countries will pick up the transmissions, of course, but I don't want the Americans to think I am trying to bring international pressure on them to change their laws. They will do it because it is the right and moral thing to do."

"Or they won't," I said dubiously.

He looked directly at me. "Or they won't," he agreed.

"Your Holiness," I said, "that legal decision has been in force for a very long time. It's been more than two centuries since abortion was illegal."

He continued staring at me. "And your point, Richard?"

"It's very awkward," I said uncomfortably.

"You are among friends," he said more gently. "And I have asked for your honest opinion."

"Your Holiness, the United States was founded on the principle of the separation of church and state. I think injecting yourself into their politics will be resented by a large majority of the people."

"Pius XII listened to similar advice in 1940," he said. "The result was Nazi Germany."

"There would have been a Nazi Germany with or without him," I blurted, and then immediately began to apologize. "I am sorry, Your Holiness. I have no right to—"

"It is all right, Richard," he said. "You are quite right when you say there would have been a Nazi Germany regardless of Pius's actions." He looked at all of us. "But the Church would not have been accused to looking the other way, or, worse still, of being complicit."

"But we weren't!" said Carciofo. "Those are vile slanders voiced by the ignorant and the bigoted."

"I know we weren't," replied Sixtus calmly. "But it was our initial inaction that gave birth to those slanders." He paused once more, and I realized that, more than with any other speaker, his pauses were for emphasis, because they usually proceeded something important. "We have been inactive on *this* front long enough, and if you are inactive long enough, it is indistinguishable from complicity." He turned back to me. "Richard?"

"Yes, Your Holiness?" I said.

"You know America better than anyone else in this room. Will my canceling the trip precipitate an attack on the Vatican?"

"Of course not," I said.

"Will it lead to anti-Catholic pogroms?"

"Certainly not."

"Will they burn churches because I choose to remain at home?"

"No."

"That makes it very easy to take a moral stand then, does it not?" he said, and his mechanical lips curled into an amused smile.

"You would take one regardless, Your Holiness," I said.

"Yes, I would. But I hope this little talk will encourage the doubters to take it with me."

"Where you lead, we will follow," said Asciuga, and everyone in the room nodded or voiced their agreement.

"I never doubted it," said Sixtus in his most tranquil tones, and then he was gone.

"What do you think?" asked Cardinal Ortiz, who had been silent for most of the discussion.

No one answered.

"I'm asking *you*, Richard," he persisted. "You grew up there. What will happen? Will their Supreme Court ever reverse itself?"

I shook my head. "It's been settled law for centuries. I can't imagine a case getting all the way up to the Supreme Court with the number of decisions that have already been laid down."

"Would they change the Constitution?" he asked. "Add an amendment outlawing abortion?"

"It's harder to pass an amendment than you think," I told him. "Besides, I think most Americans are in favor of abortion."

"That's insane!" chimed in Carciofo.

"I stated that poorly," I apologized. "No, of course most Americans don't actively favor abortion. What they favor is not telling someone else whether or not *she* can have an abortion."

"That doesn't make any sense," continued Carciofo. "That's like saying they don't believe in murder, but they don't mind if their neighbor goes on a killing spree."

"Then I must still be wording it poorly," I said. "But I do know one thing: Americans don't like anyone else telling them what to do, whether those suggestions come from another country or a religion."

"I just don't understand how such a barbaric practice can still be happening in a civilized country," said Ortiz.

"Let's be honest," I said. "People have been performing abortions since before the birth of Our Lord. And most Americans feel that by making it legal, it's relatively safe. What I mean is, abortions aren't going to stop, but at least this way it's done in sterile surroundings by doctors, not in back alleys by midwives."

"I've heard this all before," said Carciofo. "Civilized nations don't buy into it."

I was about to point out how many times in the past three centuries my uncivilized nation had saved his civilized nation's ass—but I immediately began blushing in shame, not only for the thought but for the words I would have used.

"The Pope has spoken," I said. "Let us pray that men of goodwill and better judgment listen to him."

Bishop FitzPatrick spoke up for the first time. "But he hasn't really spoken at all," he said in troubled tones. "He cancelled a trip, that's all. And he urged people not to have abortions, which Popes have been doing probably all the way back to Peter. But he didn't *do* anything."

"Such as?" asked Asciuga.

FitzPatrick shrugged. "I don't know. *Something.*"

"He is a spiritual leader, not a political one," said Asciuga.

*And who knows?* I thought. *With all those other physical attributes that we once thought impossible, for all I know he's listening to every word of this from six rooms away.* Then I thought further. *Actually, that might not be a bad idea. Not that he needs consensus, but it can't hurt for him to know what we say frankly to each other in his absence.*

We spoke a little further, solved nothing, went off to our evening prayers, and returned to our quarters.

I'd been in Rome for a long time, and in truth I didn't know very much about President Egan, so I sat at my desk and ordered my computer to bring up his biography.

"There have been seven full-length biographies of Bradford Egan, plus nine holographic documentaries," said the machine promptly. "Which would you prefer?"

"Just tell me very briefly what his history and accomplishments are."

"Define 'briefly'."

I grimaced. "Less than ten minutes," I said. "Just the most important facts."

It was interesting, to say the least. Egan had been a star football player in college, as well as being Phi Beta Kappa. He was an entrepreneur who'd started three businesses, all totally different, all wildly innovative and successful, and he was a self-made multi-millionaire before he was thirty.

Then came the incident that changed his life. Thieves broke into his house—one of his bodyguards was in their employ—killed his two other bodyguards, and demanded the code to his safe and the computer ID and password to his main bank account. He refused. They roughed him up pretty badly, but he was adamant. One of them actually gouged his left eye out. He remained silent. Then, frightened that he would bleed to death, the thieves fled. A neighbor noticed them, alerted the police, the thieves were apprehended, and Egan was rushed to the hospital, where he was patched up and given a prosthetic left hand and a new eye.

When he emerged a few weeks later, he decided to use the attendant publicity to run for Congress. He was up against a popular nine-term incumbent, and was given no chance at all. He won in a landslide.

Four years later he ran against the Senate Majority leader, who happened to be from his state, and beat him handily. He spent twelve years in the Senate, retired to run for governor, served a couple of terms, and decided to retire from public life.

Public life wouldn't hear of it, and when the Presidential nominating convention deadlocked between two candidates, his name came up and he was drafted—and won.

"Thank you, computer," I said. "You may deactivate now."

I began pacing the room, considering what I'd learned. Bradford Egan was a remarkable man, no question about it. He'd been a winner in sports, in education, in business, and in politics. The man had never lost at anything, so he had no reason to assume he ever would.

But the thing that stood out even more was the incident with the thieves. He was filthy rich. What would it have cost him to give them what they wanted? Most of his money was in the market, not the bank. Probably he was insured. Even if not, he'd make his millions back in months, maybe weeks. But he lost a hand and an eye before he would give in, and that did not sound like the kind of man who would give in to whatever moral pressure Sisto Settimo bought to bear on him.

I was conflicted. I knew abortion was wrong, a sin. There was no doubt about that. And Sixtus was my Pope, my spiritual leader. But I suddenly had enormous admiration for Egan. There was no question that whatever Sixtus asked or gently demanded, even if Egan agreed with him, he'd look him in the eye with his one good orb and say No.

And what would the Pope do? Most Popes must have had *some* doubts about the rightness of at least some of their actions. But Sixtus had been created, programmed if you will, to *know* his beliefs were right. He was polite, he was gentle, he was compassionate, but when push came to shove he would know to the very core of his being that in matters of religious doctrine he was, as the Church insisted, infallible.

I kept waiting for the other shoe to drop. Every day I checked all the news sources, prepared to see a statement from Egan stating that the Pope had no business intervening in American politics or trying to influence American laws, but there was nothing, not even an acknowledgment that Sixtus had canceled his trip or was displeased with Egan personally or America generally.

A week passed, and then another, and then a month, and still no word came from Egan or America. Oh, a few politicians tried to capitalize on the Pope's remarks, and the Bishop of Denver and the Archbishop of Baltimore both made strong public statements, but it was nothing out of the ordinary. Indeed, it was the kind of thing that happened every couple of years, even during those long periods when the Pope, Sixtus and his predecessors, had barely acknowledged America's existence. I finally began to relax, convinced that somehow a potential crisis had been averted.

And then the other shoe dropped—and it dropped from a metal foot that had never worn a shoe.

Egan held another press conference, and this time he didn't have to wait for the last question. Right off the top, one of the California reporters asked if he'd had any further contact with the Pope.

"I've never had any initial contact with him," answered Egan.

"Has your position changed?"

"You guys have been living in my pocket since the last press conference," said Egan. "Don't you think you'd know if it had?"

"What would you say if the Pope contacted you today?"

"I'd tell him I was honored to speak to him, and I wish he'd reconsider his decision not to visit our beautiful country."

"And if he made the outlawing of abortion a condition for that visit?"

"Then I'd tell him I was sorry he felt that way, and I'd send him some postcards of our national parks."

"But if you personally are opposed to abortion…" began another reporter.

"It's settled law, and it's not going to change," said Egan. "Not for him, not for me, and not for you. Next question, and if it's not on a new subject this conference is over."

Nothing surprising. I didn't think he'd been aggressive or defensive, just straight from the shoulder, as we used to say. I made a cup of tea, decided I was too sleepy for my eyes to focus on the Bible, and had the computer start reciting the psalms in what I call its "bedtime voice." I was asleep in less than five minutes.

It was when I went to the large dining room for breakfast the next morning that I saw perhaps thirty cardinals and as many bishops in animated and very emotional conversations all over the room.

As I pulled up a chair, Cardinal Ortiz walked over to me.

"Have you heard?" he said excitedly.

"Heard what?" I asked.

"The Pope!" he said.

"He's all right, isn't he?"

"He's better than all right!" said Egan. "He just threatened to excommunicate Bradford Egan!"

"You're kidding!" I exclaimed.

"Ask anyone!"

"He *really* threatened to excommunicate him?" I said, trying to grasp what I was hearing.

"Not only that!" said Bishop FitzPatrick, who was walking by. "He gave him a two-week deadline!"

I blinked my eyes and tried to clear my head. "A deadline for *what*? Egan's already said he's against abortion."

"He's got two weeks to tell Congress he wants them to propose a constitutional amendment outlawing abortion. If he doesn't, his soul is gone."

This was the man who wouldn't reveal the combination of a safe when he had more money that he could ever spend, even at the cost of having an eye gouged out. He didn't cave in to pressure.

"He'll never do it," I said decisively. "Sixtus has to back off. He can't excommunicate a President."

"*You* convince him he's wrong," said Ortiz.

"There's 150 million Catholics in America, and they supply a third of our funding. He's going to piss it all away—them *and* the money!" I blurted.

"Cardinal!" said Ortiz sharply. "What kind of language is that!"

"I'm sorry," I said, and truly I was. "But he's made a terrible blunder."

"He cannot blunder when he speaks on matters of doctrine," replied Ortiz.

"Especially *this* Pope," added Fitzpatrick.

There followed a discussion—well, an affirmation, actually—that no one was better versed in Church doctrine than Sisto Settimo. If he thought the President of the United States deserved excommunication, then clearly he did. It was inconceivable that any Pope could be wrong on such a subject—and as Bishop FitzPatrick pointed out decisively, especially *this* Pope.

We monitored every newscast for the next two days, waiting for Egan's reaction. He made one brief comment. As he was leaving a meeting with his Secretary of Agriculture, a reporter yelled out a question, asking what he was going to do about the Pope's threat.

"I've got a country to run," he said tersely. "I can't waste my time worrying about it."

"But, Mr. President, sir, what if—?" began the reporter, but the Secret Service stepped between them, and then Egan was whisked away before he had to answer any more questions.

Still, the country and the world wanted to know his response, and next morning it was announced that he would issue a brief address from the Oval Office that evening, which of course became the only topic of conversation in the Vatican.

The general consensus was that neither of them—the Pope nor the President—wanted to push the situation to its limits. A number of the Cardinals thought that Egan would demand that Congress get to work drafting an amendment. It would never pass, but he'd have done what Sixtus had demanded.

I didn't believe it for a second. This was a man who didn't give in to pressure. I thought it more likely that he would make an accommodation—some face-saving public penance such as Henry II had done after the murder of Thomas Beckett—and that might satisfy both sides.

No one agreed with me, and as it turned out, I was indeed wrong—but so were all the other members of the Curia.

We gathered around the huge holoscreen at 2:45 AM (he was speaking at 9:00 PM Washington D.C. time). Cardinal

Cuozo—he must be 95 years old—began snoring, and we decided not to wake him until a minute before the broadcast was due to begin. I noticed that a few of the Cardinals and Bishops had elected to watch it in their rooms. The evening news had predicted than more than three billion people would watch or hear the address in one form or another.

"He *is* a practicing Catholic," Cardinal Carciofo was saying. "He will not defy the Holy Father."

"I think they will try to reach an accommodation," said Bishop Mboka, I found it comforting that at least one other person in the room agreed with me. But then he added: "I don't know if they will succeed."

"He will not oppose a Pope who speaks with the absolute authority of the Lord behind him," insisted Carciofo.

"We'll find out soon enough," said Ortiz as the screen suddenly showed Bradford Egan seated at his desk.

"Ladies and gentlemen," said an unseen voice, "the President of the United States."

"Good evening, my fellow Americans," said Egan, looking straight into the camera. "I'm sure you know why I am speaking to you this evening. By rights I shouldn't have to, since it concerns a matter between myself and my spiritual leader—but he has threatened to excommunicate me, not for any personal sin or act against God that I may have committed as a private citizen, but rather he has threatened me with excommunication for performing my duties as the President of the United States of America."

He paused and took a sip from a glass of water.

"I am sorry this has come to pass. I am a devout Catholic, and I believe that the Pope—*any* Pope—is infallible when he speaks on matters of doctrine, and that he has the right to excommunicate me." Another pause. "I'll go a step further. I believe abortion is immoral, and is, yes, a mortal sin. I have always believed that; I believe it still."

Suddenly his expression hardened. "But I am not speaking to you as a private citizen or a lifelong Catholic. I am speaking to you as the President of the United States, the President of a country that was founded on certain principles, among which is the separation of church and state. And as your President," he continued, the anger in his voice apparent to all who could hear him, "I will not be threatened by anyone for any reason. Not now, and not ever."

I looked at his hands on the desk. The prosthetic one was motionless; the real one was clenched in a fist.

"It would be easy for me to do the bidding of Sisto Settimo. I could ask Congress to craft an amendment outlawing abortion. You know and I know that it would never pass—and if it did, it would never pass the required number of states. It would certainly satisfy the Pope and get us both out of this very awkward situation. But I answer only to *you*, and that is not about to change."

He glared into the camera. "I hope you are listening, Holy Father. I bear you no malice. But I cannot and will not allow you to interfere in American domestic policy. Do what you will. My decision is made, and it is irrevocable."

The transmission went blank.

"I can't believe it!" exclaimed Carciofo. "He has practically challenged the Pope to excommunicate him. Does he think the Holy Father won't keep his word?"

"He knows he will," I said.

"Is he mad, then?" said Carciofo. "This is worse than a death wish. He is facing eternal damnation."

"The Pope was wrong," I said.

"He *cannot* be wrong when he speaks on matters of doctrine!" chimed in Asciuga.

"Let me explain," I said. "I realize that if he excommunicates President Egan he is of course doctrinally correct to do so."

"Then how can he be wrong?"

"Because *threatening* to do so, trying to pressure him into changing his position, is not doctrinal," I replied. "And President Egan is not a man who responds to threats or pressure. I said that last week, and now you have seen it for yourself. He truly believes that the Pontiff has the power to condemn him to hell, and he *still* will not yield."

"Then he will burn forever," said Ortiz.

"And the Church will lose half a billion members," said Bishop Mboka.

Everybody turned to him, most with expressions of skepticism or outright anger.

"The Holy Father's actions are in keeping with Church doctrine," continued Mboka. "We all agree that they cannot be otherwise. But to the world at large, it will look like he was meddling in the internal affairs of a great nation and threatening the President with the worst punishment imaginable if the President will not do what seems to be his political bidding."

"Nonsense," scoffed Carciofo. "Anyone can hear or read the Pope's statement. It is a straightforward statement of doctrine."

Asciuga and most of the other nodded their heads in agreement.

Finally I felt I had to speak up. "Bishop Mboka is right," I said. "Where I come from, which is the American city of Chicago, we would call this good doctrine but bad politics."

"The Holy Father is not concerned with politics," insisted Carciofo.

"I know," I said. "But 600 million Americans are. Especially tonight."

"You know," mused Mboka, "when John F. Kennedy became America's first Catholic President people wondered what would happen if he had to choose between his office and the Vatican. It never happened. It is ironic that it should finally happen during the tenure of the first robot Pope rather than the first Catholic President."

"Egan's made his choice," insisted Carciofo. "Now he must live with it."

*And Sixtus has made* his *choice,* I thought, *and now we must live with* that.

For the next eleven days the only topic of conversation in the Vatican—and, it seemed, in the world at large—was whether the Pope would keep his word. Nobody in the Curia doubted it. He was infallible, he knew it, and he would do what he knew was right.

Egan gave no more speeches or press conferences. As far as anyone could tell, he had put the incident behind him, prepared to live—and die, or worse—with its consequences, and he busied himself the massive responsibilities and duties of his office.

Twice Sixtus led us in our evening prayers. Nobody dared to bring up the subject that was on all our minds. He came, he prayed, he blessed us, and he retired to his quarters.

And the clock kept ticking.

Two days before the deadline the heads of state began showing up. Alvaro of Brazil, Mordante of Venezuela, Kobernykov of Russia, Zhao of China, even Princess Marie of England, each there to entreat the Pope to extend or totally cancel his deadline.

None of us, not even Asciuga and Carciofo, were privy to the meetings, but we knew what the outcome would be. From the Pontiff's point of view, they were well-meaning and compassionate men and women, but they were trying to convince him to give up a position that was doctrinally correct and exchange it for one that he knew was wrong. It was really as simple as that.

The one visitor we never expected was Delores Egan Montague—Egan's married daughter. A practicing Catholic herself, she came, with no press and no fanfare, to beg for her father's soul. She got no farther than any of the others, but Sixtus refused to see anyone after that, remaining alone in his quarters. Some of the Cardinals thought he was reconsidering his position. I thought he was merely emotionally drained after speaking to her, and needed some time to regain his composure. Not that we had ever seen him without it, but then we'd never seen him in this kind of situation either.

When it came, and of course it *did* come, it was like an anti-climax. It was brief, there was no fanfare, no prior announcements, no interviews when it was done. One moment the world was running along pretty much the way it had for more than a century, and the next moment the President of the United States had been excommunicated from his Church.

President Egan held a press conference the next day, announcing in advance that he had a brief statement to make. When the time came he stepped up to the podium, faced the reporters, and spoke.

"As I'm sure you all know by now, Pope Sisto Settimo and I have been unable to resolve our differences. The situation is no longer a matter of concern to the people or the government, and I will answer no questions about it, now or in the future." He paused. "Now, concerning the lunar colony..."

Every hand went up, and every reporter began shouting questions about the excommunication.

"I told you," said Egan. "The matter is now between the Pope and myself, and the subject is closed."

When they persisted, he simply left the podium and vanished into the interior of the West Wing.

"What do you think?" asked Ortiz, turning to me.

"I have enormous admiration for him," I said honestly.

"Little good it'll do him," said Ortiz. "Still, I have a sneaking respect for a man who sticks to his principles, even when they're in total opposition to my own."

"But he does so at the cost of his faith," FitzPatrick chimed in. "Don't forget that this is a man who thinks abortion is a mortal sin and does nothing to stop the millions of abortions they perform in his country every year."

"Perhaps he thinks ignoring the law of the land he's been elected to uphold is an even greater sin," I said gently.

"Rubbish!" snapped FitzPatrick. "Wasn't it one of the Roosevelts, centuries ago, who spoke of the bully pulpit. Has he ever even *tried* to convince the people to repeal the law?"

"I truly don't know," I admitted.

"Well, I checked, and *I* know," answered FitzPatrick. "The answer is no."

Somehow I didn't think it was that simple, but I didn't know what to say. Besides, I was aware that as a Cardinal who had grown up in America, whatever I said would be considered through a prism of suspicion if I seemed to be siding with Egan against the Pope. And in truth I wasn't.

I was trying to side with reason and understanding, but it didn't seem to be working, nor could I be sure I was right. After all, if Sixtus said something was true and he was speaking on matters of doctrine, it *was* true. Period. No ifs, ands or buts. All I could think was that maybe a human Pope would have been imbued with a little more self-doubt. In fact, strike the word "more." Doubt was neither in his programming nor his lexicon.

He was my Pope, and I knew that in the long run I supported him. But I couldn't get over the feeling that he was doing enormous damage to the Church. Then I remembered that he was also steeped in religious and (probably) secular history, since the two weren't always separated, and if he felt this was not only necessary but beneficial, then it must be.

Or was he so certain of what it took to be a Catholic that he was willing to wipe hundreds of millions off the rolls? And if so, was that beneficial or detrimental—and did it depend on whether it was doctrinal or not? I didn't know, and I had a feeling that no one else did either, except maybe Sixtus.

The next three weeks were hectic beyond belief. Only Somalia, Indonesia, and Uzbekistan out-and-out condemned the decision, but country after country officially regretted it, and kept sending emissaries to try to convince the Pontiff to change his mind. His met each of them, was polite and gracious, and refused to change or moderate his decision.

Then the President of Norway asked the question that was on all of our minds—would Sixtus revoke the excommunication if President Egan asked Congress to craft an anti-abortion amendment to the Constitution? Sixtus answered that he had spoken to Egan privately twice since the announcement and the President was adamant: he would take full responsibility for his actions in the confessional, he would do any personal penance required, but he would brook no interference in the running of the country. The issue, said Sixtus, was closed.

But it wasn't. Exactly.

It was four months later that Sixtus asked for a list of Catholics in the United States Senate and House of Representatives.

Shortly after he received it he summoned me to his office. It was my first audience there.

"Your Holiness," I said, bowing as I entered.

He was standing by a window, looking out across a plaza. "Good morning, Richard. Please be seated."

"But you are standing, Your Holiness," I noted.

"I am as comfortable standing as sitting," he answered. "Now please sit down."

I sat on a chair facing his ornate desk, and he walked around it and stood behind it, facing me.

"I have summoned you, Richard, because at the moment you are the one Cardinal in the Vatican who is most conversant with American politics."

"You're going to revoke the excommunication?" I blurted.

"No, I am not," he said in a tone of infinite sadness.

"Then—?"

"I have not yet resolved the situation in America," he said, holding up a hand to silence me. "The Church cannot turn its back on twenty million abortions a year. I cannot merely say, 'Well, I tried', and let it go at that. It would not only make my actions meaningless, but it would make President Egan's punishment even more so. If I condemn one soul to hell without changing the law, then despite all the public furor—yes, I know it's been going on—the sum total of my actions is to lose one soul to Satan without saving a single aborted infant. This is unacceptable."

"This has something to do with the list you asked for," I said. It was not a question.

"Richard, there are 27 Catholics in the Senate, and 119 more in the House of Representatives. Are their positions in any danger because of President Egan's excommunication?"

"In danger, Your Holiness?"

"In your opinion, based on the half century or more than you lived there, will the electorate be so enraged that I have actually tried to take steps to outlaw abortion that they will vote these Catholic Senators and Representatives out of office solely because they *are* Catholic?"

"Ah!" I said. "Now I see. I had feared you might ask the same of them that you asked of President Egan. No, I don't think the American public will vote anyone out of office based on his religion and your actions against the President."

"That is comforting in a way," he said.

"In a way, Your Holiness?"

"I would not want to see Catholic office holders suffer for their religious beliefs." He paused, but I could tell he wasn't quite through. "If those *are* their religious beliefs."

And then I knew what he was going to do.

"Your Holiness," I said quickly, "I must point out that they are a minority in both houses of Congress. Even if they were to vote unanimously for the amendment you want, they would be totally ineffective."

He stared at me through those prismatic eyes that seemed to peer into my soul.

"Surely you are not suggesting that they should not take a stand, simply because they are outnumbered," he said mildly. "We have been outnumbered throughout our history."

"No, Your Holiness," I stammered. "I meant…I merely meant…"

He walked around the desk and laid a metal hand on my shoulder. "It's all right, Richard."

I looked at him gratefully but made no reply.

"We want to eradicate this terrible practice," he continued. "The Church has stood by long enough. It is not sufficient that we have spoken out against it, because centuries later it is still with us. I cannot believe God put me here to ignore this endless slaughter of the innocent."

"I don't know what to say, Your Holiness."

A smile appeared on his metal face. "You might say that you agree with me."

"I do, Your Holiness."

"Then we must put our heads together to see how to eradicate abortion, and as a first step we must make certain that it is no longer given legal cover."

"I agree, Your Holiness."

"How many of these men and women do you know anything about?" he asked.

"I keep up with the news," I said. "I know some of their accomplishments, I know their party affiliation—well, the Senators, anyway—and I know that three of them are in the hierarchy of the Senate leadership and I think five are members of the House leadership."

He shook his head gently. "That is not what I meant."

"If you meant, am I aware of the strength of their faith, the answer is no, Your Holiness."

Another gentle smile. "Let me ask my questions before you answer them, Richard."

"I apologize."

"If I were to ask the five American Cardinals and all the Bishops and Archbishops to sign a joint statement condemning abortion, would the Catholic members of Congress support it?"

"I think their reactions would be very much the same as President Egan's, Your Holiness," I answered. "I think that almost all of them would say they agree with the Church and that they themselves would never condone an abortion for any member of their family. I think every President for the past three centuries has said the same. But I think they would then say that their decisions were private and personal decisions, and they would not force their religious beliefs on anyone else, especially when it would eradicate a right that every court case has said is inherent in the Constitution."

"I was afraid that would be your conclusion," said Sixtus.

"I could be wrong," I said hastily.

He shook his head. "It is my own conclusion as well." He walked back to the window and stared out. "This will be harder than it should be. It will take more time than I had hoped. The world will destroy still more innocent lives. But we must start somewhere." He turned to me. "What kind of Pope would I be if I turned my back on it, just because my predecessors have failed to solve it?"

"They used to say, back when I lived in America, that we got the government we deserved." I inclined my head toward him. "In you, Your Holiness, I think we have gotten better than we deserve."

*And I don't know if we're ready for you yet*, I added silently.

He dismissed me, and I went back to my room. I should have picked up the Bible, or had my computer start reciting it, but instead I had the computer bring up some of the speeches of the Senators we had just discussed. Then I had it excerpt their remarks on abortion. It was as I had said: they were all against it personally, and they all acknowledged that it was the law of the land.

Then, just out of curiosity, I had the computer supply me with any remarks they had made about President Egan's excommunication. To a man (and a woman) they supported his unwillingness to let any outside influence try to dictate domestic policy. They were upset, or angered, or saddened, or noncommittal about the excommunication, but they were unanimous about Egan's refusal to let his spiritual leader dictate his political actions.

I did not discuss my meeting with Sixtus with any of the other Cardinals. What was there to say? I knew what was coming. I just didn't know when.

It took five months. He waited until there a mid-term election was ten days away, and then gave the Catholic Senators and Representatives the same kind of ultimatum he'd given Egan, but this time the deadline was eight weeks. It showed some political acumen on his part: if they refused to do as he asked, at least there wouldn't be a sympathy vote for officeholders who refused to yield to foreign and religious influence, yet there could be no doubt that 122 members of Congress—24 were either retiring or were Senators were not up for reelection this year—were facing excommunication, just as surely as Egan had.

"What's next?" demanded Asciuga. "If he doesn't get what he wants, will he excommunicate all 150 million American Catholics?"

"I wouldn't put it past him," said Mboka.

"Hold your tongue!" snapped Carciofo.

"Oh, shut up!" said Asciuga. "That's what we're all thinking."

"Not me!" Carciofo shot back.

"Then you are blind to what's going on," said Asciuga, lowering his voice. "Think about it. This is the 24th Century—and we have a Pope who just excommunicated an American President, is threatening to do the same to 112 members of the House and Senate, and if that doesn't get him what he wants, who knows what's next? Will he threaten to excommunicate Catholic governors, or perhaps a few hundred thousand Catholic doctors?"

"He won't," said Carciofo.

"Why not?" demanded Asciuga.

"It isn't rational."

"A year ago would you have said it was rational to excommunicate a President?" He learned forward. "Look me in the eye and tell me you truly don't believe that he'll excommunicate all those Senators and Representatives if they don't try to craft an amendment."

Carciofo stared at him but made no reply.

"At least you're honest," said Asciuga.

"But *why*?" said Carciofo in frustration. "He could turn the entire country and half its allies against us."

"Because he is *too* perfect," suggested Mboka.

Everyone turned to him.

"What do you mean?" asked Ortiz.

"He has no fear of the political consequences, because unlike the rest of us, he is not concerned with politics. His function as Pope is to run the Church and promote its doctrine, and to say his knowledge of doctrine is profound is an understatement. When he speaks as our spiritual leader, on matters of Church doctrine, he is truly infallible. But because his training—his programming, if you will—does not extend beyond matters pertaining to the faith, he looks no farther when he acts."

"But he has lived all over the world!" said Ortiz. "Surely you are not suggesting that he is incapable of learning!"

"It is *what* he learns," replied Mboka. "He is brilliant, and he is compassionate, he is everything he was planned to be, but even when he was abroad, even when he saved Pius from the gunman Breque, he did it as a religious leader. He never asked for Breque to stand trial for his previous crimes. He saw a spark of decency in him—and he was right, of course; the man's behavior has been exemplary ever since—but he never asked him to stand trial. He never allowed the police to arrest him, he took the law into his own hands because he was serving a higher law."

Mboka looked around the room at the various Cardinals and Bishops. "Other Popes might have forgiven Breque. A few might have interceded on his behalf in court, or asked for a mitigation of part of his sentence. But ask yourselves if any other Pope would have behaved with the compassion—and the disdain for secular law—that Sixtus did?"

A lot of Cardinals, including myself, had been serving and observing Sisto Settimo from the day he had become Pope, and for many years before that, but it had taken a Bishop from distant Zambia, a newcomer among us, to illuminate our dilemma. We had been alarmed by his recent actions, but the more we studied him and them, the more difficult it became to disagree or find fault with him. It took Mboka to realize that his singular fault was that he was totally faultless in his capacity as a spiritual leader, but that we lived in a political world and actions—even right actions—have political consequences.

And at that moment I think we all understood what had to be done.

Sixtus was waiting for us when we arrived at his quarters.

"I know why you have come," he said. "When you are finished, you will find a document in my safe. I urge you to use it."

That took us aback, and we just stopped and stood there, staring at him.

"I bear you no ill will," he continued. "Your vision is limited, but you are still God's children. I love you no less for what you are about to do, and I will pray for your souls to the very last second of my existence." He stretched his arms out. "Do what must be done," were his final words.

I think if he had implored God to forgive us for we knew not what we were doing, we might have fled the room in guilt and shame, but he did not say another word. He remained motionless, and the tiny light in the back of his eyes vanished.

When we were finished, someone remembered the document, and we took it from the safe. It read as follows:

*"My Children:*

*There can be no higher honor or privilege than serving as your Pope. As you know, the Pope is the Pope for life—but in my case, that is a meaningless term, because I am for all practical purposes eternal. For you to have but a single spiritual father until the end of all things is surely not God's will. Therefore, I have decided to resign as of the date on this missive, and go into total seclusion to commune with God for as much time as remains to me. Far from feeling sorrow, I hope you will share my joy with me."*

And at the bottom, signed not in ink or with the standard stamp of his office, was the clearly discernable seal of the leaden Papal bull.

When we were finished we moved him to a sealed, unmarked crypt, and those of us who were in the room declared ten days of very private mourning. At the same time we gave the letter to the press, which studied it, had it examined by experts, and declared it to be authentic.

Then came the election of a new Pope. Most outsiders thought the likely winner would be either Asciuga or Carciofo. Black smoke was seen after the first two ballots, but on the third the smoke was white, and shortly thereafter we had our very first Zambian Pope, Thomas Mboka, who took the name of John XXV.

His very first Papal act was to revoke the excommunication. His second was to assure the American Congress that the Vatican would never again interfere with their deliberations. His third will take a little longer, but I don't think anyone doubts that it will be accomplished, and that is the canonization of Sisto Settimo.

No one has said it aloud, and no one ever will, but I think everyone who served in the Vatican during his reign will agree that he makes a better Saint than Pope.

# The Jetsam of Disremembered Mechanics

## Caitlín R. Kiernan

Caitlín R. Kiernan is the acclaimed author of several novels, including *The Red Tree* (nominated for the Shirley Jackson and World Fantasy awards) and, most recently, *The Drowning Girl: A Memoir* (winner of the Bram Stoker and James Tiptree, Jr. awards, nominated for the Nebula, British Fantasy, World Fantasy, Mythopoeic, Locus, and Shirley Jackson awards). Her tales of the weird, fantastic, and macabre have been collected in several volumes, including *Tales of Pain and Wonder*; *From Weird and Distant Shores*; *To Charles Fort, With Love*; *Alabaster*; *A is for Alien*; *The Ammonite Violin & Others*; *Confessions of a Five-Chambered Heart*; *Two Worlds and In Between: The Best of Caitlín R. Kiernan (Volume One)*; and, most recently, *The Ape's Wife and Other Stories*. She has also recently returned to comics with the critically-acclaimed *Alabaster* for Dark Horse. She lives in Providence, Rhode Island.

Caitlín R. Kiernan says: "There are authors you discover at just the right time, at just the right age, that they affect you in a way that stays with you your entire life. That even shape you. For me, authors such as Ray Bradbury, Ursula K. LeGuin, Harlan Ellison, Michael Moorcock—and Robert Silverberg. There are these authors, and they produce gems, and if you're lucky, you find those gems, which shine for you, and never cease to shine, no matter how many hundreds of book you're made to read afterwards. For me, Silverberg's *Nightwings* was one such book. Looking back, those works of science fiction that mean the most to me, and I think always will, are the works of the "New Wave" authors and those who set the stage for the New Wave. I number Silverberg among those writers. *Nightwings* is a book about *humanity*—no matter how alien to current concepts of human beings. Few characters in SF have ever stayed with me the way Avulea has. Which is what brought me, when asked to write a short story based on a work of Silverberg's, back to *Nightwings*. I only hope I've done the source justice. These gems are too rare to subject to cheap counterfeits. They're too precious."

# 1.

At sunrise, the Flier stands alone on a beach whose gritty, fine sand is the color of slate. There are dunes piled up behind her, high wind-shaped mounds overgrown with stunted conifers and mad tangles of briars. Sometime in the night, the briars blossomed, and the air smells almost as much of their sugary yellow-orange blooms as it does of the sea. The Flier is nude, as she has spent a long summer's night riding the currents of this unfamiliar sky, and it is the custom of her guild to remove their clothing whenever they go aloft. It is a tradition born of necessity, as the added weight of even the most flimsy clothing is sufficient to hobble their wings and keep them earthbound. In the light of this new day, her skin, pale almost as chalk, glimmers with faint iridescence.

To one who has never seen a Flier, this small, gaunt woman might appear stricken by some terrible wasting illness. Her body is spindly and lean, almost entirely devoid of the luxury of fatty tissue. She is all taut musculature stretched over hollow bones, a skeletal physiology fashioned after birds by the genetic surgeons who, at the end of the Second Cycle, sculpted her race. Her chest is flat, and her buttocks, too. She might easily be mistaken for a young, malnourished boy, were it not for the ready evidence of her sex.

But, despite her size and seeming frailty, it would be a mistake to ever think her weak; that her strength is not at once apparent should not be taken for weakness. She is merely of a race of humanity adapted to an entirely different existence than are the cumbersome, wingless men and woman who will never sail between the clouds and gaze down at the earth from a thousand feet up. She has folded her exhausted wings, and they lie collapsed now into twin lumps on her back, nestled over her knobby spine and between the sinewy humps of broad shoulder blades. Unfurled, they are each almost a dozen times again the width of her small body, and they are veined and delicate, patterned colorfully as the motley of a butterfly's wings. The specific colors and configuration of markings vary from one Flier to another, from Flier family to family.

This Flier is named Aelita, which was also the name of her mother. And this lagoon and its fringe of charcoal-gray beach lie at the end of a long and arduous journey that began across the sea in the ancient city of Perris. She did not, of course, fly across Earth Ocean, as the distance was too great and there would have been nowhere for Aelita to rest when the sun was in the sky, during those day-lit hours when the charged electrons and protons of the solar winds keep all Fliers grounded. Rather, she crossed from Eyrop on a great watership, a glittering, golden vessel built and operated by the Guild of Transporters, presently leased to the service of the Rememberers.

No other Fliers number among the members of the expedition, only Aelita, who joined this company in its quest to survey a poorly mapped region of the sunken western lands, the Lost Continents that had once, thousands of years past, girdled Earth Ocean from pole to pole. All that now remains are scattered islands, none even half so large as Strayla. A year ago, rumors reached Parris, by way of the Guild of Merchants, of a great unexplored archipelago where the partially submerged ruins of a Second Cycle city known as Ares might still be viewed. This string of tropical islands is situated roughly where the easternmost shores of Sud-amerik had lain, in those distant ages prior to the global cataclysms triggered by foolish but well-intended men who'd only hoped to create a paradise. But their vast weather machines brought drought and famine, and upheaval and floods, played havoc with the planet's magnetosphere and tectonics, sundering and sinking the Lost Continents and signaling the end of the glorious civilization of the Second Cycle of humankind.

However, Aelita is no Rememberer, no Indexer, no Scribe, and it is not so much the past that has brought her to this beach—a full-night's flight from the ruins of Ares—as it is the possibilities of the present. She has come seeking after a thing that has been deemed lost to time and extinction by the scholars of Eyrop and Afreek and Ais. She stands here in the warm briar-scented wind, staring down at her thin bare feet, her toes half buried in the dark sand. Her bright eyes take in the strands of rubbery seaweed and the various species of snails, starfish, and mussels cast up on the shore. In this moment, she appreciates fully the unlikely folds of luck and happenstance that have propelled her so far from her home in the snowy mountains of Hind. In truth, the secretive organizers of this expedition would have preferred not to have her among them, but she is a Flier with skills they knew could prove invaluable to their endeavors. And she was in the proper place at the proper time, with all the right contacts. Aelita raises her head and glances over her left shoulder, towards the place where she landed, the spot just past the dunes where her footprints begin.

"Take care out there," a Rememberer named Carver advised, at sunset the previous evening, as Aelita was undressing and readying to leave the deck of the golden watership. "These are wild lands, and there is always the threat of dangerous beasts."

"I will be cautious," she promised.

"One may never be too cautious," the Rememberer said.

Slipping out of her silvery jacket, exposing her small breasts to the twilight, she eyed the man, smiling very softly at his concern. He was unlike so many of the others aboard the ship, who had looked upon her, at best, as a sort of useful nuisance, not so very different from the Changelings and neuters who served as the crew.

"Don't fear for me," she told him. "I have flown over scorched deserts, across the Arban wastelands to Somalyemen and Thiopia, all the way to Agupt. When others sought the easy passage and security of Land Bridge, I flew high above Lake Medit. So, don't fear for me. Instead, wish me luck, that I find what I have come so far to find."

"If you should not return—" the Rememberer began, but Aelita interrupted and finished the warning for him.

"—the expedition's interests will not be served in expending its resources searching for me."

He nodded solemnly and watched as she carefully folded her leggings and jacket and set them together inside a locker slot in the metal plating of the deck.

"I meant no offense," he said.

"I have taken none," Aelita replied, shutting the locker, smiling for the tall man in his shawl spun from silk and copper. The silken weft threads have been dyed the deepest shade of blue, and Aelita wondered if the abyssal reaches of the sea were that same shade of blue, or if waters that far down were only black, permitting no visible light and so entirely bereft of color.

"Then I shall wish you success in your quest, Flier, though you have chosen to keep the object of your inquiry a mystery, hidden from us."

Aelita had begun to spread her filmy wings, and they sparkled vividly in the last rays of the fading day. The salty wind tugged insistently at them, and for a moment it seemed to the Rememberer that she would be plucked from off the deck and hurled tumbling into the air. But Aelita hardly budged from the spot where she stood, having instinctively braced herself against the wind. Her smile wavered only slightly as she leaned towards him, shifting her center of gravity as powerful scapular ligaments repositioned her wings so they formed less effective aerofoils.

"I should go now," she told him, and again he nodded.

Aelita genuflected then, in the manner of the Guild of Fliers, her forehead bending to meet her knees, her hard little knuckles pressed against the deck of the watership. She sighed and whispered a ceremonial invocation, shaping each word, each syllable with the utmost precision, for (as the Rememberer well knew) more than the hard facts of biology and physics were required to lift a Flier and keep it airborne. It is an old mysticism, harking back to elder gods of the First Cycle, a catechism in which every Flier child is instructed before they may leave the snow-shrouded temples of Hind. And when these words were finished, Aelita smiled once more to the Rememberer who had not been unkind to her, then flapped her wings and rose suddenly from the vessel. Soon enough, it was only a streamlined smudge on the blue-green plain of Earth Ocean stretched out hundreds of feet below her. She circled above the watership twice, three times, gaining her bearings, working the stiffness from her wings, and then turned southward.

And now the night has passed, and she is standing alone on this sun-drenched beach, and the Rememberer and the ship are both far, far away. Often, she has flown without companions, and her flights have carried her frequently to remote and lonely places. She is no stranger to this solitude. And yet she feels a strange, disorienting unease, and allows herself to wish for the company of others.

*I'm very tired*, she thinks. *I ache, and my eyes and mind are weary. That is all it is.* And Aelita glances back at the dunes again, the snarl of briars and jutting kauri branches, and wishes she might seek sanctuary in those shadows and even sleep a few hours. Better to be rested, when she confronts whatever ghosts her dreams have brought her all the way from the streets and comforts of Perris to find. And then she thinks, as she has thought countless times already, *Perhaps I am a lunatic and nothing more, and there are no revelations awaiting me here. Perhaps there is only kelp and sand and stranded starfish, and I will return empty-handed to the Council.* She knows that the possibility of failure should not seem like solace, but it does, and Aelita does not turn it away.

# 2.

More than a year has passed since the first dream. It was late winter, and the streets of Perris were frozen and caked with filthy layers of ice and stale snow. There were weeks on end when the sun seemed unwilling to reveal itself for even a meager few seconds, and the low steel-blue clouds lay heavily upon the city, muffling all sound, discouraging all movement. Aelita had business with the Rememberers, which, in the more agreeable season of early autumn, had brought her there from Stanbool to the east, and which had kept her there many months longer than she had intended.

She'd come seeking certain arcane data regarding the origin of her guild, of her people. As is always the case with such studies, merely framing the *questions* for requisition from the access banks was, by far, the most difficult part of the endeavor. What seemed innumerable days and nights had been spent in the company of muttering Indexers, tediously trying to frame her questions in just such a way that they might yield the optimal return for her very finite resources. The greater portion of her energy was squandered struggling to articulate the requisitions, and beginning, necessarily, with searches so peripheral to her main purpose as to seem almost irrelevant. True, the fruits of the Rememberers and the labors of the Indexers were open to all who came asking, but open in such a limited and often counterintuitive capacity as to prove all but useless to anyone but the most dedicated and wealthy. She was one lone, inquisitive Flier, and her queries were far too ambitious for her means.

In the end, she'd had to content herself with superficial half-answers, and by then it was mid-winter, and she passed long, gloomy afternoons in the Flier's Lodge. She would not dare attempt the flight back to Stanbool until spring and fairer weather.

And it was during one of these interminable days that the first dream came. She was sitting by herself at a wide and drafty window looking down on the narrow, snow-scabbed avenue below, watching the halting progress of an elderly Watcher as he tried to drag his cart of mechanical instruments through frozen drifts and over the ice-slicked pavement. A retinue of burly, ivory-furred outworlders, evidently at home in these cold and inclement conditions, paused to observe the Watcher's plight. One of the aliens pointed a long triple-jointed arm at the cart and the man, and they all made rude, hitching noises that Aelita interpreted as laughter, but none among them moved to help. After a time, both the Watcher and the furry outworlders rounded a corner and were lost to her sight. And she closed her eyelids and drifted off, there in the window seat, feeling vaguely guilty that she'd been offended by the jeering throng, but had not herself gone down to assist the beleaguered old Watcher with his burden.

Near the beginning of the dream, she was talking with another Flier, a woman named Mapiya whom she had met in Stanbool. Aelita was unsure how or why Mapiya had come to Perris, but Mapiya was telling Aelita she should not feel so badly for not having assisted the Watcher.

"They're fools, all of them," Mapiya scoffed. "Keeping vigil against an offworlder invasion that's never coming, devoting their whole lives to guard us from a mythical threat. Do not waste your pity for the likes of a Watcher."

And Aelita frowned and admitted to harboring suspicions that Mapiya was right, that the invasion might well be no more than myth. But still, it seemed cruel to treat an old man with such flagrant disrespect. Then she undressed, and Mapiya undressed, and they gave one another pleasure, in those secret ways that only one Flier may pleasure another. It seemed to Aelita that they were no longer in the lodge then, but removed to a chamber of immense stone columns carved from reddish sandstone and rising towards a vaulted ceiling half-obscured by the thick, aromatic smoke of smoldering braziers. Their naked, gangling bodies were slippery with sweat, and the air smelled of frankincense and vetiver, sandalwood and dragon's blood. The chamber was dimly lit by the spicules of slave lights, imported to earth from some far-flung Brightstar world.

"I do not know this place," Aelita whispered to her lover, and Mapiya replied, "It is a place of remembering, but also a place unknown and forbidden to all among the Rememberers."

Aelita considered the words—individually and in concert—and also the indistinct fresco painted on the high ceiling of the chamber. It seemed to her like a sort of riddle, what Mapiya had said, but Aelita was reluctant to ask for clarification, in case it *wasn't* a riddle after all. She lay back among the satin and velvet cushions, still puzzling over how a place of remembering could be off limits to the Guild of Rememberers, and after a time she realized that Mapiya had slipped quietly away and left her alone.

*No, not alone,* she thought, *not alone at all,* for Aelita was suddenly aware of the excited mumbling of many other voices all around her. It was impossible, though, to separate any single voice from the low din of that unseen crowd. She could not even be sure what language was being spoken, except that it seemed to be no tongue she herself could speak or understand. But she did try, straining to wrestle meaning from the voices, and as she tried, it occurred to her that the smoky air of the chamber was no longer smoky air, that it had been transmuted somehow into murky water. The glow of the slave lights had been replaced by the far more peculiar light cast by bioluminescent creatures—toothsome eels with bulging eyes and photophores arrayed along their sides and also by boneless, gelatinous creatures that drifted above her, moving between the sandstone columns like living chandeliers.

In truth, this new light was far more pleasant, and for a time it did not even occur to Aelita to wonder how she could be breathing, or when the chamber had flooded, or if she should try to find a way out and back to the surface. There was such a profound *peace* in this place, a serenity she'd only ever found in flight, and she had no wish for it to end. She rose from the cushions, only to discover that the pillows of satin and velvet had become masses of coral and silt. A school of small fish approached and swirled frenetically about her, like a rain of copper coins, and then was gone again. And meanwhile, the multitude of voices continued to whisper their incoherent conversations. Perhaps it wasn't anything she was supposed to overhear, much less understand; maybe she was eavesdropping without even meaning to eavesdrop. So she made a conscious effort *not* to listen, but this only seemed to encourage the voices to speak louder and more insistently.

This is when Aelita realized that she was drifting upwards, rising with exquisite slowness through a swaying forest of seaweed, sponges, and what appeared to be fantastic forms of marine fungi. Transfixed, she watched as glassy trails of bubbles bled from her mouth and nostrils and rushed upwards towards the ceiling of the flooded chamber.

*I will not drown*, she thought with absolute certainty, and no small degree of determination. *I am meant to see something here, and there would be no point in having seen it, in having it shown to me, if I were then allowed to drown.*

Comforted and buoyed by these thoughts, the Flier continued her ascent, though, in truth, she was beginning to believe the painted vault above her wasn't getting any closer. Could it be, she wondered, that one may never reach it and whatever insights or affirmations it might bestow, through so mundane a process as physical approach?

Then an especially bright eel passed directly in front of Aelita, its flanks blazing with splotches of cobalt light. The fish regarded her with an eye as black and smooth as any night sky through which she had ever flown. The eye was, she saw, not actually an eye at all, but a living portal or doorway, and so she seemed presented with an option: to either allow that empty stare to draw her from here to somewhere else, or permit the eel to slither past and hope to eventually arrive at the painted vault, by one course or another. It was then that she felt strong hands seize her about the ankles and begin to pull her backwards. Aelita kicked and flailed her skinny arms, but could not manage to shake off her attacker. Startled, the eel sped away into the gloom. And so she was deprived of making a choice between one path and another, and growing furious, she kicked more violently, hoping not only to free herself, but wound whoever had dared to interfere.

*Thief!* her mind screamed, and her lips shaped the same word, though nothing escaped her mouth but more bubbles.

All at once, the indecipherable muttering fell silent, and was replaced by a single, oddly lilting voice, clearly speaking words Aelita understood.

*Look at me, Flier. Look down.*

And so she *did* look down, reluctantly taking her eyes from the fresco and squinting into the murk below. But she could see no farther than her narrow waist and hips, and the thing that has seized her remained hidden in shadows that the cold radiance of fish could not hope to penetrate.

*Release me,* Aelita commanded, but the grip on her ankles did not loosen; if anything, it grew tighter. Her feet were beginning to go numb, the blood flow constricted by this unseen assailant. *You have no right to hold me back. You have no right to hinder me.*

And the voice replied, *No, milady. Neither any right, nor any wish.*

*Then release me!* And for the first time since the dream took this dark, diluvial turn, she felt her lungs starting to ache, and knew that too soon she would need to breathe. She was growing lightheaded and did her best not to panic. She recalled the elders in Hind who had instructed her and helped her master her wings, their warnings of errant winds and admonitions that panic was a greater threat than any unexpected downdraft.

*But this is not my dream, milady. It is not for me to release you.*

*I'm suffocating,* she replied. *You are suffocating me. I'm dying, and I'll never see what is painted on the ceiling or follow the path through the eye of the eel.*

Again, that voice billowed up from the concealing darkness. *There is not breath here, nor any need of breath. There is only the beginning of a path to the questions you've been trying to ask since coming to this city. There is no death. This is a region where nothing ends, milady, unless that ending be ignorance and forgetfulness.*

She'd stopped kicking and floated limply now in the water, defeated, still sure that death hovered somewhere very nearby. All the phosphorescent fishes and worms and jellies were withdrawing to sheltering niches in the coral and stone, taking their illumination with them, and soon she would be lost in a blackness as absolute as the eye of an eel.

*You wish to know how the Fliers began, and by what hand they were fashioned, and to what end, but you fail, because the question you ask is not whole.*

She closed her eyes, squeezing them shut against the dizziness and terror threatening to overwhelm her. *Then tell me, demon, what question do I ask?*

*You do not ask me,* it replied, that lilting voice flowing directly into her skull. *No, you ask the ones who were made to speak from dreams, and to speak truths that may be found only in sleeping hours.*

*Somnambulists?* she asked the voice. *You mean that I should ask my questions of the Somnambulists?*

But before the thing below her could reply, the water around Aelita abruptly dissolved into a freezing whirlwind of snowflakes, and for the briefest time she was falling. It is a fear born into her race, the fear of falling. And at that she opened her eyes and sat up, gasping for breath as though she had never breathed before, as if this were the first inhalation after the moment of her birth. Her back ached from having drifted off on the window ledge, and she rubbed the sleep from her eyes and stared down at the icy avenue, clothed now all in night.

# 3.

The dream returned to Aelita—or her to it—many times during that long Perrisian winter. It was never precisely the same dream twice, though sometimes the differences between one incarnation and the next were so insignificant as to resemble skillful forgeries, betrayed only by the least consequential of deviations. A dropped stitch here, a clumsy brushstroke there, fish that glowed with amber light instead of blue. For the better part of two months she rarely left the lodge, or spoke to her fellow lodgers or to the hostellers, and she almost always took her small meals alone rather than endure the company of others. She had come to dislike the feel of their eyes upon her, and usually prickled at their well-intentioned, if misguided attempts at conversation. Aelita wanted to fly away home and leave this crowded, stinking city behind her, but the weather remained too treacherous for flight. She prayed to the Will for strength and understanding and that the dreams might end. But prayer seemed increasingly hollow, as though the Will were no less mythical than the outworlder invasion the Watchers guarded against.

Finally, with great reluctance and misgiving, she sought the services of a pair of Somnambulists who plied their trade not far from the Flier's Lodge. Aelita had never trusted the soothsayers' guild, though she could not have said whether their unsavory reputation was entirely warranted. They tended to serve—or take advantage of, depending upon one's view—the members of the lower, more menial guilds, and even the guildless. But the unrelenting, persistant dreams, and what they almost but never quite revealed, had taken a toll on her, and Aelita had begun to doubt her sanity. Spring was still a month away—a month or more—and the Flier had come to know desperation as she had never known it before.

The Somnambulists' dingy, ramshackle booth gave every indication of having been hastily cobbled together from cast-off scraps of metal, wood, and plastic, and it sat, listing to one side, very near the banks of the Senn. Aelita lingered at the entryway, watching the cold black river moving slowly by on its way to the excavations at Roen and then the Normand coast beyond. But the river was a dreary sight, and somehow much too reminiscent of the dreams, and she soon slipped through the thick draperies hung across the entrance.

Inside, the air was redolent of sweat and dust, and a bit too warm after the chilly streets. Aelita was greeted by a girl, dressed in somber rags, so rawboned that she might almost have passed for a Flier herself.

"I am Pratima," she said, speaking hardly above a whisper and not meeting Aelita's gaze. "You have come for an audience with my mistress, yes?"

"I have," Aelita admitted, blinking as her eyes adjusted to the dim interior of the booth. There were no slave lights here, only a number of flickering beeswax candles. "You are her acolyte?"

"I am," the girl said, keeping her eyes on the threadbare carpet. "From the depths of her reveries, my mistress saw your approach and sent me to greet you. If you will follow, Simone is waiting. You have coin?"

"Of course," Aelita replied, though she wondered if she could afford to pay even half what these two might require to divulge the information she sought. Assuming, of course, they knew anything at all. Aelita produced four silver coins and gave them to the acolyte.

"You have no more than this?" Pratima asked.

"No, that is all I have."

"You can only expect so much for so little. You should understand that in advance. If you had, say, twice again this sum, I am sure—"

"That is all I *have*," Aelita said again, impatiently and with greater force. "If it is not sufficient, I will leave your mistress to her reveries."

"No, no," the acolyte said. "But you can only expect so much—"

"—for so little. Yes, I know."

"Well, then follow me, Flier, and we shall soon see what we shall see," and Pratima led Aelita out of the anteroom, through more draperies and candlelight, and into the booth proper (which seemed somewhat larger inside than the Flier had guessed from the street).

Her first impression of the Somnambulist was that she had been led not to a living woman, but to a hunched and crooked sort of mummification, propped up on a tattered divan amid a discrepant assortment of cushions. The Flier had always assumed the soothsayers' work to be more profitable, and the squalor of the booth was disorienting. The malformed figure whom the acolyte had called Simone was swaddled in overlapping layers of linen bandages, stained here and there with food and human filth. Her eyes were tightly shut, her lips parted slightly. Pratima pointed to a stool, and Aelita promptly sat.

"She is a *great* seer," the acolyte said, a hint of reproach in her voice now. "A *very* great seer, and it is a shame your offering is insufficient to the magnificence of her abilities. She might have shown you much. But for *this*," and Pratima paused to jingle the silver coins in her palm, "I fear she will show you very little, indeed."

Before Aelita could reply, a rattling sound gurgled forth from the lips of the Somnambulist, neither quite a belch nor a cough, and she began to mutter in the rasping language of her guild. Pratima stared at her mistress a moment, then turned towards Aelita, her eyes going again to the floor.

"There are *many* things Simone would say to you," the acolyte said. "You are certain this is the limit of what you may afford?"

"If you ask me that again," Aelita answered, speaking as sternly as she dared, "I'll take my coin and leave. It may be a *less* talented Somnambulist would prove sufficient to the needs of a pauper."

Again, Simone spoke, pausing once or twice in the labyrinth of her trance to draw and let out a wheezing breath. Aelita thought there was an urgency to the sleeping woman's words, but could not be sure. When Simone was done, Pratima nodded and nervously licked her thin, chapped lips.

"Visions may seem as dreams," she said, "to those untrained in their interpretation. You only believe you are haunted by nightmares. Rather, you have been chosen—"

"By whom," Aelita asked. "By whom have I been chosen."

"Four coins is not much," Pratima reminded her. "I will speak. You will listen. Simone, who sees all, who understands that which is hidden from waking minds, she will speak, and I will speak on her behalf. You should not interrupt. You have not purchased that privilege."

"No," Aelita relented. "I have not."

Again, Simone wheezed and spoke in that tongue she and Pratima shared, and again Pratima translated. "You are being sought after," she told the Flier. "A thing that has been lost for ages wishes to be found, to be found by you, for it has questions. A thing which might almost be your brother, or your sister, as your race and its were conceived during the Years of Magic, and from not dissimilar desires."

A third time, Simone spoke, and at greater length than before. When she was done, Pratima bowed slightly before interpreting the Somnambulist's message for the Flier.

"The thing that seeks you is far west from here, across the wide expanse of Earth Ocean. Were you nearer the messenger, then less distorted would its communications be. This mind is strong. This mind, or *these* minds, yes? By closing distance, you would find clarity. All the world might marvel at what you would be shown." Here Pratima paused and glanced briefly at her mistress.

"You are indeed honored, Flier. For what I am bidden to say next is worth a hundred times what you have paid."

"I have *asked* for no more than I can afford. Keep it to yourself."

"Oh, I *would* do that, most assuredly. But I serve Simone, and Simone tells me that I am forbidden to withhold. So… you return to the Guild of Rememberers. Go to them at once. They will soon cross the ocean and have need of a Flier. At the confluence of your needs and theirs may you find your route west."

# 4.

And so Aelita had gone to the Hall of Rememberers and offered her services to that guild—an offer that was greeted with surprise and suspicion, but eventually also with acceptance. And so she joined this expedition to find the ruins of Ares amid the island chains that are all that remain of the continent of Sud-amerik and of nations lost at the end of the Second Cycle. And so, too, she stands on this gray beach as the sun passes overhead and begins the long descent towards evening. She stands where, so far as she knows, no human being has stood for untold millennia. And the equatorial sun shines down and washes over her exposed flesh, a constant reminder that she cannot hope to return to the watership until dusk. Hours have passed since her arrival here, unremarkable hours, and Aelita has begun to wonder if she has made some mistake, a miscalculation of one sort or another, if possibly she has misunderstood a very small but crucial portion of the instructions conveyed in her dreams. Or maybe it is not a mistake on her part. Maybe *they* have changed their minds about this contact. Upon reconsideration, maybe they have decided it is unwise. *To come so far and fail,* she thinks, but finds the thought intolerable and pushes it away.

She sits only a little distance from the reach of the calm but simultaneously restless sea, those low, frothing waves that rush up the sand and then, all forward energy spent, immediately withdraw, colliding with the next line of incoming swells in their hasty retreat. The sun burns her skin, and she is thirsty, thirsty and hungry and wondering if she will even have the strength to make the flight back once the sun has set. Her body has no overpocket, and she was, of course, unable to carry provisions. It may be there is freshwater somewhere on this island, and it may be there are edible fruits. But Aelita has been too afraid of missing what she has come to find to set off into the dunes foraging for food.

*What if they came and I was not here to greet them? There would not ever be a second chance.*

So she sits in the sun and waits. When the heat becomes too painful, she spreads her wings, then holds them close together and over herself, making a sort of canopy of that delicately veined flesh to cast a stingy pool of half-shadow. She huddles there and watches the sea, trying not to dwell on her parched throat and rumbling stomach. The heat is making her sleepy, but she doesn't dare close her eyes for longer than the space of a blink, for fear of nodding off. Surely, if she dozed, they would wake her. But then she thinks, they might take it as an insult, if they come up and find her napping. One of the larger waves rushes in, coming within mere inches of her toes, and it leaves a small fish stranded when it recedes. The fish flops about on the wet sand, the opercular flaps at either side of its head rising and falling as its feathery gills struggle to draw oxygen from gas instead of liquid. Aelita is about to stand up and go to its rescue, when another wave carries it back out into the lagoon.

Aelita lowers her head, uncertain whether what she has just witnessed should be taken as evidence of a merciful or a merciless sea. A drop of sweat runs from her brow, down the bridge of her nose, and falls to the sand. It leaves a dimple amid the granules of quartz and olivine and basalt, and she thinks the loss of that drop of sweat is not so unlike the blood sacrifices offered up by First and early Second Cycle men to their invisible gods—a precious trickle of her personal, internal ocean to merge with the relative infinity of salt water laid stretching out before her. And then Aelita hears something splashing in the surf, and she looks up.

The Swimmer is wading towards dry land, towards her, and the sun glimmers off its sleek, hairless body. Its skin is the color of a mid-winter sky hanging low over Perris, she thinks, that exact same gray gone almost to the outskirts of violet. She never saw it in her dreams, the one who spoke to her, and no images of the Swimmers survive, at least none that she has been able to retrieve from the access banks of the Rememberers. It is not what she expected, but Aelita is not sure she could say what she might have expected instead. It is tall, with thick webbing between its greatly elongated fingers. Much of the Swimmer's face is obscured behind what Aelita takes to be a sort of breathing apparatus, and she is immediately reminded of that beached fish, gasping for air. The Swimmer is as naked as she, save the black metallic angles of its respiratory machinery and an assortment of fine gold chains worn about its throat. There is a heavy bracelet, also gold, clamped about its right wrist. Despite the Swimmer's nakedness, it is impossible for her to determine gender; it has neither breasts nor any visible genitalia, and the general build is neither particularly male nor particularly female. Its face is hidden behind the breathing apparatus, which makes a soft gurgling sound, punctuated by an occasional loud *click*. She wishes that she could see its eyes, then wonders if the Swimmers even have eyes.

It raises its right arm, as if in greeting, and the gold bracelet flashes brilliantly, reflected sunlight almost blinding Aelita for a moment. She folds her wings and gets slowly to her feet, blinking back the yellow-orange afterimages. When the Swimmer speaks, its voice is flat and tinny, filtered through speakers somewhere on the breathing apparatus.

"Most of us did not believe that you would come," it says, and then there is a sound like a long wet sigh.

"I *had* to come," she replies, and is surprised by the tremble in her voice. It is not fear, because she is not afraid of this strange being, and so she thinks that maybe it is awe. Awe, and relief that she is not insane. "You *touched* me," she says and presses a finger to her forehead. "You showed me so many things. I had to come. I had to find a way to be here."

"Most do not," the Swimmer replies. It is standing very near her now, the sea lapping about its bare ankles. Aelita, who is accustomed to feeling small (for few are as slight of build as the Guild of Fliers), has never felt so completely diminished by the physical presence of another person, not even by some of the hulking Changelings she has met. "Most hear, when we call, but they do not choose to listen," the Swimmer adds. The valves and cogs of the breathing machine sigh, and the blades of a miniscule fan beneath its chin whir loudly.

"You would die without that?" she asks, and the Swimmer cocks its head to one side, but does not answer the question. Its skull is narrow, from what she can see, the lower jaw jutting out slightly. A high bony or cartilaginous crest projects from the back of the Swimmer's head, and the skin covering the crest appears to have been elaborately tattooed with symbols that mean nothing to her.

"I do not have long with you, milady," the Swimmer says, and Aelita wonders if the mechanism it wears not only aids in breathing, but translates the wearer's words into a language she can understand. "There is much I would say, and much more I would hear, but I have only a short time."

Aelita does not ask the Swimmer *why* there is not more time; the question seems irrelevant.

"I will listen," she says, "and will do my best to answer whatever questions you would ask me."

"First, Flier, there *must* be a covenant," the Swimmer says, "for I need to be certain you will never speak of this meeting with anyone. You will not record or relate it in any way beyond your own memories. Such a thing is not permitted."

And she is only surprised that she is *not* surprised.

"Half the world now believes that you are extinct," she replies, "the other half that you have never existed. Would you not be known again?"

The Swimmer's breathing machine wheezes and clicks, and then it slowly shakes its oddly proportioned head from side to side. "No, milady. We would not and must not."

"Am I at least permitted to ask why you have chosen to hide yourselves away? And if such secrecy is so important, why risk it like this?"

The Swimmer seems to watch her for a moment, though Aelita cannot be sure, as she cannot see its eyes. Perhaps it is staring at the dunes behind her, or at the cloudless blue-white sky above the island. She is about to retract the question, having thought better of it, when there is an especially loud *click* from the breathing apparatus, and also a distinct *pop*. The Swimmer takes one step nearer Aelita, so that it has almost completely crossed that shifting threshold from its element into hers.

"When our minds found you, Flier, you were searching for the origins of your own guild. Your curiosity attracted our attention." It pauses briefly, then continues. "I can say that it is in the creation of the Swimmers by the flesh crafters of the old and fallen world that the need for this covenant lies. In their surgeries, long ago, were we shaped, though not from any mere whim or scientific thirst for knowledge. From a need, they would have said, for a race of servants who could venture where they themselves could not. Human beings who could live and work in the abyssal depths beyond the margins of the continents, whose anatomies would be able to withstand such terrible pressure and cold as is found there, and who would have no need of the air. So, this is not how, but why I exist as I do, for servitude soon proved not so different from slavery, Flier Who Is Named Aelita. In the rebellion that followed, my people almost *were* driven to extinction, as our makers would rather have wiped us from the face of the world than see us free."

Aelita stares a moment, then asks, speaking hardly above a whisper, "You *know* these things?"

"Yes," it replies, "I know these things, milady, for unlike you we have not forgotten." And the apparatus hiding its face echoes these words with an urgent series of clicks.

"It was very long ago," Aelita says. "Surely, the world has changed."

"All things do not change with time. Are there not still human slaves?" the Swimmer asks. "What of your Neuters? What of the Changelings and guildless ones?"

And because these are fair questions, and there is no denying the enduring cruelty of humanity, Aelita offers no further argument. She nods her head and sits back down in the damp sand near the Swimmer's broad webbed feet. Each toe ends in a small ebony claw, sharp as any dagger. Out in the lagoon, something leaps clear of the water and falls back with a splash.

"I have your word?" the Swimmer asks. "Our mysteries will be safe with you?"

"Yes, you have my word, though I came seeking answers, and not the weight of such a confidence."

"It is your choice, Flier," the Swimmer says, and now it bends low, kneeling beside her. Somehow, she thinks, it smells more of the sea than the sea itself. "I would never rob you of that. Like so many others, you could have *refused* the dreams, ignored the call."

"But I didn't," she tells it, and, in truth, the dreams never felt like something she could have turned her back on.

"I do not have long," the Swimmer reminds her.

"And I may not fly away until the sun is down," she replies and glances up at the Swimmer. She smiles, squinting, trying to get a better impression of the face hidden beneath the bulky mask.

"Then we shall talk, milady," it says. And so they do, trading stories of the world above for secrets of the world below. Aelita learns of a war the Swimmers fought and almost lost against their makers, in the chaos near the end of Second Cycle. She learns of leviathans that still dwell above submarine mountains, and of the cities the Swimmers have built in the most lightless and inaccessible canyons of the hadopelagic zone. And, in turn, she tells of the surface, and what she knows of the affairs of other guilds. She speaks of Perris and Roum, Stanbool and many other great cities she has visited in her travels. And then, before the Swimmer goes and leaves her alone on the sand, they sit together silently, and watch the white gulls soaring above the retreating tide.

# Silverberg, Satan, and Me
# or
# Where I Got the Idea for My Silverberg Story for This Anthology

Connie Willis

Connie Willis lives with her husband in Greeley, Colorado. She first attracted attention as a writer in the late '70s with a number of stories for the now-defunct magazine *Galileo*, and went on to establish herself as one of the most popular and critically-acclaimed writers of the 1980s. In 1982, she won two Nebula Awards, one for her novelette "Fire Watch", and one for her short story "A Letter from the Clearys"; a few months later, "Fire Watch" went on to win her a Hugo Award as well. In 1989, her novella "The Last of the Winnebagoes" won both the Nebula and the Hugo, and she won another Nebula in 1990 for her novelette, "At The Rialto." In 1993, her landmark novel, *Doomsday Book* won both the Nebula Award and the Hugo Award, *as* did her short story "Even the Queen." She won another Hugo in 1994 for her story, "Death on the Nile," another in 1997 for her story, "The Soul Selects Her Own Society," another in 1999 for her novel, *To Say Nothing of the Dog*, another for her novella, "The Winds of Marble Arch" in 2000, another in 2006 for her novella, "Inside Job," and yet *another* in

2008 for her novella, "All Seated On the Ground"—capped off in 2011 by her novel, *Blackout/All Clear* winning *both* the Nebula and the Hugo Awards. In 2009 she was voted into The Science Fiction Hall of Fame, and in 2011 she received the SFWA Grand Master Award. All of which makes her the most honored writer in the history of science fiction, and the only person ever to win *two* Nebulas and *two* Hugos in the same year. Her other books include the novels *Water Witch, Light Raid*, and *Promised Land*, all written in collaboration with Cynthia Felice, *Lincoln's Dreams, To Say Nothing of the Dog, Bellwether, Uncharted Territory, Remake*, and *Passage*, and, as editor, the anthologies *The New Hugo Winners, Volume III, Nebula Awards 33*, and (with Sheila Williams), *A Woman's Liberation: A Choice of Futures By and About Women*. Her short fiction has been gathered in the collections, *Fire Watch, Impossible Dreams*, and *Miracle and Other Christmas Stories*. Her most recent books are the massive two-volume novel, *Blackout/All Clear*, and a huge retrospective collection, *The Best of Connie Willis*.

Connie Willis says: "My first contact with the inimitable Mr. Silverberg was *Revolt on Alpha C*. My second was watching him do his amazing presenter thing at my first Worldcon, and my third was reading his terrific "Good News From the Vatican." And then I read his "When We Went to See the End of the World," a story which promptly went onto my list of Best SF Stories Ever list (and has remained there) and then the astonishing *Dying Inside*.

But none of his stories or novels meant as much to me as the man himself, and his wit and charm and unflappability. I was immediately jealous of them and have only gotten more so as I realized I would *never* be as good a writer, emcee, or conversationalist as he is. And as I've realized how difficult it is to pull off that whole calm, cool, possessed-of-a-rapier-wit thing and make it look effortless. Fred Astaire has always been a hero of mine for making the impossibly difficult look easy. Robert Silverberg is another.

He's wonderful, that's all there is to it. But on occasion, it strikes me as unfair that he got *all* the talent and charm and humor and is handsome besides. And well-dressed. And sometimes I even think that there must be something nefarious behind it, that it all has to be the result of some deep, dark plot.

Which of course is completely, tin-foil-hat-conspiracy-theory ridiculous. Although..."

I was at a science fiction convention, and I'd just gotten off a panel on "How to Break Into Science Fiction." On the panel I'd said I'd gotten my start writing short stories and mentioned that I was currently writing one for a collection honoring Robert Silverberg, whom I adored and whose short stories had inspired me when I was starting out. I'd named some of them—"Sailing to Byzantium" and "The Pope of the Chimps" and "The Man Who Never Forgot"—and suggested that reading and learning from them was a good way to break into the field.

Anyway, the panel'd ended, and I'd made it safely out of the room only to be trapped in the hall by two aspiring young writers who thought the way to break in to science fiction was to force me to read their manuscripts. When I explained that it wouldn't do any good because I wasn't an editor, the first one said, "But you could tell your editor to buy it," and the second chimed in, "And you could write us a cover blurb."

At which point I said, "I'm sort of in a hurry," fled into the bathroom, and hid in one of the stalls, hoping that if I waited a few minutes, they'd have attached themselves to one of the other writers, and reminding myself not to do another "How to Break Into Science Fiction" panel.

It may just be my advancing age, but it seems to me new writers are more aggressive than they were when I broke in: demanding you read their eight-volume fantasy series, introduce them to your agent, and get them in to see your editor. If action isn't taken, they'll be holding a gun on you and dictating the glowing recommendation they want you to write for their novel.

I half-expected my two to follow me into the bathroom and slide their manuscripts under the stall door, which happened recently to an editor of mine. They didn't, but when I came cautiously out of the bathroom ten minutes later, a young woman stepped out in front of me from behind a pillar.

*Oh, no,* I thought, bracing myself, but she made no move to give me the envelope.

Instead, she said, "On that panel you just did, you said you were going to be in the Robert Silverberg anthology. Do you know him?"

"Yes," I said warily. Was she going to ask me to give her manuscript to Bob? "But I doubt if he'd have time to read your—"

"Is he as cool as he seems?" she cut in.

I was relieved. She wanted info on her favorite writer, that was all. "Yes, he's very cool," I said. "And very nice. He—"

"How long have you known him?" she demanded. Her manner was a bit abrupt, but I was used to that. Science fiction fans are apt to come up to you at conventions and ask all sorts of things—"Have you ever read H.P. Lovecraft?" and "Did you know the plague is endemic to prairie dog burrows?" and "Why did you kill off my favorite character?"—without any preamble at all.

So, instead of asking her why she wanted to know, I said, "Oh, gosh, I've known Robert Silverberg forever. I met him at the first Worldcon I ever went to. I was up for a Hugo Award, and he was *so* nice to me. When I said this was what I'd dreamed of since I was a teenager, he said, 'It was what I dreamed of, too. We're two of a kind, my dear,' and I thought, this is even better than winning a Hugo. Robert Silverberg is standing here talking to *me*, a nobody, and—"

"When was that?" she cut in.

"I don't know. It had to be thirty years ago at least. 1980, maybe? I remember it was in Boston and—"

"How old was he?"

"How *old* was he? Thirty years younger than he is now, I guess."

"Which is how old?"

"I don't know," I said, trying to figure out where this was going. "Sixty? Sixty-five?"

"He doesn't *look* sixty-five."

"I know. He never seems to age. He's as handsome as when I first met him."

"That's what I thought," she said. "When you first met him, was he as good a public speaker as he is now?"

"Yes. He's always been terrific at giving speeches and being a master-of-ceremonies. He's wonderful on stage, the best emcee science fiction has ever had, as a matter of fact— very witty, with this cool, suave delivery that—"

"What about his writing?" she cut in. "Was he always good? From the beginning?"

"Yes." His first book had been *Revolt on Alpha C*, which I'd read when I was a teenager and loved. I told her that.

"And you don't think there's something odd about that?"

"Odd?" I said, surprised. "No. There have been lots of science fiction writers who wrote terrific stuff when they were really young. Peter Beagle wrote *A Fine and Private Place* when he was only twenty, and there's Samuel R. Delany and Harlan Ellison and—"

"But none of them look like Silverberg."

True. Robert Silverberg was one of the nicest-looking men in science fiction and certainly the most debonair. And the best-dressed, though there wasn't much of a bar in a field dominated by ratty T-shirts with "Beam Me Up, Scotty" and "What Part of BwaHaHa Don't You Understand?" on them. But even if he'd been a stockbroker, or a movie star, he'd have been well-dressed.

"How rich is he, do you think?" the young woman was asking. "As rich as J. K. Rowling?"

"No writer is as rich as J. K. Rowling. Except possibly Stephenie Meyer. Who I heard was supposed to be here," I said, looking vaguely around in the hope she'd say, "Where?" and go darting off. This conversation was starting to make me uncomfortable. Why did she want to know how much money he had? Was she some sort of stalker instead of a fan?

She wasn't interested in *Twilight*. "How many awards has Robert Silverberg won?" she asked.

"I don't know. Tons. I imagine you could look them up on Wikipedia," I said, staring pointedly at my watch. "Look, I'm sorry, I've got to get to my next panel—"

"Here," she said, suddenly thrusting the manila envelope at me. "Read this."

"I'm afraid I don't—" I began, but she was already halfway down the hallway.

"Wait!" I called, waving the envelope, and started after her, only to run into a crowd surrounding Neil Gaiman. By the time I extricated myself from it, she was gone.

*I should have known it,* I thought disgustedly. All those questions had been nothing but a pretext for giving me the manuscript of her novel, no doubt with a note attached saying, "Send blurb to this address."

I started toward the nearest trashcan to get rid of the envelope, but halfway there a woman with a book to have signed (something a writer's always willing to do) stopped me, and I jammed everything I was holding in my tote bag so I could fish for a pen.

It turned out she thought I was Lois McMasters Bujold, and by the time I'd explained that and handed her back *The Vor Game,* I'd forgotten all about the envelope.

I didn't think of it again till I got home and found it while unpacking. I dumped it in the wastebasket, and as I did, it broke open, and the contents fell out.

It wasn't a manuscript. It was a bunch of Xeroxed photos. There was a Xeroxed copy of his short story, "Born with the Dead," a literary analysis of Silverberg's short stories by a Dr. Herrenhorn at the University of Idaho which began, "His output and artistry from the beginning were amazing, even superhuman;" a link to a YouTube video, which, when I tried to link to it, said, "This site is no longer available;" and a handwritten letter. There was also an unmarked old-fashioned VHS tape. When I stuck it in the player it was, inexplicably, the musical *Seven Brides for Seven Brothers.* I decided I'd better read the letter.

It was addressed to me, and the first line said in all caps, "*DO NOT* READ UNTIL YOU'VE LOOKED AT THE PHOTOS," which were all of Robert Silverberg in his younger days—at writers' workshops and SF conventions and parties.

Attached to it was a bibliography of his novels, short stories, and essays, and a list of all his awards—he'd won four
Hugos, four Nebulas, and a Jupiter Award and been named
a Grand Master of Science Fiction. She'd even included
a biography.

It turned out he was older than I'd thought: seventy-
eight. But why had she asked me how old he was and all
those questions if she already knew the answers to them?
And what were the photos supposed to mean? They were all
group shots—Silverberg with Isaac Asimov and Charles N.
Brown and Harlan Ellison or with Frederik Pohl and Alfred
Bester and Harry Harrison. They weren't captioned except
for the date and location: Milford, Summer 1962; World SF
Convention, 1957; Boston, 1959; and there was no indication
of what I was supposed to be looking for.

I turned back to the letter, which wasn't a letter. It was
another list, which read:

"1. Youth

2. Handsome

3. Rich

4. Beautiful wife

5. Republican

6. Fame

7. Historical precedent (See videotape)"

Historical precedent? The only precedent in *Seven Brides
for Seven Brothers* that I remembered was that the brothers
had carried off their brides like the Romans had kidnapped
the Sabine women, and in spite of the reference to Bob's wife,
I couldn't imagine the letter-writer was accusing Bob of carrying Karen off against her will. I turned the page.

"8. Talent

9. Fire
10. Bestsellers
11. Famous
What do you think?
(Signed) Janine Sammael"

What did I think? I thought Janine—and people nowadays in general—do not understand how to write a list—the items in it are supposed to be parallel—or how to make themselves clear. What did "fire" mean? The only fire I knew about involving Bob was the one that had burned down his house a number of years back, destroying several of his manuscripts in the process. And what did Bob's political affiliation have to do with anything?

I also thought I'd better watch *Seven Brides for Seven Brothers*. Janine was obviously hinting at something, but I had no idea what. Maybe the movie would tell me. Besides, I love it, especially that great dance number at the barn-raising. And Howard Keel singing, "Bless Your Beautiful Hide." So I made some popcorn, hunted up our old VHS player, and settled down to watch.

It wasn't *Seven Brides for Seven Brothers*. That turned out to be an ad from AMC or Turner Classics or whatever Janine had taped it from. It was another musical—*Damn Yankees*—and five minutes in, it suddenly hit me: Janine thought Silverberg had sold his soul to the Devil.

That was why she'd asked me how long I'd known him and whether he'd always been a good writer, because she thought his youthful appearance and talent were due to Satanic intervention.

You could actually make a case for that. Silverberg *was* rich, acclaimed, extremely good-looking, had been a prodigy, and, unlike everyone else in those photos, had aged hardly at all. You could almost believe he'd made a pact with the Devil. If there was such a thing as the Devil to make a pact with. Which there wasn't, except in Goethe. And *Damn Yankees*.

And apparently in Janine's fevered imagination. Which meant I needed to warn Bob. I tried calling him, but all I got was his answering machine. And when I called our editor at *Asimov's* (in case Janine had Bob tied up somewhere à la *Misery* and was insisting he conjure up the Devil so she could make a deal with him herself or something), Sheila said he was at a conference in Tokyo and wouldn't be back till the beginning of the month.

I debated waiting and then decided I'd better not and sent off an e-mail to Janine saying, "There's no chance Robert Silverberg made a deal with the Devil like the one Joe made in *Damn Yankees*. In the first place, I've known Bob for years, and he's a lovely person—charming, witty, and gracious. The first time I met him I was a new writer and so thrilled to meet him I could hardly speak, and he was wonderful to me, extremely kind and generous. Which are hardly the qualities he'd have if he'd sold his soul to the Devil. In the second place, THERE IS NO SUCH THING AS THE DEVIL. You've been reading too much science fiction."

Then I made copies of everything, including the tape, and sent it off to Bob's home address with an explanatory note, and then sent him an e-mail, giving him the short version of what had happened, just in case she showed up in Tokyo, and asking him to call me when he got back.

He called the next morning.

"I thought you weren't due back till next month," I said.

"I'm not back. I'm calling from Tokyo."

"Tokyo? Good heavens, isn't it the middle of the night there?"

"Yes. Yesterday. Or tomorrow. I'm not certain which. What's this fan's name?"

"I don't know. Janine Something. She's not there, is she?"

"No. Janine what?"

"I don't remember. It's on the letter," I said. I explained I'd sent it and copies of the rest of the stuff in the packet to him at home. "She's obviously a wacko. I wouldn't worry. She'll probably have forgotten all about you by the time you get home and will have moved on to someone else. Like Neil Gaiman," but he wasn't listening.

"Did you keep a copy of the letter?" he asked, and when I said yes, made me go get it and read him her name.

"Janine Sammael," I said.

"Janine Sammael," he repeated. "How do you spell that?"

I spelled it for him. "Do you know her?"

"No. Is she a writer or a fan?"

"I don't know. She was at the 'How to Break Into Science Fiction' panel, but she didn't ask me to read her manuscript or give her a blurb."

"Not a writer then," he said dryly. "Read me the letter."

"Wouldn't it be cheaper for me to e-mail it to you?" I suggested. "Aren't international calls expensive?"

"Never mind that. Read it."

I did.

"Republican?" he said. "How does my being a Republican prove that I've sold my soul to the devil? Abraham Lincoln was a Republican. And I don't even like Sarah Palin."

I kept reading.

"Fire?" he said, outraged. "I was the victim of a fire, not the one who *set* it."

"Do you want me to finish this or not?" I said and read the rest of the list and the "What do you think?"

"Her theory won't hold water, even to a hardened Democrat like yourself. In the first place a lot of writers have more awards than I do—"

"You *are* a Grand Master of Science Fiction," I noted. "And you're in the Science Fiction Hall of Fame."

"*And*," he went on as if he hadn't heard me, "there are any number who have more money, like Dan Brown. And he writes novels directly attacking established religion, besides which his writing style is execrable. In fact, a pact with the Devil may well be the only explanation for his popularity. Did you point that out to this Janine person?"

"No," I said. "I didn't have the chance to say anything at the time, and anything we say now will just encourage her. Besides, you wrote a story about a robot becoming Pope. And one about building a new Tower of Babel."

"But *they* were well-written."

"That's another one of Janine's arguments," I reminded him. "The fact that you write so well. She thinks 'Passengers' and *Up the Line* are too good to have been written without supernatural assistance, and I have to agree with her."

"Thank you," he said. "But do I really seem the sort of person foolish enough to enter into a pact with Satan?"

"No," I said, thinking of the innocent hero Joe in *Damn Yankees*. Bob would never have been naïve enough to fall for Ray Walston's pitch or his talk of an "escape clause" or have believed the Devil would actually let the Washington Senators win the pennant. He was far too savvy.

"Did this Janine person provide any proof of her extraordinary theory?" he asked.

"Only some photographs of you at conventions and workshops in the fifties and sixties," I said. "There's one of you with a bunch of people at Milford—Damon Knight and Ed Bryant and Harlan Ellison—"

"Is Gardner Dozois in the picture?"

"Yes. At least I think it's him. He's got long hair, and he's wearing—"

"White bell-bottomed trousers?"

"Yes," I said. "Why? Is there something in the picture that—?"

"No wonder Janine person thought there was evil afoot," he said with a shudder in his voice. "White bell-bottoms are in fact a cardinal sin, and Gardner was also wearing a shirt with large daisies on it, as I recall. The photo's not in color, is it?"

"No, at least not the copy she sent me."

"Thank God. The daisy-covered shirt was, as I recall, Day-Glo orange with sulfurous yellow leaves, which would have completely convinced her it could only have come from a boutique in the Ninth Circle of Hell. Though that was the sixties, when even virtuous men were guilty of all sorts of sins—psychedelic ties and fringe and polyester leisure suits."

*You* weren't, I thought. He'd been well-dressed even in the sixties, and he still was, the very picture of sartorial elegance.

"Did this Janine person specify what it was I am supposed to have obtained from this infernal contract I signed?" Bob was asking. "Surely not the few shekels I get paid for my column in *Asimov's*. My wife, perhaps? I'll admit Karen resembles Helen of Troy, but pacts with the Devil don't usually involve *marrying* the object of one's desire, do they?"

"No," I said. "But they *do* involve eternal youth, and looking at those photos, you have to admit you look younger than the other people in them—"

"That would be more likely attributable to my parents' bequeathing me good genes than to Satanic intervention," he said. "And as to the other authors depicted therein, several of them had no handsome youth to lose."

Which was true. Some of the writers and fans who'd ended up looking like warthogs and toads had started out looking like warthogs and toads.

"And if this Janine person thinks I sold my soul for financial remuneration," Bob was saying, "why is she not accusing Stephenie Meyer? Or Sarah Palin? They make more off their books than I do, and their success is far more suspicious."

"I know—"

"And everyone knows a pact with the Devil is unwinnable. If I *had* sold my soul to the Devil, he'd surely have collected long since."

"You don't have to convince me," I said. But I realized with a shock that that was exactly what he'd been trying to do. From Tokyo. In the middle of the night. Why? He no more needed to persuade me he hadn't made a pact with the Devil than that a UFO hadn't crashed in Roswell.

And why did he sound so nervous? I had seen him hundreds of times through the years, on contentious panels and in shouting-match meetings and at awards ceremonies, and he'd never once lost his cool, no matter what had happened. And some pretty spectacular things had happened, especially at the Hugo Awards—the wrong winner's name read, the wrong award handed out, assorted interruptions and eruptions— yet Silverberg had maintained his unruffled, wryly-amused demeanor throughout. So why would a ridiculous letter from an obviously delusional fan send him into a tizzy?

"Methinks he doth protest too much," I muttered after I hung up and went to look at the photographs again.

Silverberg's beard was whiter and his hairline a fraction of a millimeter farther back on the noble brow now than they had been in the photos, but otherwise he looked almost exactly the same as he had back in 1956, expecially when compared to his contemporaries. All of them were either fatter, more stooped, more wrinkled, balder, or all of the above, and a couple of them I couldn't even recognize in their younger incarnations, while Silverberg looked like something out of *Dorian Gray*.

And he was as talented as he was good-looking and, according to the bio Janine had given me, had been from the very beginning: first novel at twenty, first Hugo at twenty-one. And prolific. He'd published over a hundred novels, and during his first five years written over five million words, and produced a best-selling series in his *Majipoor* novels.

And then there were the short stories, classic after classic: "The Pope of the Chimps" and "Nightwings" and "Enter a Soldier. Later, Enter Another," all of them good enough to make one suspect Satanic intervention.

But even if there *were* such a thing as the Devil and you could sell your soul to it, Bob was right—he was rich but not that rich, famous but not that famous, like, say Robert James Waller of *Bridges of Madison County* fame. And he was just too good a writer for the Devil to have had anything to do with it.

Satan might be capable of giving someone bestseller status, fame, fortune, even a silver tongue. But good writing isn't just about a facility for words. It's also about telling the truth—never the Devil's strong suit—and about having insights about people and the world. And the Devil has never had any interest in understanding things, only in controlling and manipulating them. And Bob was right—he would never have fallen for such an obvious trick. I could see him convincing someone else to sell their soul to *him*, but—

I looked at his photograph again—at his thin, pointed goatee, at his mockingly-arched eyebrows, at the devilish twinkle in his eyes.

What if Janine had it backwards, and instead of selling his soul to the Devil, he *was* the Devil? And he was—what? Buying up souls? In science *fiction?*

Sure, there were lots of people in the field who'd sell their souls for a Nebula. Or even a short story sale. But science fiction was slim pickings when it came to opportunities for making mischief. There were lots of other places where the stakes were much higher. Wall Street. Or Congress. Or professional sports, like in *Damn Yankees.*

And if the Devil was busy trying to corrupt SF writers, there should have been a falling off in wickedness in all those other areas, and I hadn't noticed any downturn at all. Look at Karl Rove and Enron and AIG. And Lance Armstrong.

Unless…

I called Sheila again and found out Bob wasn't due back till the twenty-fourth, which gave me a few days to do some research of my own. I spent it reading *Paradise Lost* and Marlowe's *Dr. Faustus*, listening to the Charlie Daniels band's rendition of "The Devil Went Down to Georgia," and looking up "Satan," "soul-selling," and "Ray Walston" on Wikipedia.

As I'd expected, the descriptions I found of the Devil varied widely, from Milton's noble fallen angel to the vomit-inducing monster of *The Exorcist* to the traditional red-horned and triangle-tailed guy with the pitchfork in the comic strips. Sometimes the Devil was described as having huge leather wings and being wrapped around Bald Mountain (Disney) or encased in ice (Dante), and sometimes he wore red socks and wanted the Yankees to win the Series.

What if those discrepancies in his description weren't an accident? What if the discrepancies were because there was more than one devil, and that accounted for why he had so many different names—Lucifer and Beelzebub and the Prince of Darkness and Old Nick (not to be confused with Old *Saint* Nick) and Azazel? What if there were different names because there were different devils—the yellow-eyed hairy guy who impregnated Mia Farrow, and the one who palled around with God and made bets involving boils; the one in charge of wars and other forms of wholesale slaughter, and the one in charge of dirty tricks. And the one in charge of nice, elegant forms of evil, who was tall and debonair and looked like Charles Boyer—or Robert Silverberg? And what if they split up the wickedness territory amongst them?

There'd definitely been a shortage of elegant evil in the last fifty-five years. The sophisticated seduction of innocent young girls has given way in recent years to "So You Want to Be a Hooker," and "The Jersey Shore," and none of the evil-doers in recent memory have shown any tragic nobility at all, or even remorse. Instead, Tom Delay is dancing with the stars, Eliot Spitzer's call girl has an advice-to-the-lovelorn column, and Bernie Madoff's wife is refusing to return the mink.

Whoever was in charge of classy evil had definitely taken a leave of absence. Or was busy working his wiles somewhere else. Like in science fiction.

Bob would be back in two days. I spent them looking up articles by evangelical preachers who'd written diatribes about *Harry Potter* and who claimed that reading science fiction would lead to witchcraft, sex, drugs, and human sacrifice, and the day Silverberg was due back, flew to California to confront him.

"Connie! What a pleasant surprise," he said, though he didn't look it. What he looked was distinctly taken aback. And very nervous. "Is something wrong?" he asked warily. "That person with the soul-selling theory—what was her name? Janice?—hasn't contacted you again, has she?"

"Her name was Janine," I said. "No, I needed to ask you some questions for the story I'm writing about you for the anthology," and there was no mistaking his expression. He looked distinctly relieved. More importantly, he didn't ask why I'd found it necessary to fly all the way out to California to ask him instead of phoning him.

"Of course," he said as if my flying out was the most natural thing in the world. "Come in. What is it you need to know?"

"I've been thinking about using an idea Janine's letter gave me."

"You're writing a story in which I sell my soul to the Devil in order to get published?"

"No. A story in which you *are* the Devil. Or rather, one of them." I told him about my Devil, Inc., theory.

"Highly improbable," he said. "Still, a rather intriguing idea. An organization like the Holy Trinity, only with—how many manifestations did you imagine? Five for the points of the pentacle? Or seven for the seven deadly sins? And which one of these many—or perhaps I should say legion—devils do you see me as?"

"I—"

He put up a warning hand. "If you say Ray Walston, I shall be forced to kill myself. Thus disproving your theory that I'm the Devil, by the way."

"I don't see you as Ray Walston," I said. "I see you as Mephistopheles."

"Ah, from *Faust*," he said, arching an eyebrow. "Well, at least you've chosen a demon who's good-looking."

"And suave and sophisticated. And he has a silver tongue."

"And an excellent tailor," Bob said. "Though I'm deeply wounded to think you envision me as the personification of Evil. But let's set that aside for the moment and assume— just for your story's sake—that I *am* Mephistopheles. What dark deeds do you suspect me of using science fiction to commit? Surely you can't believe the argument that science fiction turns its readers into warlocks and Satan-worshippers?"

"No," I said.

"Then what is it you see me as doing? Expanding readers' horizons beyond their own planet? Encouraging them to be scientifically literate—or simply literate? Exposing them to corrupting works like *1984* or *Fahrenheit 451?*"

He was right. Science fiction wasn't dangerous—except to those rigid ideologies and religions which, in order to survive, had to keep their flocks from questioning anything at all. Or, heaven forfend, thinking for themselves. But that didn't mean Bob/Mephistopheles wasn't up to something.

"I haven't worked that part out yet," I said. "For my story. Maybe you got stuck with science fiction because you drew the short straw or something. Or lost a wager with Beelzebub."

"Or God, as in the Book of Job. Though Mephistopheles has never seemed to me to be the sort to make bets he cannot win. Or to draw the short straw, for that matter."

"Well, then, maybe you picked science fiction for the challenge of the thing. You thought it would be fun to try to corrupt people more interested in playing World of Warcraft and drawing to-scale maps of the *Enterprise* than in obtaining fame, fortune, and power."

"Trust me, *everyone* is interested in obtaining fame, fortune, and power, even if it only consists of getting to the fifth level of Halo. But where are these poor SF souls I've corrupted? Where are their vast fortunes and masses of awards? Speaking of which, *you* have an inordinately large number of Hugos and Nebulas. Are you certain you're not—?"

"Don't change the subject," I said. "We're talking about you and the souls you've bought. Or intend to buy. You might not have done it yet. Maybe you're waiting till everything's in place, like one of those Russian moles."

"My dear child, I have been in science fiction for fifty-nine years. That seems excessively long even for a deep-cover spy. And what is it I've been doing in the meantime? Putting Satanic subliminal messages in my stories, or writing my *Asimov's* columns so that when they're read backwards, they say, 'Paul is dead?' Another conspiracy theory, I might add, which turned out to be false."

"You're right," I said. "It was a silly idea. I'll have to come up with some other plot for my story." I stood up. "Or maybe I'd better just tell Gardner I don't have a story for the anthology. The deadline's next month. I'm not sure I can come up with another story idea by then." I picked up my coat. "I'd better go. I have a plane to catch." I put my coat on. "I didn't really think you were the Devil. You were much too nice to me that night at the Hugo Awards." I put on my coat. "And you write much too well." I started toward the door.

"Wait," he said. "It seems a pity for you not to have a story in the anthology. Perhaps I can think of a way to make your Mephistopheles idea work."

"Like what?" I asked.

"Well, suppose Mephistopheles had heard an evangelist discoursing on the evil-working powers of science fiction, and he decided to investigate the field to investigate its possibilities."

"*What* possibilities?" I asked. "As you said yourself, science fiction's not evil. The only reason evangelists hate it is because they're afraid their flock might be exposed to new ideas and begin doubting what they've been told."

"*I* know that, and *you* know that, but Mephistopheles might not have known that. Science fiction is an obscure enough field it might have escaped his notice till then. Or perhaps he knew it wasn't dangerous, but he thought he might be able to do something by drumming up fear of it. After all, Devil, Inc., had already had excellent success with Communism, comic books, and those witches in Salem. And suppose, to that end, Mephistopheles disguised himself as a callow (though still tall, good-looking and witty) teenaged science fiction writer."

"The plot sounds plausible so far," I said carefully.

Bob went on, "But suppose in order to make his disguise believable, he decided to write several SF stories of his own. And in order to do so, he read the stories in print at that time."

"Which would have been what?" I said dryly. "Robert Bloch's 'The Hell-Bound Train?'"

"Yes. And Theodore Sturgeon's 'The Man Who Lost the Sea,'" he said, "and Philip K. Dick's 'Minority Report,' and 'Flowers for Algernon.'" A strange, softened expression came over his face as he named them, as if he were remembering not only the stories, but how he'd felt when he read them for the first time. And as if he'd completely forgotten I was there. "And 'Surface Tension,'" he said, "and 'Fondly Fahrenheit' and 'A Canticle for Leibowitz.'"

"And he fell in love with them," I said wonderingly. "Like Lola fell in love with Joe in *Damn Yankees*. She was supposed to seduce him, but instead, she fell in love with him, and—"

"What *is* this ridiculous obsession of yours with *Damn Yankees*?" Silverberg spluttered. "I am talking about Mephistopheles, not that badly-dressed little runt Ray Walston."

"Sorry," I said. "Go on? What happens then? In the story?"

"It turns out the evangelist was right—science fiction is a corrupting influence. Instead of using it to corrupt others, Mephistopheles becomes corrupted himself. He is, as you said, introduced to new ideas. He begins to think for himself, and what he thinks is, he wants more than anything else in the world to write science fiction. It would create a nice irony, don't you think? Evil being seduced by good instead of the other way around? Though I'll admit the idea's far-fetched."

"Not necessarily," I said. "'The Man Who Lost the Sea,' could seduce anyone."

"True," he said, and smiled, a reminiscent, almost beatific smile.

"I'm glad you—"

"Glad I what?" he said sharply.

"Glad you gave me that story idea," I said. "And glad you picked science fiction as a career."

"So am I," he said.

I looked at him thoughtfully. "Did you renounce evil or did science fiction make you lose your powers?"

"You're writing the story. You'll have to determine that for yourself. Perhaps Mephistopheles is a reformed character. Or perhaps he's only taking a holiday."

"Like Brad Pitt in the remake of *Death Takes a Holiday?*" I said. "Fifty-five years is a pretty long holiday."

"For a mortal," he said. "Perhaps he went AWOL and has been afraid an outbreak of evil would alert the other members of Devil, Inc., to his whereabouts. Or perhaps he had to give up evil for the duration to avoid giving the company a bad name."

"Or you had to strike a bargain, like in *The Little Mermaid,* where Ariel had to give up her voice to get legs."

"You keep forgetting we are discussing the character of Mephistopheles, not me. And I refuse to discuss anything with an author whose literary allusions all come from the movies and/or Disney cartoons. Be off with you. Go and write your story."

"I'm not sure I should," I said. "What if Janine reads it, and she gets ideas?"

"I assure you there's no reason to worry about Janine. And besides, if it's in a story, people will assume it's science *fiction*, not reality."

"But Janine already thinks—" A horrible thought occurred to me. "You're not planning to do anything to her, are you? Like turn her into a frog or something?" I said and realized too late that that was another allusion to a Disney cartoon.

But he apparently hadn't seen *The Princess and the Frog.* "I assure you, I won't touch a hair of her head," he said. "It won't be necessary. Janine has something else in mind besides exposing me."

He was right. When I got home, there was an e-mail waiting for me from her, advertising *Book One* of Janine's new series,

*Jane Austen Demon Hunter: Satan and Sensibility,* with a note attached that said, "Thanks for the blurb, Connie."

Blurb? I clicked to a photo of the cover, on which was prominently displayed, "'Lovely...charming, witty...wonderful science fiction!' Connie Willis."

*I'll sue her for false representation,* I thought, and then went back and looked at the words again. They were all from the e-mail I'd sent Janine.

I called Bob. "Those words were about *you,*" I spluttered to him, "not her stupid book."

"I always wonder why the Devil gets such a bad rap," he said, "when it's clear he's no match for humans when it comes to sheer wickedness."

"You're right," I said. "It's too bad you renounced evil."

"I never said that," he said, and the next day I read Janine had been sued for several million dollars by Dan Brown and Stephenie Meyer's publishers for having lifted *Satan and Sensibility* straight from *Angels and Demons* and *New Moon,* merely substituting "demon" everywhere the words "Illuminati" or "vampire" appeared, and is facing thirty years to life.

I can't say I'm sorry. And I'm sure Bob had nothing to do with it, although I didn't think plagiarism charges usually got you sent to a maximum security prison. But these aggressive blurb-getting tactics by new writers have *got* to stop.

And if Robert Silverberg is in fact Mephistopheles, it sure would explain a lot. And it would prove what I've always thought—that science fiction has the power to change lives for good. I know it changed mine. Especially stories like "When We Went to See the End of the World" and *Dying Inside.* By Robert Silverberg.

# The Hand is Quicker—

## Elizabeth Bear

Elizabeth Bear was born in Connecticut, and now lives in Brookfield, Massachusetts after several years living in the Mohave Desert near Las Vegas. She won the John W. Campbell Award for Best New Writer in 2005, and in 2008 took home a Hugo Award for her short story "Tideline," which also won her the Theodore Sturgeon Memorial Award (shared with David Moles). In 2009, she won another Hugo Award for her novelette "Shoggoths in Bloom." Her short work has appeared in *Asimov's, Subterranean, SCI FICTION, Interzone, The Third Alternative, Strange Horizons, On Spec,* and elsewhere, and has been collected in *The Chains That You Refuse* and *New Amsterdam.* She is the author of three highly acclaimed SF novels, *Hammered, Scardown,* and *Worldwired,* and of the Alternate History Fantasy "Promethean Age" series, which includes the novels *Blood and Iron, Whiskey and Water, Ink and Steel,* and *Hell and Earth.* Her other books include the novels *Carnival, Undertow, Chill, Dust, All the Windwracked Stars, By the Mountain Bound, Range of Ghosts,* a novel in collaboration with Sarah Monette, *The Tempering of Men,* and two chapbook novellas, *Bone and Jewel Creatures* and *ad eternum.* Her most recent book is a new collection, *Shoggoths in Bloom.* Coming up are two new novels, *Shattered Pillars* and *One-Eyed Jack,* and a new novella, *Book of Iron.*

Elizabeth Bear says: ""The Hand is Quicker—" was inspired by a pair of Silverberg stories that rely heavily for their impact on the idea of the unknowability of reality, the unreliability of human perceptions, and the ability of technology to mediate and filter the world, and in so doing reinforce our biases and preconceptions. Those stories are "Enter a Soldier. Later: Enter Another," and "Sailing to Byzantium." This view of the world as being of essentially unparsable complexity, which humans struggle to filter down into something small and tame enough to compass, has influenced my work heavily for years. Reality tunnels, virtual filtering, skinning perceptions—concepts that appear in my own work as well as that of Charles Stross and Hannu Rajaniemi—find a great deal of their early expression in genre in Silverberg's work."

Rose and I used to come down to the river together last summer. It was over semester break, and my time was my own—between obligatory work on the paper I hoped would serve as the core of my first book and occasional consultations with my grad students.

Rose wore long dark hair and green-hazel eyes for me. I wore what I always did—a slightly idealized version of the meat I was born with. I wanted to be myself for her. I wondered if she was herself for me, but the one time I gathered up the courage to ask, she laughed and swept me aside. "I thought historians understood that narratives are subjective and imposed!"

I loved her because she challenged me. I thought she loved me too, until one day she disappeared. No answer to my pings, no trace of her in our usual haunts. She'd blocked me.

I didn't handle it well. I was in trouble at the university. I was drinking. I wasn't maintaining my citizenship status. With Rose gone, I realized slowly how much my life had come to revolve around her.

No matter how she felt about me, I knew she loved the river-edge promenade, bordered by weeping willows and her namesake flowers. Those willows were yellow as I walked the path now, long leaves clinging to their trailing branches. The last few roses hadn't yet fallen to the frost, but the flowers looked sparse, dwarfed by the memory of summer's blossoms.

The scent was even different now than it had been at the height of summer. Crisper, thin. The change was probably volunteer work; I didn't think the city budget would stretch to skinning unique seasonal scents for the rose gardens. I knew Rose was older than I, no matter how her skin looked, because she used to say that when she was a girl, individual cultivars of *roses* had different odors, so walking around a rose garden was a tapestry of scents. Real roses probably still did that.

I didn't know if I'd ever smelled them.

Other people walked the path—all skins. The city charged your palm chip just to get through the gate. I didn't begrudge the debit. It wasn't as if I was ever going to get to pay it off. Or as if I was ever going to get to come back here. This was a last hurrah.

I edited out the others. I wanted to be alone, and if I couldn't see them, they couldn't see me. That was good, because I knew I didn't look happy, and the last thing I wanted was some random stranger reading my emotional signature and coming over to offer well-meaning advice.

Since this was my last time, I thought about jumping skins—running up the charges, seeing some of the other ways the river promenade could look—fantasyland, or Rio, or a moon colony. Rose and I had done that when we first started coming here, but it turned out we both preferred the naturalist view. With seasons.

We'd met in winter. I supposed it was fitting that I lost her—and everything else that mattered—in the fall.

———

Everything changed at midnight.

Not *my* midnight, as if honoring the mystical claptrap in some dead fairy tale. But about the dinner hour, which would be midnight Greenwich Standard Time—honoring the mystical claptrap of a dead empire, instead. I suppose you have to draw the line somewhere. The world is full of the markers of abandoned empires, from Hadrian's Wall to the Great Wall of China, from the remnants of the one in Arizona to the remnants of the one in Berlin.

My name is Ozymandias, King of Kings.

I was thinking about that poem as I crossed Henderson—with the light: I knew somebody who jaywalked and got hit by an unskinned vehicle. The driver got jail time for manslaughter, but that doesn't bring back the dead. It was a gorgeous October evening, the sun just setting and the trees still full of leaves in all shades of gold and orange. I barely noticed them, or the cool breeze as I waited, rocking nervously from foot to foot on the cobblestones.

I was meeting my friend Numair at Gary's Olympic Pizza and I was running a little late, so he was already waiting for me in our usual corner booth. He'd ordered beers and garlic bread. They waited on the tabletop, the beers shedding rings of moisture into paper napkins.

I slid onto the hard bench opposite him, trying to hide the apprehension souring my gut. The vinyl was artistically cracked and the rough edges caught on my jeans. It wasn't Numair making me so anxious. It was finances. I shouldn't be here, by rights—I knew I couldn't afford even pizza and beer—but I needed to see him. If anything could clear my head, it was Numair.

One of the things I liked about Numair is how unpretentious he was. I didn't skin heavily—not like some people, who wandered through underwater seascapes full of sentient octopuses or dressed up as dragons and pretended they live in Elfland—but he was so down to earth I'd have bet his default skin looked just like him. He was a big guy, strapping and barrel-bodied, with curly dark brown hair that was going gray at the temples. And he liked his garlic bread.

So it was extra-nice that there were still two pieces left when I pulled the plate over.

"Hey, Charlie," he said.

"Hey, Numair." Garlic bread crunched between my teeth, butter and olive oil dripping down my chin. I swiped at it with a napkin. I didn't recognize the beer, dark and malty, although I drank off a third of it making sure. "What's the brew?"

"Trois Draggonnes." He shrugged. "Microbrew license out of…Shreveport.com, I think? Cheers."

"Here's mud in your eye," I answered, and drained the glass.

He sipped his more moderately and put it back on the napkin. "You sounded upset."

I nodded. Gary's was an old-style place, and a real-looking waitress came by about thirty seconds later and replaced my beer. I didn't know if she was an employee or a sim, but she was good at her job. The pizza showed up almost instantly after that, balanced on a metal tripod with a plastic spatula for serving. Greek-style, with flecks of green oregano visible in the sweet, oozing sauce. I always got the same thing: meatball, spinach, garlic, mushrooms. Delicious. I'd never asked Numair what he was eating.

The smell turned my stomach.

"I may not be around much for a while." I stuffed the rest of the garlic bread into my mouth to make room. And buy time. "This is embarrassing—"

"Hey." He paused with a slice in midair, perfect strings of mozzarella stretching twelve inches from pie to spatula. They glistened. The booth creaked when he shifted. "This is me."

"Right. I've got financial trouble. Bigtime."

He put the slice down on his plate and offered me the spatula. I waved it away. The smell was bad enough. Belatedly, I turned it off. Might as well use the filters as long as I had them. The beer still looked appealing, though, and I drank a little more.

"Okay," he said. "How bigtime?"

The beer tasted like humiliation and soap suds. "Tax trouble. I'm going to lose everything," I said. "All assets, all the virtuals. I thought I could pay it down, you know—but then I got dropped by the U., and there wasn't a replacement income stream. As soon as they catch up with me—" I thought of Rose, to whom Numair had introduced me. They'd been Friday-night gaming buddies, until she'd vanished without a word. I'd kept meaning to look her up offline and check in, but… It was easier to let her go than know for certain she'd dumped me. Amazing how easy it was to lose track of people when they didn't show up at the usual places and times. "I got registered mail this morning. They're pulling my taxpayer I.D. I'll be as gone as Rose. Except I came to say goodbye before I ditched you."

He blinked. Now it was his turn to set the pizza down and push the plate away with his fingertips. "Rose died," he said.

I rubbed the back of my neck. It didn't ease the sudden nauseating tightness in my gut as all that bitterness converted to something sharp and horrible. "Died? *Died* died?"

"Died and was cremated. Her family's not linked, so I only heard because she and Bill went to school together, and he caught a link for her memorial service on some network site. You didn't know?"

I blinked at him.

He shook his head. "Stupid question. If you knew—Anyway. I guess you've tried everything, so I'll save the stupid advice."

"Thank you." I hope he picked up from my tone how fervently glad I was. Nothing like netfriends to pile on with the incredibly obvious—or incredibly crackpot—advice when you're in a pickle. "So anyway—"

"Give me your offline contact info?" He held up his phone and I sent it over. It was a pleasantry. I knew what the odds were that I'd ever hear from him. And it wasn't like I could keep my apartment without a tax identification number.

However good his intentions.

Right then, a quarter of the way around the planet, midnight tolled. And I fell out of the skin.

It was sharp and sudden, as somewhere a line of code went into effect and the last few online chits in my account were levied. I blinked twice, trying to shake the dizziness that accompanied the abrupt transition, eyes now scratchy and dry.

Numair was still there in the booth across from me. It was weird seeing him there, unskinned. I'd been right about his unpretentiousness: he looked pretty much as he'd always done—maybe a little more unkempt—though his clothes were different.

Since he was skinned, I knew I'd dropped right out of his filters. I might as well not exist anymore. And Gary's Olympic, unlike Numair, had really suffered in the transition.

The pizza that congealed on the table before me was fake cheese, lumpy and dry looking. Healthier than the gooey pie my filters had been providing a moment before, but gray and depressing. I was suddenly glad I hadn't been chewing on it when the transition hit.

The grimy floor was scattered with napkins. The waitress was real, go figure, but a shadow of her buxom virtual self—no, she was a guy, I realized. Maybe working in drag brought in better tips? Or maybe the skin was a uniform. I'd never know.

And there was me.

I was not as comfortable with myself as Numair. I didn't skin heavily, as I said—just tuning. But my skins did make me a hair taller, a hair younger. My hair...a hair brighter. And so on. With them gone, I was skinny and undersized in a track suit that bagged at the shoulders and ass.

Falling into myself stung.

I reached out left-handed for my beer, since Numair was going to get stuck for the tab anyway. It was pale yellow and tasted of dish soap. So maybe the off flavor in the second glass had been something other than my misery. Whatever.

I chugged it and got out.

The glass door was dirty, one broken pane repaired with duct tape. On the way in, it had been spotless and decorated with blue and white decal maps of Greece. I pushed it open with the tips of my fingers and moved on.

Outside, the street lay dark and dank. Uncollected garbage humped against the curb. Some of it smelled organic, rotten. A real violation of the composting laws. Maybe they didn't get enforced as much against businesses. I picked my way across broken cement to the corner and waited there.

There were more people on the street than there had been. Or maybe they'd been there all along, just skinned out. You could tell who was wearing filters by the way they moved— backs straight, enjoying the evening. The rest of us shuffled, heads bowed. Trying not to see too much. The evening I walked through was full of bad smells and crumbling buildings that looked to be mostly held together by graffiti.

"Aw, crap."

The light changed. I crossed. Of course, I couldn't get a taxi home, or even a bus. Skinned-in drivers would never see me, and my chips were cancelled. I wouldn't get through a chip-locked door to take the tube.

I wondered how the poor got around. I guessed I'd be finding out.

———

I didn't know my way home.

I was used to the guidance my skins gave me, the subtle recognition cues. All I was getting now was the cold wind cutting through a windbreaker that wasn't warm enough for the job I expected it to do, and a pair of sore feet. Everything stank. Everything was dirty. There were steel bars on every window and chip locks on every door.

I'd known that intellectually, but it had never really sunk in before what a bleak urban landscape that made for. Straggling trees lined unmaintained streets, and at every corner I picked my way through drifts of rubbish. I knew there wasn't a lot of money for upkeep of infrastructure, and what there was had to be assigned to critical projects. But it didn't matter; you could always drop a skin over anything that needed a little cosmetic help.

Sure, I'd seen news stories. But it was one thing to vid it and another to wade through it.

About fifteen minutes after I'd realized how lost I was, I also realized somebody was following me. Nobody bothers the skinned: an instantaneous, direct voice and vid line to police services meant Patrol guardian-bots could be at our sides in seconds. It was a desperate criminal who'd tackle one of us. One of *them*. But that was another service I couldn't pay for, along with a pleasanter reality and access to mass transit.

I wasn't skinned anymore, and I bet anybody following me could tell. Of course, I didn't have any credit, either—or any cash. I guessed unskinned folks still used cash, palm-sized magnetic cards with swipe strips. A lot of places wouldn't take it anymore. But if you didn't have accounts or a working palm chip, what else were you going to do?

Well, if you were the guy behind me, apparently the answer was, *take it from somebody else.*

I was short and I was skinny, but living skinned kept me in pretty good shape. There were all kinds of built-in work-out programs, after all, so clever that you hardly even noticed they were healthy. And skinning food kept the blood pressure down no matter how many greasy pizzas you enjoyed.

My pursuer was two thirds of a block back. I waited until I'd put a corner between me and him. As soon as I lost sight of him, I broke into a run.

It was a pretty good run, too. I was wearing my Toesers, because I liked them, and if they were skinned nobody could tell how dumb they looked. Also, they were comfortable. And supposedly scientifically designed for natural running posture, so you landed on the ball of your foot and didn't make a thump with every stride. Breath coming fast, feet scissoring—I turned at the first corner I came to, then quickly turned again.

Unskinned folks looked up in surprise as I pelted past. One made a grab for me, and another one shouted something after, but I was already gone. And then I was on a side street all by myself, running down a narrow path kicked in the piles of trash.

Maybe this was an even more desolate street, and maybe most of the lights were burned out, but I kept on running. It felt good, all of a sudden, like positive action. Like something I could do other than wallowing. Like *progress*.

It kept on feeling like progress all the way down to the river's edge. And then, as I stopped beside a hole snipped-and-bent in the chain link, it felt like a very bad idea instead.

The river was a sewer. When I'd been here before—okay, not down here under the bridge, but on the bank above—it had been all sunshine and rolling blue water. What I saw now was floating milk jugs and what I smelled was a sour, fecal carrion stench.

———

I put a hand out to the fence, the wire gritty, greasy where my fingers touched. It dented when I leaned on it, but I needed it to bear my weight up. A stitch burned in my side, and every breath of air scoured my lungs. I didn't know if that was from running, or because the air was bad. But it was the same air I'd been breathing all along. The filters didn't change the outside world. Just our perceptions of it. So how could the air choke me now when before, I breathed it perfectly well?

Shouts behind me suggested that maybe my earlier pursuer had friends. Or that my flight had drawn attention. I was in shadow—but the yellow track suit wasn't anyone's idea of good camouflage.

Gravel crunched and turned under my feet. I pushed the top of the bent chain triangle up and ducked through, into the moist darkness under the bridge.

Things moved in the night. Rats, I imagined, but some sounded bigger than rats. What else could live in this filth? I imagined feral dogs, stray cats—companion animals abandoned to make their own fate. Would they attack something as large as a man?

If they did, how would I fight them?

I groped along the bridge abutment, feeling with my toes for a stick. The old stones swept down low, the arch broad and flat. I kept my hand up to keep from hitting my head on an invisible buttress. The masonry was slick with paint and damp, mortar crumbling to the touch. I couldn't see my hand in front of my face, but light concentrated by the oily river reflected up, and I could see the stones of the bridge's underside clearly.

I crept into that dank, ruinous beauty until the flicker of lights against the chain fence told me that my pursuers had found me, and they had come in force. My chest squeezed, stomach flipping in apprehension. I crouched down, tucked myself into the lowest part of the arch, and fumbled out my phone.

"Police," I said. Even if my contract had been cancelled, that should work. I'd heard somewhere that any phone can always dial emergency. And there it was, a distant buzz, and then a calm voice answering.

"Emergency services. Your taxpayer identification number, please?"

My voice stuck in my throat. I'd never been asked that before. But then, I'd never been calling from an unskinned

phone before. Without thinking, I rattled off the fourteen dig-
its of my old number, the one that had been revoked. I held
my breath afterward. Maybe the change hadn't propagated
yet. Maybe—

"That number is not valid," the operator said.

"Look," I whispered, "I'm in a dispute with Revenue
Services. It's all going to be sorted out, I'm sure, but right now
I'm about to be mugged—"

"I'm sorry," said the consummate professional on the other
end of the line. "Emergency services are for taxpayers only."

Before I could protest, the line went dead. Leaving me
crouched alone in the dark, with a glowing phone pressed to
my ear. Not for long, however: in less than a second, the dazzle of flashlight beams found me. Instinctively, I ducked my
head and covered my eyes—with the hand with the phone.

"Well hey. What's this?" The voice was deceptively pleasant, that seductive mildness employed by schoolyard bullies
since first Romulus beat up Remus. The flashlight didn't waver
from my eyes.

I flinched. I didn't answer. Not because I didn't want to,
but because I didn't have a voice.

I tried to find the part of myself that managed unruly
students and lecture-hall hecklers, but it had vanished along
with my credit accounts and the protection of the police. I
ducked further, squinting around my hand, but he was just
a shadow through the glare of his light. At least three other
lights surrounded him.

He plucked the phone from my hand with a sharp twist
that stabbed pain through my wrist. I snatched the hand back.

"Huh," he said. "Guess you didn't pay your taxes, huh?
What else have you got?"

"Nothing," I said. The RFID chip embedded in my palm was useless. Would they cut it out anyway? I had no cash, no anything. Just the phone, which had my whole life on it—all my research, all my photos. Three mostly-finished articles. There were backups, of course, but they were on the wire, and I couldn't get there without being skinned.

I wasn't a skin anymore. Objects, I realized, had utility. Had value. They were more than ways to get at your data.

"Your jacket," the baseline said. "And your shoes."

My toes gripped the gravel. "I need my shoes—"

The dazzle of lights shifted. I knew I should duck, but the knowledge didn't translate into action.

At first there wasn't any pain. Just the shock of impact, and an exhale that seemed to start in my toes and never stop. *Then* the pain, radiating stars out of my solar plexus, with waves of nausea for dessert.

"Jacket," he said.

I would have given it to him. But I couldn't talk. Couldn't even inhale. I raised my hand. I think I shook my head.

I think he would have hit me anyway. I think he wanted to hit me. Because when I fell down, he kept hitting me. Hitting and kicking. And not just him, some of his friends.

It's a blur, mostly. I remember some particulars. The stomp that crushed my left hand. The kick that broke my tailbone. I got my knees up and tucked my head, so they kicked me in the kidneys instead. Gravel gouged the side where kicks didn't land. If I could burrow into it, I'd be safe. If I could just fall through it, I might survive. I thought about being small and hard and sharp, like those stones.

After a while, I didn't have the breath to scream anymore.

———

At first the cold hurt too, but after a while it became a friend. I noticed that they had stopped hitting me. I noticed that the cuts and bruises stung, the broken bones ached with a deep, sick throb. My hand felt fragile, gelatinous. Like a balloon full of water, I imagined that a single pinprick could make the stretched skin explode back from the contents. I prodded a loosened tooth with my tongue.

But then the cold got into the hurts and they numbed. Little by little, starting from the extremities. Working in. It mattered less that the hard points of gravel stabbed my ribs. I couldn't feel that floppy, useless hand. The throb in my head slowly became less demanding than the throb of thirst in my throat.

In the fullness of time, I sat up. It was natural, like sitting up after a full night's sleep, when you've lain in bed so long your body just naturally rises without consulting you. I thought about water. There was the river, but it smelled like poison. I'd probably get thirsty enough to drink it sooner or later. I wondered what diseases I'd contract. Hepatitis. Probably not cholera.

My cheekbones were numb, along with my nose, but I could still breathe normally. So the nose probably wasn't broken. The moving air brought me a tapestry of cold odors: sour garbage, rancid meat, urine. That oil-tang from the river. Frost rimed the gravel around me, and in noticing that I noticed that the morning was graying, the heavy arch of the bridge a silhouette against the sky. There was pink and silver along the horizon, and I knew which direction was east because the sun's light glossed a contrail that must have sat high enough to reach out of the Earth's moving shadow.

Footsteps crunched toward me. I was too dreamy and snug to move. *I'm in shock*, I thought, but it didn't seem important.

"What's this?" somebody said.

I flinched, but didn't look up. His shadow couldn't fall across me. We were both under the shadow of the bridge.

"Oh, dear," he said. The crunch of shifting gravel told me he crouched down beside me. When he turned my chin with his fingers and I saw his face, I was surprised he was limber enough to crouch. He looked like the bad end of a lot of winters. "And you lost your shoes too. What a pity."

He didn't seem surprised when I cringed, but it didn't light his eyes up, either. So that wasn't a bully's mocking.

"Can you walk?" He took my arm gently. He inspected my broken hand. When he unzipped my jacket, I would have pulled away, but the pain was bad enough that I couldn't move against him. When he slid the hand inside the jacket and the buttons of my shirt, I realized he was improvising a sling.

As if his touch were the opposite of an analgesic, all my hurts reawakened. I meant to shake my head, but just thinking about moving unscrolled ribbons of pain through my muscles.

"I don't think so." My words were creaky and blood-flavored.

"If you can," he said, "I've got a fire. And tea. And food."

I closed my eyes. When I opened them again, his hand was extended. The left one, as my right hand was clawed up against my chest like a surgical glove stuffed overfull with twigs and raspberry jam.

Food. Warmth. I might have given up, but somewhere in the back of my mind was an animal that did not want to die. I watched as it made a determined, raspy sound and reached out with its unbroken hand.

Letting him pull me to my feet was a special kind of agony. I swayed, vision blacking at the edges. His steadying hand kept me upright. It hurt worse than anything. "Come on," he said.

I remember walking, but I don't remember where or for how long. It felt like forever. I had always been walking. I would be walking forever. There was no end. No surcease.

Pain is an eternity.

———

His fire was trash and sticks ringed with broken bricks and chunks of asphalt. It smoldered fitfully, and pinprick by pinprick, the heat reawakened my pains. The soles of my feet seeped blood from walking across the gravel. I couldn't sit, because of the tailbone, but I figured out how to lie on my side. It hurt, but so did anything else.

There was tea, as promised, Lipton in bags stewed in a rusty can. I hoped he hadn't used river water. It had sugar in it, though, and I drank cautiously.

The food was dumpster-sourced chicken and biscuits, cold and lumpy with congealed grease. I ate it with my good hand, small bites. The inside of my mouth was cut from being slammed against my teeth. If I chewed carefully, on one side, the loose tooth only throbbed. I hoped it might reseat itself eventually.

Why was I thinking about the future?

The sun had beaten back the gloom enough for even my swollen eyes to make out the old man across from me. He had draped stiff, stinking blankets around my shoulders, but as the sun warmed the riverbank, he seemed comfortable in several layers of shirts and pants. A yellowed beard surrounded his sunken mouth. His hands were spare claws in ragged gloves. He drank the tea fearlessly, and warmed his share of the chicken on the rocks beside the trash fire. I thought about plastic fumes and kept gnawing mine cold.

After a while, he said, "You'll get used to it."

I looked up. He was looking right at me, his greasy silver ponytail dull in the sunlight. "Get used to being beaten up?" My voice sounded better than I'd feared. My nose really wasn't broken. One small miracle.

"Get used to being a baseline." He bit into a biscuit, grimacing in appreciation.

I winced, wondering how long it would take me to start savoring day-old fast food fat and carbohydrates. Then I winced in pain from the wincing.

The old man chewed and swallowed. "It's honest, at least. Not like putting frosting all over the cake so nobody with any economic power can tell it's rotten. What's your name?"

"Charlie," I said.

He nodded and didn't ask for a surname. "Jean-Khalil." I wondered if first names only was part of the social customs of the baseline community.

The shock was wearing off. Maybe the sugar in the tea was working its neurochemical magic. My broken hand lay against my belly, warmed by my skin, and the sweat running across my midsection felt as syrupy as blood.

I kind of wanted the shock back. I looked at the chicken, and the chicken looked back at me. My gorge rose. Bitterness filled my mouth, but I swallowed it. I knew how badly I needed the food inside me.

I balanced the meat on the fire ring next to Jean-Khalil's. "You eat that."

He wiped the back of his hand across his beard. "I will. And you need to get to a clinic."

I put my head down on the unbroken arm. If I didn't get the hand seen too, even if I survived—even if I didn't have internal injuries—what were the chances it would be usuable when it healed? "I don't have a tax number."

"There's a free clinic at St. Francis," he said. "But it's Tuesdays and Thursdays."

I managed to work out that if I normally met Numair on Tuesdays, it would be just after dawn on Wednesday. Which meant, depending on when the clinic opened, something over 24 hours to wait. I could wait 24 hours. Could I *sleep* 24 hours? Maybe I'd die of blood poisoning before then. That might be a relief.

I had heard of St. Francis, but I didn't know where it was. Somewhere in this neighborhood? If it offered a clinic for baselines, it would have to be. They couldn't get through the chip gates uptown.

Despite the blankets heaped over me, I thought I could feel the ground sucking the heat out of my body. The old man nudged me. I opened my eyes. "Edge over onto this," he said.

He'd made a pallet of more filthy blankets, just beside where I lay. With his help, I was able to kind of wriggle and flop onto it. I couldn't lie on my back, because of the tailbone, and I couldn't use the hand to pillow my head or turn myself.

He rearranged the blankets over me. Something touched my lips: his gaunt fingers, protruding from those filthy gloves. I turned my head.

"Take it. It's methadone. It's also a pain killer."

"You lost your tax number for drug addiction?" I had to cover my mouth with my unbroken hand.

"I'm a dropout," he said. "Take the wafer."

"I don't want to get hooked."

He sighed like somebody's mother. "I'm a medical doctor. It's methadone, it's 60 milligrams. It won't do much more than take the edge off, but it might help you sleep."

I didn't believe him about being a dropout. Who'd pick this? But I did believe him about being a doctor. Maybe it was the way he specified *medical*. "I was a history teacher," I said. I couldn't bring myself to say *professor*. "Why do you have methadone if you're not an addict?"

"I told you," he said. "I'm a doctor."

"And you dropped out."

"Of a corrupt system." His voice throbbed with disdain, and maybe conviction. "How many people were invisible to you, before? How much of this was invisible?"

If I could have had my way, I would have made it all invisible again. This time, when he pressed his hand to my mouth, I took the papery wafer into my mouth and chewed it. It tasted like fake fruit. I closed my eyes again and tried to breathe deeply. It hurt, but more an ache than the deep stabbing I associated with broken ribs. So that was something else to consider myself fortunate for.

I knew it was just the placebo effect and exhaustion making me sleepy so fast, but I wasn't about to argue with it.

I said, "What made you decide to come live on the street?"

"There was a girl—" His voice choked off through the constriction of his throat. "My daughter. Cancer. She was twenty. Maybe if she hadn't been skinning so much, in so much denial—"

I put my good hand on his shoulder and felt it rise and fall. "I'm sorry."

He shrugged.

It was a minute and a half before I had the courage to ask the thing I was suddenly thinking. "If you're a dropout, then you have a tax number. And you don't use it."

"That's right," the old man said. "It's a filthy system. Eventually, you'll see what I mean."

"If you don't want it, give it to me."

He laughed. "If I were willing to do that, I'd just sell it on the black market. The clinic could use the money. Now rest, and we'll get your hand looked at tomorrow."

———

I don't know how I got to the clinic. I didn't walk—not on those bare cut-up feet—and I don't remember being carried. I do remember the waiting room full of men and women I never would have seen before I lost my tax number. Jean-Khalil had given me another methadone wafer, and that kept me just this side of coherent. But I couldn't sit, couldn't walk, couldn't lean against the wall. He got somebody to bring me a gurney, and I lay on my side and tried to doze, blissfully happy there weren't any rocks or dog feces on the surface I was lying on.

It doesn't take long to lower your standards.

I realized later that I was one of the lucky ones, and because of the broken bones I got triaged higher than a lot of others. But it was still four hours before I was wheeled into one of the curtained alcoves that served as an examining room and a woman in mismatched scrubs and a white lab coat came in to check on me. "Hi," she said. "I'm Dr. Tankovitch. Dr. Samure said you had a bad night. Charlie, is it?"

"The worst," I said. She was cute—Asian, plump, with bright eyes behind her glasses—and I caught myself flirting before a flood of shame washed me back into into myself. She was a contributing member of society, here to do charity work. And I was a bum.

"Honestly, there's not much you can do for a broken tail-bone except—" she laughed in commiseration "—stay off it. So let's start with the hand."

I held it out, and she took it gently by the wrist. Even that made me gasp.

She made a sympathetic face. "I'd guessing by the bruises on your face you didn't get this punching a brick wall."

"The cops don't come if you're not in the system."

She touched my shoulder. "I know."

———

I got lucky. For the first time in weeks, I got lucky. The hand didn't need surgery, which meant I didn't have to wait until the clinic's surgical hours, which were something like midnight to four AM at the city hospital. Instead, Dr. Tankovitch shot me full of Novocaine and wrapped my hand up with primitive plaster of Paris, a technology so obsolete I had never actually seen it. Or if I had seen it, I'd skinned it out. She gave me some pain pills that didn't work as well as the methadone and didn't have a street value, and told me to come back in a week and have it all checked out. The cast was so white it sparkled. Guess how long that was going to last, if I was sleeping under bridges?

She didn't offer me the clinic's contact information, and I didn't ask for it. How was I supposed to call them without a phone? But I was feeling less sorry for myself when I staggered out of the alcove. I planned to find Jean-Khalil again, and ask him if he'd show me where he looked for food and safe drinking water. I was clear-headed enough now to know it was an imposition, but I didn't have anywhere else to turn. And he'd sort of volunteered, hadn't he, by picking me out of the gutter?

*If you pick up a starving dog and make him prosperous, he will not bite you. This is the principal difference between a dog and a man.*

It was Mark Twain. But then, so were a lot of true things. And I was determined to prove myself more like the dog than the man. Jean-Khalil was an old man. Surely he could use my help. And I knew I needed his. I didn't see Jean-Khalil. But just as the waves of panic and abandonment—again, just like after Rose—were cresting in me, I spotted someone. Leaning against the wall by the door was Numair.

Numair had seen me first—I'd been moving, and he'd been looking for me—so he saw me stop dead and stare. He raised his hand hesitantly.

"Buy you dinner?" he asked. He didn't flinch when he looked at me.

From the angle of the light outside, I realized it was nearly sunset. "As long as we can get it someplace standing up."

———

That meant street meat, and three hotdogs with everything were the best food I'd ever tasted. Numair drank beer but he didn't eat pork, so he ate potato chips and watched me lean forward so the chili and onions didn't drip down my filthy shirt. I knew it was ridiculous, but I did it anyway. It felt like preserving my dignity to care. What dignity? I wasn't sure. But it still mattered.

"I'm sorry," Numair said. "I'm really sorry. If I'd realized you didn't know about Rose—I just never imagined. You two were so close. And you never mentioned her—I figured you didn't want to talk about her."

"I didn't." We'd had a fight, I wanted to say. Something to absolve myself of not checking. But when she stopped logging in, I figured she'd just decided to cut me off. She wouldn't be the first, and I knew she had another life. A wife. We'd talked about telling her she was having an affair.

And then she'd just…stopped messaging. People fall out of social groups all the time. It happens. I guess somebody more secure wouldn't have assumed they were the problem. But I was used to being the problem. Numair's the only friend I have left from the gang I hung around with all the time in grad school.

I swallowed hot dog, half-chewed. It hurt. He handed me an open can of soda, and I washed the lump down. "How'd she die?"

She hadn't been old. I mean, she hadn't skinned old. But who knew what the hell that meant, in the real world.

"She killed herself," Numair said, bluff and forthright. Which was just like him.

I staggered. Literally, sideways two steps. I couldn't catch myself because the last hotdog was balanced against my chest on the pristine cast. I already had the instinct to protect that food. I guess you don't have to get too hungry to learn fast.

"Jesus," I said, and felt bad.

He made a comforting face. And that was when I realized that if he could see me, he wasn't skinning. "Numair. You came all the way down here for me?"

"Charlie. Like I'd let an old friend go down without some help." He put a hand on my shoulder and pulled it back, frowning. He looked around, disgusted. "You know, you hear on the news how bad it is out here. But you never really get it until you see it. Poisoned environment, whatever. But this is astounding. Look, we can get you a hearing. Appeal your status. Maybe get you a new number. You can stay with Ilona and me until it's settled."

There were horror vids about this sort of thing. The baselines lived outside of social controls, after all. There was nothing to keep them from committing horrible crimes. "You're going to take in a baseline? That's a lot of trust. I'm a desperate woman."

He smiled. "I know you."

—————

Ilona only knew me as a skin, but when I showed up at her house in the unadorned flesh, she couldn't have been nicer. She, too, had turned off her skinning so she could see me and interact. I could tell she was uncomfortable with it, though—her eyes kept flicking off my face to look for the hypertext or chase a link pursuant to the conversation, and of course there was nothing there. So after a bit she just showed me the bathroom, brought me clean clothes and a towel, and went back to her phone, where (she said) she was working on a deadline. She was an advertising copywriter, and she and Numair had converted one corner of their old house's parlor into an office space. I could hear her clicking away as I stripped off my filthy clothing and dropped it piece by piece into the bathroom waste pail. It was hard, one-handed, and it was even harder to tape the plastic bag around my cast.

It had never bothered me to discard ruined clothing before, but now I found it anxiety-inducing. *That's still good. Somebody could wear that.* I set the shower for hot and climbed in. The water I got fell in a lukewarm trickle; barely wetting me.

They probably skinned it hotter when they showered.

I tried to linger, to savor the cleanliness, but the chill of the water in a chilly room drove me out to stand dripping on the rug. As I was dressing in Ilona's jeans and sweatshirt, the sound of a child crying filtered through.

I came out to find Numair up from his desk, changing a diaper in the nook beside the kitchen. His daughter's name was Mercedes; she'd always been something of a little pink blob to me. I came up to hand him the grease for her diaper rash and saw the spotted blood on the diaper he had pushed aside.

"Christ," I said. "Is she all right?"

"She's nine months old, and she's starting her menses," he said, lower lip thrust out in worry. I noticed because I was looking up at the underside of his chin. "It's getting more common in very young girls."

*"Common?"*

With practiced hands, he attached the diaper tabs and sealed up Mercedes' onesie. He folded the soiled diaper and stuck it closed. "The doctor says it's environmental hormones. It can be skinned for—they'll make her look normal to herself and everyone else until she's old enough to start developing." He shrugged and picked up his child. "He says he treats a couple of toddlers with developing breasts, and the cosmetic option works for them."

He looked at me, brown eyes warm with worry.

I looked down. "You think that's a good enough answer?"

He shook his head. I didn't push it any farther.

———

They put me to sleep in their guest room, and fed me—unskinned, the food was slop, but it was food, and I got used to them not being able to see or talk to me at mealtimes. After a week, I felt much stronger. And as it was obvious that Numair and Ilona's intervention was not going to win me any favors from Revenue, I slowly came up with another plan.

I couldn't find Jean-Khalil under the bridge. His fire circle was abandoned, his blankets packed up. He'd moved on, and I didn't know where. Good deed delivered.

You'd think, right? Until it clicked what I was missing.

I showed up at the free clinic first thing next Tuesday morning, just as Dr. Tankovitch had suggested. And I waited there until Dr. Tankovitch walked in and with her, his gaunt hand curved around a cup of coffee, Dr. Jean-Khalil Samure.

He didn't look surprised to see me. My clothes were clean, and the cast was only a little dingy. I'd shaved, and I was surprised he recognized me without the split lip and the swelling.

"Jean-Khalil," I said.

I guessed accosting the clinic doctors wasn't what you did, because Dr. Tankovitch looked as if she might intercept me, or call for security. But Jean-Khalil held out a hand to pause her.

He smiled. "Charlie. You look like you're finding your feet."

"I got help from a friend." I frowned and looked down at my borrowed tennis shoes. Ilona's, and too big for me. "I can't do this, Jean-Khalil. You've got to help me."

I'm sure the clinic had all sorts of problems with drug addicts. Because now Dr. Tankovitch was actively backing away, and I saw her summoning hand gestures. I leaned in and talked faster. "I need your tax number," I said. "You're not using it. Look, all I need is to get back on my feet, and I can help you in all sorts of ways. Money. Publicity. I'll come volunteer at your clinic—"

"Charlie," he said. "You know that's not enough. The way you live—the way you have been living. That's a lie. It's not sustainable. It's addictive behavior. If everybody could see the damage they're doing, they'd behave differently."

I pressed my lips together. I looked away. Down at the floor. At anything but Jean-Khalil. "There's a girl. Her name is Rose."

He looked at me. I wondered if he knew I was lying. Maybe I wasn't lying. I could find somebody else, skin her into Rose. Maybe she'd have a different name. But I could fix this. Do better. If he would only give me the chance.

"You're not using it," I said.

"A girl," he said. "Your daughter?"

"My lover," I said.

I said, "Please."

He shook his head, eyes rolled up and away. Then he yanked his hand out of his pocket brusquely. "On your head be it."

I was not prepared for the naked relief that filled me. I looked down, abjectly, and folded my hands. "Thank you so much."

"You can't save people from themselves," he said.

# Eaters

## Nancy Kress

Nancy Kress began selling her elegant and incisive stories in the mid-seventies. Her books include the novel version of her Hugo and Nebula-winning story, *Beggars in Spain*, and a sequel, *Beggars and Choosers*, as well as *The Prince Of Morning Bells*, *The Golden Grove*, *The White Pipes*, *An Alien Light*, *Brain Rose*, *Oaths & Miracles*, *Stinger*, *Maximum Light*, *Crossfire*, *Nothing Human*, *The Floweres of Aulit Prison*, *Crucible*, *Dogs*, and *Steal Across the Sky*, as well as the Space Opera trilogy *Probability Moon*, *Probability Sun.*, and *Probability Space*. Her short work has been collected in *Trinity And Other Stories*, *The Aliens of Earth*, *Beaker's Dozen*, *Nano Comes to Clifford Falls and Other Stories*, *The Fountain of Age*, *Future Perfect*, *AI Unbound*, and *The Body Human*. Her most recent book is the novel *Flash Point*. In addition to the awards for "Beggars in Spain," she has also won Nebula Awards for her stories "Out Of All Them Bright Stars," "Fountain of Age" and "The Flowers of Aulit Prison," the John W. Campbell Memorial Award in 2003 for her novel *Probability Space*, and another Hugo in 2009 for "The Erdmann Nexus." Most recently, she just won another Nebula Award in 2013 for her novella "After the Fall, Before the Fall, During the Fall." She lives in Seattle, Washington with her husband, writer Jack Skillingstead.

Nancy Kress says: "The first Robert Silverberg story I ever read was the Hugo-winning "Nightwings," in 1968. I was suitably awed by the story's breadth, daring, and lyricism. At that time, I was in college and had no thoughts of ever becoming a writer myself; I planned on being a fourth-grade teacher. And so it came to pass. In the fullness of time, however, the fourth-grade thing fell apart, I began writing stories, and Robert Silverberg—without ever diminishing his own astonishing output—became the editor of the anthology series *New Dimensions*.

I have in my files a yellowing piece of typewriter paper dated March 22, 1978. It's a rejection from Bob of one of my first, never-to-be-published, truly dreadful stories. Bob wrote, in part: "You write very well, apart from a habit of reaching too far for prose effects (like that "exhausted" sunlight lying on the rug on page one). But I don't see much of a plot manifesting itself here." He was right on both counts: there was no plot, and sunlight is seldom exhausted (I mean, what has it been doing all day to get so tired?) But the most thrilling part of the rejection letter was that he asked to see more of my work. I didn't have any more, but I immediately set to work creating some.

A few years later, I met Bob, at the 1983 Worldcon in Baltimore. Unlike all the other writers I met that memorable weekend, Robert Silverberg looked exactly as I'd imagined. He looked like Mephistopheles, and his graceful elegance intimidated me so much that after the first introduction I never went near him again for about ten years.

And now I have the opportunity to write in one of Bob Silverberg's universes. I read "Sundance" in a graduate course on science fiction. When I began writing the story's sequel, I decided that I would not try to duplicate Bob's pyrotechnics with point of view. His story was narrated by a man on the edge of mental collapse; mine is narrated by a woman who suspects she's been all too sane. But they share a planet, and a history, and it was great fun borrowing those things from Bob. I'm grateful for the opportunity."

The girl is two days early.

Ellen first sees Josie Two Ribbons crossing the staff mess trailer, several moments before Josie sees her. Ellen's belly goes cold. This is going to be even worse than she has dreaded. Josie wears military fatigues; she scowls so hard that her eyebrows nearly meet. She looks far too much like her father: short, with wide shoulders, spreading nose, glossy black hair cropped into bristles.

Jim Herndon, seated beside Ellen, touches her arm. "Do you want me to—"

"No. No." Ellen has to do this herself. She rises and holds out her hand as the girl stops beside the table. "Corporal Two Ribbons?"

The girl ignores the outstretched hand. Her eyes, as dark as Tom's, sweep away from Ellen, over the other scientists, back again. Ellen drops her hand.

"You bastards," Josie Two Ribbons says.

———

"She wants to go out alone," Carlos Sanchez says, "but of course I can't let her do that. Corporate would have my head if she damaged one of our copters. Or herself."

"I know," Ellen says.

"For her to even get permits to come here—just how *did* she do that?"

"I don't know." Although Ellen has her suspicions.

Carlos has called her into his office, which is just as make-shift as everything else human on the base. The office had, a decade ago, been a fuel tank on the ship that brought the first team from Earth. The fuel tank had been flown down-stairs, fitted with electronics and with foamcast furniture newly sprayed into existence, and now serves as command station for the Second Terraforming Team of SettlerHome Corporation on Janus 4. The rest of the base, housed in other bits of the ship or in pre-dropped trailers, consists of twenty-four of Ellen's fellow scientists and a great number of very large, very expensive machines, some stationary and some mobile. Twenty-four people to remake a planet for the hordes of colonists to follow.

Not that Janus 4 needs very much remaking. Unlike some other worlds, the profit margin on this one would be large. The atmosphere is already breathable, there is enough fresh water, the small planetary tilt means a fairly stable climate. The gravity is .93 Terran, just enough difference to put a spring in one's step. Janus 4 could be a very popular settlement world. The team's only real problem has been the soil—at least, until Tom Two Ribbons, the junior xenobiologist, had gone out into the bush. And gone, and gone, and gone.

Carlos runs his hand through his hair, which immediately flops back over his forehead. "Ellen, there's no reason for you to be the one to go with her to look for him. In fact, anybody else would be better."

"No, it has to be me."

"So you said. Why?"

Carlos looks straight at her, his no-nonsense-give-me-a-real-answer look. Ellen has always liked Carlos. Whoever said that a team leader needs either charisma or an iron hand was dead wrong. What a team leader needs is a nose for truth, and Carlos—quiet, skinny, occasionally dithering Carlos—has it.

Ellen says quietly, "Because I didn't love Tom. If I had, I'd have tried harder to find out what was driving him, and I didn't. It was all just good-time light-hearted fucking for me. I treated him with the same carelessness that—"

She breaks off, knowing that Carlos knows the rest of the sentence: *with the same carelessness that we treated the Eaters.*

Carlos says, "I really wish you wouldn't go, Ellen."

"I have to."

"I don't think she's dangerous—no history of that, although Chang will run a psych check—but she's completely unedited. Primal."

"I know."

"Also, she's mad as hell."

"Well," Ellen says, shifting her gaze to the window, where two Eaters have wandered too close to the force fence, "she has reason to be. He's her father, he's out there someplace alone, and he's crazy."

"But *not*," Carlos says, with an emphasis unusual for him, "because of us."

Ellen doesn't answer.

———

It takes two days for Josie to pass Chang's mandatory health exam, psych check, and gene scan. After the two days, Chang tells Ellen that Josie is a remarkable physical specimen, that Josie psych-tests as sane, and that none of the medical team can stand her. "I've never seen an angrier human being," Chang says, "and she absolutely refuses editing. It's a good thing that she only has a ten-day planetary permit. Still, it's going to be unpleasant for you." Ellen agrees, thinking it's also good that Josie was not allowed to bring any weapons to a Corporate planet. A second later she's ashamed of this thought; Josie is not a threat, merely "unpleasant."

They leave at dawn of Josie's third day planetside. As the two-seater copter lifts off from the base with Ellen piloting, a herd of Eaters wanders across the ground below, just outside the fence. The alien creatures are spherical, bulky, slow-moving, covered with masses of coarse orange fur.

From this angle Ellen cannot see their legs, which are thin and scaly as a chicken's although they end in broad, hard hooves. She can barely see the Eaters' arms, thin and short and held close to their silly-looking bodies. Furry beach balls bobbing along. Those beach balls are delaying a multi-trillion-credit project by at least a decade.

Ellen knows what will happen next, and it does. The left flank of the herd brushes the force-field fence, and half a dozen Eaters crumple to the ground. The rest move on a little more quickly. The copter makes so little noise and flies so low that Ellen can hear their hoofs on the hard ground. How do creatures that are basically sacks of protoplasm on ungulated sticks manage to make so much noise? She braces herself for Josie's rant about the fence deaths, but instead the girl directs her hostility in another direction.

"You're very pretty."

It sounds like a curse. Ellen, not knowing how to respond, says nothing.

"You're exactly the type my father always favored. Soft, feminine. Weak. In fact, you look like a blonde version of my mother."

Ellen says dryly, "One can't be all that weak and still belong to a terraforming team."

"I meant emotionally weak. Yielding."

Ellen puts the copter on autopilot and turns to face Josie. "Look, I know you don't like me, or any of us. You resent that we edited your father's memories of what happened. And you resent that until he told us different, we *did* think the Eaters were non-sentient and we did try to exterminate them so they would stop eating the nitrogen-fixing plants. I realize that with your ethnic heritage—"

"Fuck my ethnic heritage."

Ellen stares at her.

"Do you think I give a shit that two hundred years ago your ancestors tried to exterminate the Sioux? Give me a break. Chances are your particular ancestors hadn't even yet emigrated to North America—right, Ellen *Jenssen*? That whole anguish-of-the-Indians thing was my father's bag, not mine. I got off the res as soon as I could and joined the Space Force. The white man won over the Sioux because he had all that advanced tech and so deserved to win. You think I'm going to cry for the losers, just because I carry around some of their genes? It's nothing to do with me. I'm not my great-great-grandparents, and I'm not that sentimental."

Certainly Josie Two Ribbons doesn't look sentimental. She looks hard as the granite boulders forty feet below. The girl still wears military fatigues, boots, and her habitual scowl. Even her bristly dark hair looks aggressive. Ellen feels confused and—yes, admit it!—a little afraid of this ferocious young woman fifteen years her junior.

She says haltingly, "So...why...why are you here?"

Josie turns the scowl full force on Ellen. "He's my *father*. In the same circumstances wouldn't you go out after your father?"

No. Ellen would not go across town, let alone half a galaxy away, to search for the man who calls himself her father. But she doesn't say it aloud.

"Christ, you people," Josie says, turns her back, and scans the ground.

The base is now out of sight. The copter flies around it in widening spirals, so Josie can look for—what? Ellen doesn't know. But the terrain below is varied and beautiful. Tree-analogues, never more than twenty feet high but full and bushy, purple with the rhodopsin-like photosynthesizer the plants use instead of chlorophyll. Wide slow rivers, which will grow narrower and swifter when they near the mountains, blue among the purple. Outcroppings of pale rock. The tiny, barely visible blue flowers of the native plants, almost lost among the larger white and pink blooms of the bushes introduced by humans. Flora 1 and Flora 2.

Josie says, "So which ones are hallucinogenic?"

"The white ones."

"Those are the ones you guys put here originally? That the Eaters ate?"

"Yes." The Eaters, and Tom. Ellen doesn't want to talk about this. *We didn't know.* But Josie has the right to information—doesn't she? Or is Ellen just doing what she always does, giving in to the stronger personality? She has always felt more comfortable with genes than with their carriers.

"And you're the geneticist who designed the plants, right?"

"Yes."

"What were the plants supposed to do?"

"They do it. They fix nitrogen from the atmosphere into the soil. Without more fixed nitrogen than is native to Janus 4, agriculture would be impossible here."

"And the Eaters lunched on your precious plants, so you guys decided to wipe out the aliens."

"Before we knew they were sentient, yes." The neural pellets falling from the sky—how many drops had Ellen herself made? Although they possess high-phylum nervous systems, the Eaters have no blood. What they have instead is a kind of lymph fluid that permeates every tissue. It transmits nourishment osmotically throughout those beach-ball bodies, as in Terran low-phylum amoebae or sponges. This evolutionary path had made extermination particularly easy. Within an hour of ingestion, the poison had reached all sections of an Eater's body. Then came a rapid breakdown of cellular matter as the lymph-like fluid became an acid bath. The Eater literally fell apart molecule by molecule. Flesh and cartilaginous bones dissolved. In two hours, there was a puddle on the ground. In four hours, nothing left at all.

*We didn't know.*

Josie smiles. Her smile is just as angry as her scowl. "I guess my father screwed up your big plan, huh? What did he discover about aliens that convinced you all that they're sentient?"

"They communicate through pheromone analogs. They—maybe—pray to some sort of sun god, or at least have rituals that look like prayer. They dance."

"Bees can dance. And so you stopped exterminating the Eaters and instead changed the plant's genes so that the Eaters don't like the taste?"

"Yes."

"Why didn't you just do that in the first place?"

"It's not as easy as you make it sound." Josie probably knows all these answers already, or she wouldn't know what questions to ask. Ellen jabs at the copter's controls.

"You hate this conversation, don't you, Ellen? Just like you hate me."

"I don't hate you."

Josie snorts. "The hell you don't. You hate me for coming here and stirring up your big mistake all over again, all that white-man guilt. Well, I don't give a fuck for your guilt or your big mistake. You moved into the Eaters' ecological niche, and if you can take it over, more power to you. Law of the jungle."

"That's a pretty simplistic view. The moral—"

"Yeah, right. Your guilt is dumb but your hypocrisy is criminal. The weaker culture always goes under, that's just evolution in action. If you're going to participate in evolution, you don't get to also cry about it. Didn't expect philosophy from a dumb Indian soldier, did you? You think—"

"Don't tell me what I think. And don't tell me that your heritage doesn't matter to you."

"It doesn't. I'm an individual, not a defunct tribe."

"Really? How did you get permission to visit a planet in stage II terraforming? You went to the authorities and played the race card, didn't you?"

Josie doesn't reply, and all at once Ellen is afraid she's gone too far. What does she know about the ethnic feelings of a Native American? Even if Josie is caught in some sort of Stockholm Syndrome, identifying with the victors who destroyed the Sioux, she's still a daughter searching for her lost father. Ellen is contemplating an apology when Josie points to the ground below. "Land there."

It's an oxbow in a river, a U-shaped bend so sharp that only a narrow neck of land protrudes into the river. Eventually the neck will become an island, when the river cuts it off entirely. Dense purple tree-analogs cover the future island. Ellen lands the copter in the closest clearing, and Josie jumps lightly out and disappears into the trees.

An hour later she is back. "Nope. Fly."

Seething, Ellen lifts the copter. She can't think what to say to Josie Two Ribbons: not about her peremptory tone, her rudeness, her astonishingly cold view of what humans on Janus 4 had almost done to the Eaters. Stockholm Syndrome or not, is that callous indifference normal…especially coming from a Native American? Or is the girl only pretending indifference, putting on a protective see-if-I-care shell to hide what must be complicated identification with the Eaters' near fate?

Ellen has never been comfortable with tense silence. Despite herself, she tries again. "Growing up on the reservation must have been tough, especially after your parents divorced and—"

"You don't know anything about the res," Josie says, scanning the ground, "or about me. So don't pretend you do. Land there."

"Look, Josie, while we're on this expedition together I insist that at least you treat me with minimal courtesy. Or else don't say anything at all."

Josie says nothing at all.

Ellen lands *there*.

They investigate four more oxbows before nightfall. When Josie wants to land, she flips her wrist in a gesture both indicative and insulting. Ellen swallows her anger and concentrates on the terrain below. The base uses satellite mapping, of course, but as they leave Sector A she is surprised to see how widely both Flora 1 and Flora 2 have spread. The white flowers and the pink both flourish beneath tree-analog canopies and in the shade of boulders. They must have adapted, even mutated, more quickly than she'd counted on. The Eaters are still devouring Flora 1—Ellen sees them doing it—but the hardy plant is flourishing anyway, seeding itself faster than its predator can consume it.

Just before the abrupt sunset of a planet with negligible axial tilt, they make camp. The copter, whose design demands lightness, can sleep two uncomfortably, but the back seats have been removed in order to store equipment and supplies. Ellen sleeps in the copter, curled across two front seats joined by a piece of removable foam. She can't stretch out, but she feels calmer here. Josie pitches a tent beside the copter.

Josie has still not said a single word to her.

———

*She is dancing, surrounded by vague shapes under a hot sun. Her bare feet move joyously, her arms wave. The vague shapes are also dancing, pressing close to her...closer...then away. She laughs. Her feet pound out complex rhythms that she never knew, on a grassy purplish ground that her toes never touched before. She dances faster, they all dance faster, whirling and jumping and shouting in frenzied joy, and still she doesn't tire, she dances and dances and—*

A shot, followed by a high inhuman scream.

Ellen jerks awake and fumbles for the copter's floodlights. In their harsh glare she sees Josie, legs apart and braced, lowering the barrel of a gun. How could Josie have a *gun*? It takes a moment for Ellen to recognize the weapon. She throws open the copter door.

"You stole that! From the base!"

"Of course I did."

"What in hell did you fire at?"

"An Eater." Josie points at her tent. Something has gashed one side of the tough plasticanvas. Ellen drops to her knees to examine the rip. Impossible that it could come from an Eater, they are herbivorous and at the top of the simple Janus 4 food chain, with no predators. However, Dave Schwartz, the team zoologist, has described Eater mating rituals. Two males kick each other viciously, sometime inflicting considerable damage, until one or the other gives up. This gash could have been made by an Eater hoof, doing...what?

Ellen feels dizzy. No Eater has ever attacked a human. If Tom was to be believed, the Eaters didn't even mind when he joined their herd, running with them, dancing with them, feeding with them on Flora 1, the unintended hallucinogenic that destroyed his mind. Ellen herself has seen Eaters ignore the deaths of their fellows who brush against the force-field fence that is the Corporation's grudging, expensive alternative to exterminating the creatures blocking agribusiness on Janus 4. The Eaters may be sentient, but it is a very primitive sentience, and it is not aggressive.

Josie is watching her closely. Ellen raises her head to stare back, but cannot keep it up. Not against that cool, amused disdain. Josie says, "Surprised you, did they?"

"Yes. No Eater has…has acted like that before."

"Well, they do now."

Ellen stands. "Give me the gun."

"Do you know how to use it?"

Ellen doesn't, or at least not very well. She says, hating the slight tremor in her voice, "It's Corporate property."

Josie laughs. "It's my property now. We're out here in the bush, Ellen. You can't control me, and you can't edit me to remove any behavior you happen to not like."

Editing removes memories, not behavior, but Ellen doesn't argue the point. "Give me the gun or I'll fly the copter back to base."

"No, you won't." Almost casually, Josie points the gun at her, smiles, lowers the barrel. Oddly, Ellen isn't afraid; she intuits that Josie is only playing with her. Nasty play, but not serious threat. Josie adds, "You can report this, get the second copter after me, file charges with the Space Force, whatever. But I'm not going back until I find my father, and I'm keeping the gun because I'm the one who knows how to use it. Understand?"

Ellen understands. She understands that Josie knows that Ellen will not report the incident, will not destroy Josie's life. Because Ellen has already destroyed Tom's. Guilt is driving her now, the guilt that Josie Two Ribbons so completely disavows. That she leaves to the white man, so ready to accept it, bear it, eat it.

The sky is lightening. Josie packs up her tent and climbs into the copter.

———

They spend the day investigating oxbows, and Josie actually offers an explanation: "My father used to take me camping, always on oxbows or oxbow islands. He liked them because they're easier to defend against attack."

Ellen tries to imagine this unknown Tom who was conscious of attack and defense. When she knew him, he seemed a quiet, pacific sort of man, absorbed in xenobiology. But how well had she actually tried to know him? Not very. It was Stan Michaelson whom she was in love with, and Ellen used Tom as both a convenient distraction and a (futile) ploy to incite jealousy in Stan. And when Tom presented his evidence of sentience in the Eaters and the terraforming team had to change strategy, Ellen was just as upset as anyone else. Upset and—yes!—irritated. The entire project was set back years. And then Stan took up with Julia. Ellen hated that, and she stopped sleeping with Tom, and then he went bonkers, running off to live with Eaters—three times!—and each time coming back more delusional, in need of more editing from Chang, gone just completely off the reservation—

*Off the reservation.* She never thinks in those demeaning clichés—what is wrong with her?

What has always been wrong with her? *Something—*

Josie says, "What the hell is wrong with you? You're red as a boiled lobster."

"Nothing," Ellen says. "I'm going to gather samples."

The have just landed the copter beside yet another oxbow, the sixth one today. They are farther from base than Ellen has ever gone, nearly into Sector D, and yet she can see both Flora 1 and Flora 2 flourishing here. The seeds, designed for wind-scatter, have adapted incredibly well to Janus 4. She climbs out after Josie.

"Stay near the copter," Josie says. "I'm taking the gun."

"Okay."

Ellen gathers samples of both Flora 1 and Flora 2 and brings them back to the copter. She has brought a hand-held gene scanner with her. The space in the front seat is cramped, but she prepares samples and runs them through the scanner. When the results are finally ready and she scrolls through the display on the small screen, her heart nearly stops.

There has been massive genetic drift.

Flora 1—white flowers and greenish-purple photosynthesizer, one of Ellen's best recombinant jobs—shows the most genetic mutations. Not surprising—it has been here the longest. But even Flora 2's genes have changed at an astonishing rate. Mutating, jumping, recombining to create new proteins that do...what? No way to tell, not in this copter. The scanner can record the simple facts of a shifting genome, the long strings of ATGC's, but the behavior caused by any genome is never simple.

One of her samples of Flora 1 has passed the flowering stage. Ellen touches the little lemon-colored globe of fruit, not yet fully ripe. At her touch, it releases a whiff of sweet perfume. Ingested, it is a powerful hallucinogenic. This is what destroyed Tom's mind, making him think that the terraforming team was still exterminating Eaters after the drops of neural pellets had been discontinued. Making him imagine that psychiatrists back on Earth had arranged the entire tragic extermination merely to help Tom Two Ribbons cope with anger about Indian wars two hundred years ago. Making him believe, finally, that his friends were evil enemies out to destroy him. Chang had edited and edited, trying to cut the poison out of Tom's mind, but drug-induced schizophrenic paranoia is so stubborn...

Liquid spurts onto Ellen's hand. She has clutched the lemon-colored globe so hard that it ruptured. "Damn!" She reaches for a wipe, and her gaze focuses through the copter window. A circle of Eaters surrounds her craft.

Human and aliens stare at each other. The aliens' protruding, perfectly round eyes, set above narrow rubbery lips, have no expression, or at least not that Ellen can read. But their orange fur stands straight up, in what Dave has told her is male mating aggression. A long moment passes. Then all together, as if choreographed, the Eaters rush the copter and begin kicking it furiously. Their hooves ring on the light metal. The passenger door, thin since the copter is made of light metal both to save fuel and because there was never a reason for reinforcement, caves inward. Ellen screams.

Gunfire erupts from the woods and two Eaters fall to the ground. The rest run off in a flurry of orange fur. Josie emerges from the trees. The whole episode has taken less than a minute.

This is different from Eaters ingesting neural pellets and quietly dissolving. Josie, apparently an expert shot (Ellen never doubted it), has hit both Eaters in the head. The corpses lay inert, solid, their eyes still open. They will be there until they rot.

Josie yanks open the damaged door of the copter. "What did you do?"

"Nothing!" *And I'm not hurt, thanks for asking.*

"They just attacked without provocation?"

"Yes!" Ellen remembers the juice on her hands and fumbles again for the wipe. Her fingers shake. "Eaters never acted like that before!"

"Well, they do now." Josie climbs into the copter. "Lift off."

"Just…just give me a minute!"

Josie does. Ellen cleans off the juice and tosses the wipe into the recycler. She reaches for the flight controls, but instead her hand goes to the cockpit storage compartment and pulls out a flask of whiskey. She doesn't do this very often—and she never did it before Tom's last disappearance—but there are some nights that it's the only way through. The combination of mellow and burn, as always, steadies her, and she lifts the copter. "We're returning to the base, I presume,"

Josie doesn't answer. Ellen glances over at her and finds Josie's eyes locked onto the flask. Josie has not even heard her. Ellen could not have imagined that expression on Josie Two Ribbons's face: could not have imagined that much hunger, that much despair.

Oh, Ellen thinks. *Oh.*

Eventually—and it is a long eventually—Josie again becomes aware of Ellen. The scowl returns. But Josie doesn't try to lie; lying is not her style. Attack is.

"So I'm not the only one bringing along contraband, huh? What is that supposed to be, the back-up plan, the ultimate way to control me? I'll bet Tom told you that my great-great-grandfather died of alcoholism, my great-grandfather was addicted to hallucinogens, and so on. Whiskey for the Indian, huh? What else have you got stowed away here—blankets seeded with smallpox? I thought you were more original than that."

"Fuck you," Ellen says, and immediately realizes she has never said that to anyone in her life. Never. Ashamed, she shoves the flask back into storage and slams the door close. The door bounces open. Josie reaches out and shuts it, but there is something wrong with the gesture: It is too slow and a little clumsy, as if the girl's neural timing is off. Closing that door is costing Josie every gram of will that she possesses.

Her voice comes out harsh. "Where the fuck do you think you're flying?"

"I told you. Back to the base."

"No." She faces Ellen, wrenching her gaze from the storage compartment. "We're going to find my father."

Is such determination a species of courage, or a species of delusion? Ellen can no longer tell.

———

Carlos, with his usual democratic leadership, leaves the decision up to Ellen. She suspects he is far more interested in her reports of genetic drift and Eater aggression than in Josie Two Ribbons. Ellen sends him all the data from her handheld and describes the Eater attack to the entire base, gathered in front of the linkscreen to watch and listen.

"Where are you now?" Hélène asks.

"On an open plain. I have the camera and motion detectors turned on so we won't be surprised again. Both Flora 1 and Flora 2 are everyplace, and in the morning I'll gather more samples." She is not going out onto the plain in the dark, motion detectors or no motion detectors. She spends another ten minutes being asked questions, most of which she cannot answer, by scientists concerned with their various fields. Xenobiology, zoology, geology, soil engineering. Ellen discovers that, for the moment, she doesn't care about the answers she doesn't have. She is so tired.

Josie is not present for this conference. She has set up the tent and the instabake outside and heated their meals. In the harsh glare of the copter floodlights, Ellen climbs down and sits on the ground to eat. Every little noise makes her jump. Are they out there? Of course they are. It seems to her that she can smell their hatred, feel it on her skin.

"Sleep in the copter," she says to Josie. "We'll unload enough equipment for me to squeeze back there, and you can have the front."

"Not a chance." The scowl deepens. Ellen sees that this is somehow a matter of stupid pride. Or maybe Josie is just one of those people who cannot stand being cooped up for very long. Somewhere to the east, about a mile away, is a river with a wooded oxbow. Josie will search it in the morning, possibly before Ellen even wakes.

Josie sits in the shadow cast by the copter on the floodlit ground. In that half-gloom, her heritage is somehow sharpened. Despite the military fatigues and bristly hair, she looks

Sioux. It's in the cheekbones and nose, the shape of her face, the dark eyes, the still posture. Not for the first time, Ellen wonders about Josie's mother, who had refused to follow Tom to a better life. Who had instead raised her daughter on a reservation, probably in poverty and stagnation. Ellen has read about life on what remains of Indian reservations. When the United States went into steep economic decline, Native Americans were hit even harder than most others. As usual.

Ellen picks up the plates, her excuse to go back into the copter; she puts them in the recycler. Josie stows the Instabake and then disappears into her tent. When the flap has closed, Ellen quietly opens the copter door facing away from the tent. She empties the whiskey flask onto the ground, watching the amber liquid disappear into the thick purplish grass.

It reminds her of Eaters' bodies dissolving from neural pellets.

*We didn't know. And as soon as we did know, we stopped. As soon as Tom convinced us the Eaters were sentient. That very second, we stopped.*

It is the same mantra she repeated to herself in the months that followed Tom's revelation, through all his disappearances, recaptures, therapeutic edits. *We didn't know.* It was the truth.

Too bad truth could be so inadequate.

When Ellen finally sleeps, she dreams. *She is dancing, surrounded by vague shapes under a hot sun. Her bare feet move joyously, her arms wave. The vague shapes are also dancing, pressing close to her…closer…then away. She laughs. Her feet pound out complex rhythms that she never knew, on a grassy purplish ground that her toes never touched before. She dances faster, they all dance faster, whirling and jumping and shouting in frenzied joy, and still she doesn't tire, she dances and dances and—*

Alarms shriek. Ellen cries out as she wakes. The motion detector has picked up something. Josie bolts from her tent, gun in hand. But it is not Eaters.

Walking toward the copter from the direction of the oxbow, all alone, is Tom Two Ribbons.

Almost Ellen doesn't recognize him. Although Tom's only been gone for six months, his beard and hair have grown several inches and he is much thinner. But it's not that. Tom had a certain way of walking, a tentative and careful that gait that could unexpectedly break into a brief swagger. Both tentativeness and swagger are gone. This man walks across the open plain as if across a well-known room, beyond which there might or might not be something interesting. When he is close enough, Ellen can see the lines of puzzlement cross his sunburned forehead. Something turns over in her chest. She turns off the screaming alarm, opens the copter door, and eases herself to the ground, standing behind and to the left of Josie.

Now Tom stands a few yards from his daughter. He looks from Josie to Ellen; the puzzled lines deepen. Beyond the circle of floodlight, Janus 4 is shadowy and indistinct, but in the east the sky is already paling.

Tom says, "Do I know you?"

Ellen's breath catches. He means both of them. He doesn't recognize Ellen. How much memory had Chang edited out? *"I'll need to take a lot more to cure him of his delusions,"* a somber Chang had told Ellen. She hadn't realized that "a lot more" would include her. And how much else?

Josie says, "You don't know me, no. Not since you just up and left Dakota." The girl's voice is so full of anger and hurt that Ellen winces. The very air around her seems charged. But Ellen doesn't know what to do, and so she does nothing.

"I'm Josie. Remember me, '*Dad*'?" You left when I was seven. You went on to the Space Force and a real life while my mother and me rotted away in that hellhole. And you never even contacted me again to see if I survived it."

The forehead lines deepen. Ellen sees the moment that Josie realizes that her father has no idea what she's talking about. The girl's back goes rigid. Ellen thinks wildly of an ancient Terran myth: people turned to stone by staring straight at Medusa. But that drama of deception and betrayal was Greek. What she is witnessing is an American betrayal, transplanted to the stars.

"I'm Josie," the girl says, and her voice cracks. "*Josie*."

"Josie? I can't...I don't think I know anyone named Josie."

"Y...You edited me out, didn't you? Trashed me from... from your memory..."

Ellen can't stand it. She steps out of the shadow of the copter. Maybe if Josie sees the extent of Tom's editing, she will not take it so personally. "Hello, Tom. Do you remember me? Ellen?"

He studies her—giving it a genuine effort—then shakes his head. "No, I don't think so. Have we met?"

She can't go on. Tom, who always feared editing, has been edited down to nearly nothing. Or maybe it isn't the editing; maybe it is his own fragile mind, forgetting what is too painful to remember. Behind her, in the copter, the linkscreen suddenly leaps to life. She can't see it, but she can hear Carlos's voice, both excited and weary. "Ellen? Ellen? Are you there?"

She says to Tom, "I'm Ellen Jenssen. From the base. Do you remember the base, Tom?"

"The base...no, I don't think so."

Josie says, so quietly that it's almost a prayer, "Fuck fuck fuck." Her shoulders tremble.

Carlos's voice says, "We've been up all night with your data, Ellen, along with a lot of other—the results are just—call me right away!"

Tom says politely, "Are you here to study the Eaters?"

Josie chokes out, "You really don't remember, do you? You're not...you're not you anymore. They got you."

Carlos's voice says, "Meanwhile, I'm sending you the analysis. Call!"

Josie says, somewhere between anguish and rage, "Damn you! Damn you, Daddy!" She raises the gun and fires.

"No!" Ellen screams. But by the time she reaches Tom, he is already dead. Josie lowers the gun and stares bleakly at Ellen and Tom—one alive and one dead.

"Why?" Ellen screams. "*Why?*"

Josie says nothing. She starts toward Ellen.

Fear squeezes Ellen's chest. But Josie merely hands over the gun, butt first. She holds out her two hands in a mocking mimicry of being handcuffed, then returns to the copter and climbs into the passenger seat.

The situation has been given to Ellen. She tries to think what to do, can't come up with anything, tries again. Nothing makes sense. Finally Ellen drags Josie's tent, poles and all, over to Tom's body and covers it. She weights the tent down with boxes of equipment from the copter. Carlos will have to send the other copter to retrieve it all. The sun rises.

A circle of Eaters advances toward her.

Ellen climbs in and lifts the copter. She doesn't think the Eaters will disturb the body, even if they can move the boxes and unwrap the tent. After all, Tom has lived among them for six months, unmolested. Has lived and prayed and danced with Eaters. It's Tom's dreams she has been having, not because there is any sort of psychic connection between them, but because Tom haunts Ellen's mind. And, she realizes, always will.

Josie has calmed down. As the copter skims over the ground, an Eater below munches on a bush of Flora 2. Pink flowers disappear between its rubbery lips. Josie opens the cockpit storage and takes out the whiskey flask. She says, "You thought I'd be into this by now, didn't you?"

Ellen hasn't thought about it at all. Josie is still focused on herself. But her action also reveals that she doesn't realize that Ellen emptied the flask. Ellen risks a glance at the girl. Josie is staring at the opaque flask with the same hunger that Ellen witnessed before, but also with a kind of triumph. Congratulating herself on not giving in.

Neither of them speaks the rest of the way back to the base, where Josie surrenders herself to Carlos Sanchez.

———

Ellen refuses food, a shower, comfort, discussion beyond what is necessary to tell her story. As soon as possible, she locks herself in her quarters, a Spartan room in the back corner of Trailer A, and accesses the base library. She spends the next hour studying genetic data.

In one long night of feverish work, the team has cross-indexed botanical and zoological data. Flora 1 has diverged enormously from the base genome. Ellen built plasticity into the plant's genes so that it could adapt to many soil conditions on Janus 4, fixing nitrogen over several ecological niches. But plasticity is plasticity, and there was no telling where future mutations might occur. Nor their effects.

The Eaters also possess a highly flexible genome, undoubtedly evolved so that they could digest a wide variety of plants. The lemon-colored globes of the original Flora 1 proved hallucinogenic to them, as to Tom. The mutations in Flora 1 apparently affected Eater nervous systems. It made large changes in what senior xenobiologist Stan Michaelson's previous experiments had determined were Eater processing centers for perception, memory, and communication.

Dave Scwartz has an outstanding record in zoology. He's very good, and his initial determinations ruled out sentience in the Eaters. They showed absolutely no signs of it. But aliens are alien. Eight years and four generations later, Tom observed ritual behavior, worshipping behavior, communicative behavior. Eight years and four generations of eating Flora 1.

Did humans cause that? The beginnings of sentience? *We didn't know*, we told each other, and stopped the genocide. But did we not know because, up to that point, there'd been nothing to know?

"Ellen?" A soft tap at the door, Julia's voice.

"Leave me alone," Ellen says.

"Please, honey, come on out. Don't isolate yourself."

"Go away."

She can hear Julia leave. Ellen turns back to the data. Later Eater specimens have all come from creatures killed by brushing against the force-field fence. Ellen studies the dates carefully. There are progressive changes to the Eater brains, in the areas connected to mating hormones. These are the hormones that produce aggression in Eater males. The changes correlate with the introduction of Flora 2. Flora 2 was designed to taste bad to Eaters, but only a few hours ago, Ellen herself saw Eaters munching pink flowers.

*First we trigger their evolution into sentience,* Ellen thinks, *and now into retaliation.*

Her eyes burn from reading, and she closes them. If the Eaters become more organized, the result will be the resumption of extermination. Only now it will be justified. The colonists who will be coming to Janus 4 must be protected. SettlerHome Corporation has a right to do that. In fact, it has an obligation to do so. Self-defense is always justifiable. Then, and now, and in times to come, amen.

People are back outside her door, she can hear them: Carlos and Julia and Chang and Stan and David and Hélène. Whispering, arguing, working out their concern for her. Because they care. Her family.

"Damn you, Daddy!" Josie cried just before she shot her father. But Ellen doesn't know what to call Josie's act. Not "murder." Not "mercy killing," either, because the girl had been too angry to be merciful. And Josie, no less than Tom, suffered from delusion: in her case, the belief that you could reject the past. However, to reject one's past, you first had to be able to remember it. Tom was beyond that. Josie could do nothing with the blank space that Tom had become: not confront it, not rescue it, not stand looking at it. And Josie held the gun.

*"The weaker culture always goes under."*

"Ellen," Carlos says, with what passes here for stern leadership, "open the door. Please."

Ellen rises from her chair. If she doesn't open the door, she knows, they will break it down. Carlos is not about to lose another member of his team, thus compounding his error with Tom. Everyone feeds on something: Carlos on his own competence, the scientists on their guilt, the Corporation on profits. The Eaters on Flora 1 and Flora 2. Josie Two Ribbons on her enormous anger, now about to receive a massive infusion of nutrients from a court martial and imprisonment.

"Ellen!"

"I'm coming."

No, you could not stop the clash of cultures, nor the weaker one going under. All you could do was resist. As Josie had resisted both the whiskey and thinking of herself as an ethnic victim, as Tom had resisted the base's convenient genocide of a sentient species. Ellen deplores Josie's anger, Tom's mental fragility. But they had resisted, and so were… what? Admirable, in some twisted way?

She doesn't know. This is unfamiliar territory for Ellen, and she hates having to inhabit it. But she is absolutely clear on one thing, at least.

Ellen opens the door. They are all there, huddled together, her friends and colleagues. The sharers of her guilt. They will, of course, suggest editing. She will not accept it.

Gently, but firmly enough so that there is no possibility of being misunderstood, she says to Carlos, "You need to find another botanical geneticist. I'm leaving Janus 4 tomorrow. I resign."

# The Chimp of the Popes

## James Patrick Kelly

James Patrick Kelly made his first sale in 1975, and since has gone on to become one of the most respected and popular writers to enter the field in the last twenty years. Although Kelly has had some success with novels, especially with *Wildlife*, he has perhaps had more impact to date as a writer of short fiction, with stories such as "Solstice," "The Prisoner of Chillon," "Glass Cloud," "Mr. Boy," "Pogrom," "Home Front," "Undone," and "Bernardo's House," and is often ranked among the best short story writers in the business. His story "Think Like a Dinosaur" won him a Hugo Award in 1996, as did his story "$10^{16}$ to 1," in 2000. Kelly's first solo novel, the mostly-ignored *Planet of Whispers*, came out in 1984. It was followed by *Freedom Beach*, a mosaic novel written in collaboration with John Kessel, and then by another solo novel, *Look Into the Sun*, as well as the chapbook novella, *Burn*. His short work has been collected in *Think Like a Dinosaur, Strange But Not a Stranger* and *The Wreck of the Godspeed*. His most recent book are a series of anthologies co-edited with John Kessel: *Feeling Very Strange: The Slipstream Anthology, The Secret History of Science Fiction, Digital Rapture: The Singularity Anthology, Rewired: The Post-Cyberpunk Anthology*, and *Nebula Awards Showcase 2012*. Born in Mineola, New York, Kelly now lives with his family in Nottingham, New Hampshire. He has a web site at www.jimkelly.net, and reviews internet-related matters for *Asimov's Science Fiction*.

James Patrick Kelly says: "When I was a younger, lightly-published writer I began to contemplate the prospect that I might actually be at the start of a career in science fiction.

But what kind of career did I want? I'd been reading Robert Silverberg since I was a kid, but now that I was trying to make a place for myself in our genre, I realized the scope of his accomplishment. Not only were his tales amazing, fantastic and thrilling, but they were also mature, penetrating, and (gulp) literary. He wrote science fiction for grownups and I took his success as a promise that what I hoped to accomplish might be also be acceptable to editors and readers.

I have had some success of my own since, most often a writer of short stories, and so I wanted to pay homage to one of his that excited me back when I was setting out on my career path. I am also a lapsed Catholic and my perturbed religious instincts continue to spark stories from time to time. And I've always wondered what it was about the papacy that has inspired some of my favorite Silverberg stories."

T he bot peeled from the wall. Tikko spread her fingers across its dome and opened her mind. "So, another candidate for our tribe of popes?" The day's instructions seemed to fizz behind her eyes.

Clin pushed the core of his pear into his mouth and nodded. He spat seeds into her trash.

Tikko vaulted onto her desk and squatted on its screen. "Give me a minute, then bring him in." She gave an absent-minded *hoo* as she scanned the file that the bot had brought up.

"What if he's dangerous?" Clin asked. Her sister Lola's son, Clin was ten years old and not good for much of anything as far as she could tell. Still, he was an adult now and the community had to find work for him somewhere. Tikko didn't know why it had to be with her team.

"He won't be." She tapped at the screen with her knuckle, trying to ignore him as she drilled deeper into the file. "From what I see here, he's probably too crazy to walk straight, much less hurt anyone."

"I'll stay anyway." Clin rose onto his hind legs. "In case you need help." He thrust his arms above his head in full aggression posture so that she could see his pink armpits. "You never can tell with humans." For a moment Tikko thought he might break a chair and start banging pieces against the wall. Instead he dropped back onto all fours and loped out of her office.

*Males.* Why did they always try to make everything into an adventure?

According to the bot, this human actually did think he was the Pope, and not a imam, senator, saint, prince or Nobel prize winner like the others under her care. Tikko's first patient ever had announced that he was Pope Joe, which was why the chimps called her sad and deluded tribe of humans *the popes.* This newest pope claimed he was Innocent XIV; no one had been able to coax a real name out of him. He had been discovered by loggers from a frontier community in the Great Northern Forest, one of the remnants of humanity who either had refused to join the gathered or had been left back. He had slept through the gathering in a cryovault; the chimp loggers had found him wandering near a hidden bunker with a compromised generator.

Tikko heard Clin's muffled voice just outside. "You go in here, quick, quick." She never understood why her nephew acted as if their humans barely had command of English. She cleared the screen, scooted her rump to the edge of the desk and faced the door with her legs dangling.

The new pope entered her room as if he owned it; Clin trailed close enough to grab him if he posed a threat. He appeared to be in good health and in his late thirties, although all the humans she had ever met had been juved into near immortality. She was impressed by his vestments. He seemed absolutely at ease in a white cassock, a purple chasuble that appeared to be made of silk, red slippers and purple skullcap. Very realistic—in her experience, newly-retrieved popes tended to be at once eclectic and outlandish. She had seen them wearing keffiyehs made of tablecloths, masks of aluminum foil and tape, capes and top hats and medals the size of dinner plates.

The pope puttered about her room as if it were unoccupied. She recognized this behavior as aggression but let him have his moment. He surveyed her perches and the nest that Kulki had knitted for her using broom handles, reached up and jiggled the low swing. He lingered at one of the tall windows, shielding his eyes against the sun as he took in the view of the ski slope. He leaned over her desktop and ran a finger along its edge, nodding when the screen displayed a prompt. At last he stopped and stared at her with the bad manners typical of humans. "You are in charge here?"

She held his gaze. "I'm Tikko, of the minders." She nodded toward her nephew. "He's Clin."

"Minders?"

"We study human psychology." She thought it best not to tell her patients that they were in therapy, at least until they adjusted to their new circumstances. "May I ask who you are, sir?"

The pope nodded. "Your English is excellent, Tikko Minder." He drew himself to his full height. "We are as you see." When he extended his right hand to her, Clin crouched, ready to spring to her defense. "Pope Innocent XIV. You may kiss our ring."

Tikko had been expecting this. "As you say, Innocent, I *am* in charge." She hunched forward and extended her hand, caution palm up toward her nephew, to show that she would greet the new pope on his terms. "You have no authority here." She slid off the desk and stood before him, her head just above his waist. "But I will offer you a sign of respect." She bent quickly and brushed her lips against his ring, then caught his hand in hers to examine it. He seemed surprised.

The ring was exactly as it should be: gold, no jewels. She rubbed her thumb across it, feeling the bas relief of St. Peter fishing from his boat. "You wear the Ring of the Fisherman, Innocent." She let him go.

"Cast at my coronation." Then he blessed her using the correct gesture: three fingers held up, thumb and forefinger touching. "And you may call me Your Holiness." This one might be delusional but he had done his research. "You are of the faith, Tikko?"

*Mistake.* She showed him her wide-open mouth, top teeth covered. "I am a chimpanzee, Innocent. According to your religion, I don't have a soul."

"Ah, but that doctrine was never pronounced *ex cathedra.*" He dismissed her objection with a casual wave. "Set forth by my predecessors, yes, but never infallibly. If the institution of men errs, God always sets us right. The Church now welcomes you and your kind."

"There is no Church," Clin said, his lips tight with rage. "And your god is the god of nothing."

How many times had Tikko told Clin not to taunt new arrivals? He was scarcely fit for guard duty, much less to assist in therapy. Still, she was interested to see how the pope would react.

"The Church exists as long as there are those who believe."
He raised both hands to his shoulders and glanced up. "God
exists whether you believe in Him or not." He smiled, as if
his god had confirmed that he existed, then strode to the tall
windows, rubbing his hands together. "But surely I'm not the
last?" The converted condominiums perched at the edge of
the Snowdancer trail. Even though it was late summer, the
pope eyed the chairlift carrying chimps up the mountain as
if he expected to spot human skiers. "I can't believe that all
have been gathered."

"There are just under nine hundred humans that we
know of." Tikko resisted the impulse to call them *your kind*.
"We have twenty-nine staying here with us." She vaulted to
her swing, caught the bar with one hand and hung. Now she
was looking down on him. "That's why we've brought you to
this place. We mind those who are left."

"We were not left." The pope wheeled, showing a spark
of anger. "We *chose* not to join the gathered." Then he realized
that she was studying him. "I don't mean to offend, Tikko,
but I'm not used to talking this much." He steepled his hands
and touched them to his lips. "I think it would be best if I met
with the other dissenters now."

*Dissenters?* She had never heard that one before. "I'm afraid
that isn't possible." She wasn't about to tell him that their
humans were all broken, deranged or bereft. "At least not yet."

"Not yet?" He folded his arms. "Suppose I insist?"

"Perhaps you didn't understand, Innocent." She slapped
her other hand onto the bar of the swing and kicked her legs,
swaying back and forth. "You don't give orders here."

"Ah. Would you at least tell me why I can't see them,
Tikko Minder."

She gave him nothing. The only sounds in the room were the creak of the swing and Clin's delighted panting at the human's irritation at being ignored.

"Another time then, my child." He bowed. "Is there a place where I might be alone?"

———

"Mount Washington," said her daughter Kulki. "A foolish human name." She slung herself onto a branch beneath Tikko and nestled her rump onto the collar where it joined the trunk of the beech tree. "Who was this Washington and why should geography be named after him? We should call it Mount Tikko."

"The world is big." Tikko lifted an arm as if to grasp the entire mountain range before them. "Nobody wants to rename everything in it."

"Why? Because we don't have the right? Because we don't have the time?" She slapped the trunk with a hoot. "I'll tell you why, maa. Because it's too much trouble. That pile of rocks is ours now, but we're too timid to claim it." She spat toward the Snowcrest Hotel where the retrieved humans were kept. The gob was thick and well placed, arching high into the air and falling some ten meters away. "Or too lazy."

Tikko accepted the game and spat in the same direction, but didn't get the distance her daughter had. "So, maybe we have better things to do."

"What? Mind these pathetic humans? Feed them and wipe their asses and tuck them in at night?" She spat again but the gob deflected off a branch. "The ones who were too dumb or crazy to upload?"

Tikko knew that this was about the new pope. She wrinkled her brow in frustration. Getting a new human was an honor, but it was also traumatic for the community. Even though the world belonged to the chimps now, humans had given it to them. Some still worried that they might want it back someday. Younger chimps often responded to new arrivals with belligerence displays while elders tended to hunch in submission. Tikko felt pulled in both directions but knew she had to stay centered.

"He's not crazy, dear." Tikko bent and tugged Kulki's ear. "He's the Pope."

Kulki shrieked in derision and Tikko let go. "How do you keep from laughing at them?"

"Sometimes I can't," she said. "But most don't realize that they're being laughed at." Tikko spat again, easily besting her daughter's second attempt but not quite equaling her first.

"Crazy," said Kulki . "But you like the challenge."

"Clever though, this one. He's done the research. His costume is the best I've ever seen. He must actually have belonged to a christian cult." She scratched her belly. "He used a term even I had never heard before. *Ex cathedra.*"

"What's it mean?"

"I had a bot look it up. The popes, the real ones, claimed they were never wrong. Except new popes kept having to contradict their predecessors. I mean, in the old days they thought that the sun went around the earth and that it was a sin to upload yourself."

"Sin," said Kulki. "More foolishness."

Tikko ignored her. "So the popes decided that they should only be infallible on special occasions, when they made a declaration called *ex cathedra*. It comes from Latin. Means 'from the chair.'"

"Chair? What chair?"

"The chair they were sitting on, silly." She slapped the top of Kulki's head, shrieked and scampered on all fours down the branch. *"Chase!"* she called and dropped down two branches. She caught herself and twirled away from Kulki so that the trunk was between them. By the time her daughter gathered herself to pursue, Tikko had a good ten meter lead.

They dropped around and down the tree all the way to the ground. Tikko, seeing that Kulki would soon catch up, sat abruptly in the middle of the slope and plucked at a blade of grass. She seemed not to notice anyone charging her. Just before her daughter was about the slam into her, Kulki did a sideways somersault, tumbled to rest beside her maa and gazed nonchalantly up at the sky, as if they had been idling there for hours. Tikko had changed the game and her daughter accepted it. Maybe the romp had worn the edge off Kulki's mood?

Kulki yawned. "When are you going to introduce him to the others?"

"I haven't decided yet. He'll be fine; he's so deep into his delusion that they won't be able to shake him. But I'm worried about the others. Last week Helen Calabrese told me that her lab was probably closed, so there's progress. But Ferd Mallory still thinks he's dying and has begun pestering Saint Bruce about the succession, so there's trouble. And of course, as soon as the new one announces that he's the pope, Chioma Melky will insist that she is too."

A flying grasshopper whirred between them. "Is she the tall one?"

"No, that's Uma Bhattacharjee who thinks she's the Great Mother. Chioma Melky is the one with the cross tattooed on her forehead."

"I wish my humans talked." Kulki swiped the grasshopper out of the air. "Or even grunted." She offered it to her maa to eat.

Tikko peeped a polite refusal. "Your humans are just as important as mine." She didn't actually believe this, but she had to say it. Kulki was on Lola's team minding stiffs, humans even more damaged than the popes. Their spirits seemed to have left their bodies; they never spoke, moved only when pushed and had to be fed by hand.

Her daughter brought the struggling grasshopper to her face but did not pop it into her mouth. "This bug has more personality than my humans." She released it and watched it zigzag back across the slope.

Tikko cooed in sympathy. She had minded stiffs when she was young. At least with her popes, there was a chance for improvement. "It isn't forever," she said. "Someday you'll have my job."

"You're a long way from an elders' nest." Kulki combed fingers down her mother's shoulder. "What will we do when they're gone? These humans?"

"Probably never go." Almost all of the surviving humans were functionally immortal; barring accidents, they might live for centuries.

"They will if we make them."

Tikko's ears twitched. "What are you saying? We were put on earth to mind the humans. Give them the chance to join the gathered someday."

Her daughter grabbed an imaginary human by the neck with both hands and barked. "What if I don't believe in the gathered?"

"Don't," said Tikko. "*Kulki.*"

Her daughter's grip tightened and then her hands twisted sharply. She showed Tikko all of her teeth.

———

Tikko slept badly that night. Her nest swayed whenever she wriggled to get comfortable. Its weave caught at the hair on her back. Dreams troubled her: shrieking dreams, falling dreams, dreams of the gathered. In the middle of the night she thought she heard someone whisper *my child*. But she was Bixa's child and her mother was dead. Nobody should be calling her a child.

The next morning she forced herself to nibble breakfast with her offspring, Kulki, Arfur, Soeq, and Little Bixa. She was worried about Kulki. Should she report what her favorite daughter had said? The elders all knew that the younger chimps resented minding humans, but no one in this community had ever talked about killing them. That was something that happened elsewhere. She had heard suspicious tales of accidents at the reservation town in Alabama where most of the humans who weren't crazy lived. And of course the notorious Simon Minder had let three stiffs freeze to death in Minnesota. If Tikko mentioned Kulki's threat—had it been a threat?—then her entire family would come under suspicion of human endangerment. They might be forced from the minder community to some backward frontier town.

Every morning the elders of Tikko's community met in the dark basement of the ski lodge at the center of their summer quarters. They had decorated the walls of what had once been a sports store with skis and snowshoes and skates and coats and mittens to remind themselves of winter and human folly. With the doors closed, the chimps' natural claustrophobia helped keep the meetings brief. There were five elders altogether: Tikko and Pacito led teams that minded popes, while Lola and her team cared for a dozen stiffs. Moss's chimps maintained quarters with the help of the bots, and managed the summer and winter migrations. Gamba and her team foraged, cooked the food that the farmbots grew, doctored members of the chimp community when necessary and made sure everyone got enough play.

Moss was the last to join the circle of chimps who squatted on the meeting rug. The bot peeled from the wall and she opened her mind to it and took instruction.

"We need more meat," said Gamba. "I'm calling a hunt."

"For what?"

"Rabbits. Squirrels. Turkeys, if we can find them. The humans need meat."

"Can't you just trap them?"

"Hunting will be more fun. You need fun, Pacito." Gamba reached over and tickled him.

"I'll tell you what's fun. Fun is watching Tikko's new pope change clothes."

"Vestments," Tikko said.

"Did you see? He came with three suitcases."

"How do we know what's in them?"

"Maybe he has weapons." Lola put both hands on her head in mock alarm. "He's human."

"And crazy."

"The loggers checked it out." Moss took everything too seriously. "The bots told them what to look for."

"Besides, when was the last time a crazy hurt a chimp?"

"They hurt my feelings all the time."

The room filled with breathy laughter. Only Moss and Tikko remained silent.

"So Veejay wants to go."

"Go? Go where?"

"To join another community. Someplace where there aren't any humans."

"That's most places."

"What does he have against humans?"

"Nothing. He wants to be a digger. Explore the cities."

"Moss? He's your son."

Lola draped her arms around Moss. "Let him go, dear. He hates minding stiffs." Veejay was on her team and was one of Kulki's best friends.

Although her gaze filled with sadness, Moss didn't object.

"They're digging in Montreal," Lola said. "He could go there."

"Just shipped eight bushels of peaches to Montreal and got two bushels of figs back."

"Figs? From who?"

"Diggers. Visiting from France."

"Veejay is *not* going to France.

"Walt Camlin isn't eating again."

"That's because he needs meat, dear."

"All right then." Pacito glanced around the room. "Anything else?"

Tikko knew that now was her chance to report what Kulki had said. The bots already knew because she had opened her mind, but once she spoke here there would be no taking it back. If Moss could let her offspring leave, shouldn't Tikko alert the community to the potential threat from hers? But she knew it wasn't only her offspring who were sick of the humans. It was their entire generation. This was bigger than

Tikko's family, bigger than the minders, even. It was about the duty that chimps owed humans. The debt that could never be paid.

"I've got something." Gamba, ever the clown, bowled into Pacito, knocked him onto his back and began to tickle him mercilessly. When Lola and Moss began to caper around them, hooting encouragement, Tikko knew that the moment had passed.

———

Tikko brought her entire team to observe the introduction of the new pope to their tribe. Chatta and Ash had served night duty but had agreed to stay past their shift. Tikko and the others—Clin, Peppa and Charlie—had to wait before entering the Snowcrest Hotel, while Pacito's team led her tribe of popes out for their daily hike. Today Pacito was taking his charges down the East Branch of the Pemigewasett River for a picnic near the fluxway. He claimed that they liked to watch the chains of cargo bots hurtling up and down the Northeast Main. Whether or not that was true, minder protocols called for getting the humans as much northern sun and fresh air as they could stand before the community packed up for winter quarters in Dixie. The regimen of travel and exercise and medication seemed to help keep the popes from degenerating into stiffs. Occasionally one improved enough to leave the community, either to live with the sane humans in the reservation town or make the pilgrimage to the Argonne Science Shrine to join the gathered.

There were seven popes in the tribe Tikko minded. They met each morning in the Maple Suite and stayed together until things got too chaotic. Chatta and Ash had the tribe assembled on time—a good sign. They were eager to meet their new comrade. The bots still hadn't identified him, so Tikko planned to introduce him as Innocent. She wasn't looking forward to the reactions from Chioma Melky and Saint Bruce at his claim to be the real Pope.

Chioma Melky could be either the Prophet Ezekiel or the Panchen Lama or the Matriarch of Constantinople, depending on the day of the week. The bots had never been able to identify Saint Bruce, who claimed to have worked miracles that no one else had ever witnessed. Ferd Mallory thought he was the Prince of Morocco. He often quarreled with Henrik Diesen, who spoke to the dead and the Norse gods. Uma Bhattacharjee maintained that she was the twenty-first reincarnation of Prajnaparamita, the Great Mother. Ben Brown had served one term as senator and since the rest of the Augmented Union had long since dissolved, had proclaimed himself acting Prime Minister. Helen Calabrese, their one success story, had worked on the team at the Argonne Science Shrine that had grown the cognisphere. She used to believe that she alone was to blame for the gathering of the human race and would beg Tikko to be allowed to return to her lab so that she could set them free. Now, at least, she was acknowledging that there was no lab to return to.

After opening her mind to the Maple Suite's bot, Tikko surveyed her charges, trying to take the temperature of the tribe. Some of the popes lounged in their seats around the conference table. Saint Bruce sat cross-legged on the floor; today Uma Bhattacharjee had joined him. All had dressed for the August heat in shorts and tee shirts. Prince Ferd wore his crown of fluted oak.

"Good morning," Tikko said.

"Good morning," replied Helen Calabrese, Henrik Diesen, Uma Bhattacharjee and Ben Brown with varying degrees of enthusiasm. Prince Ferd nodded regally at Tikko and Saint Bruce blessed her.

"If he's the Pope," said Chioma Melky, "then so am I."

"Really?" Helen Calabrese called the bot to her side and kept a hand in contact with the glossy surface of its dome, as if she could open her mind. "Which one are you?"

"Pope Chioma."

"You have to change your name," said Henrik Dissen. "They change their names."

"He's late," said Prince Ferd. "Do we think that's rude?"

"He's not late. I thought we'd talk among ourselves first." Tikko hopped onto the table. "So, he claims to be Pope Innocent XIV. He may ask you to call him Your Holiness but we—" she gestured at the chimps lounging along the walls "—are calling him Innocent." She noticed Clin puffing up himself into an aggression posture. "We'd like you to do the same." She stretched a caution palm toward him.

"Then call me Pope Holiness," said Chioma Melky. "No, Pope Fourteen."

"He's a miracle, this one," said Saint Bruce. "I saw him in a vision."

For weeks Tikko had been trying to get Saint Bruce to sit at the table so she could keep an eye on him. When she walked on her knuckles to the edge of the table, he gave her an enlightened smile. She had expected resistance; maybe this was going to be easier than she had expected.

"Holy, holy, holy, holiness." Chioma Melky began to chant. "Fourteen times holy, holy fourteen." She squirmed in her chair. "Fourteen o'clock, he's late, Tikko, late, holy damn late." Seeing that she was getting upset, Ash stepped forward and whispered into her ear. She shook her head but subsided.

"Tikko," said Helen Calabrese, "do I really have to be here for this?"

Ben Brown raised his index finger, as if he expected everyone to fall silent. Ignore him and he would speak anyway, raising his voice until people listened. "I had the honor of meeting the last pope." His orator's rumble carried the room. "We discussed the uploading problem for almost half an hour. It was very much on his mind."

"There is nothing wrong with uploading *per se*," said Helen Calabrese. "It's only wrong if everyone does it."

"Everyone didn't do it." Henrik Diesen pointed at each of the popes in turn. "One, two, three, four, five, six." He thumped his own chest. "And seven. Still are we here."

"Not to mention the stiffs." Chioma Melky giggled like a naughty little girl. "Do they count?"

"I never met the last pope," called Uma Bhattacharjee from her place on the floor, "but I saw him when he spoke at the Rose Bowl."

"But he wasn't the last, if this stranger is the Pope."

"If he's here with us," said Saint Bruce, "He's not a stranger anymore."

"*Tikko.*" Helen Calabrese's face was flushed. "I thought we had an understanding."

"We do, Helen. Bear with me a moment." Tikko gave a warning scream and slapped the table three times to get the popes' attention. "Humans, do you want to meet him or not?"

"Yes," said Prince Ferd. "Bring him hence."

Tikko nodded to Chatta who slipped out of the room.

"So, he might want to say something to you." Tikko strode the length of the table. She did not meet anyone's gaze directly, but rather looked at them aslant—at an ear or a neck or at the cross tattooed on Chioma Melky's forehead. "I think we should give him that chance."

"But we reserve the right to speak as well," said Ben Brown. "To have a frank and honest dialogue."

"We had another pope once, didn't we, Tikko?" Chioma Melky was twisting locks of her hair into greasy corkscrews. "Joey Ekeinde. He was the first one here, first even before me. Pope Joe."

"What happened to him?" asked Henrik Diesen.

"He died." Ash had not moved from Chioma Melky's side. "He lost track of himself and had an accident and he died." He rested a hand on her shoulder. "That's all that happened."

"And that's how we got our name, isn't it?" Chioma Melky shook him off. "Isn't it, Tikko? He said he was Pope, and I said I was Pope and you started calling us the popes. It was just the two of us, then. We were the first, the first, the first of the last."

Tikko gave her softest *hoo* and Charlie edged to Chioma Melky's other side.

"Before Ferd, before Uma and Bruce and the Senator here." Her eyes were big and there was a crackle in her voice like dry leaves. "Before Lauren What's-her-name. Before all these chimps." She cocked her head, first toward Charlie and then at Ash. "It was just Chioma and Joey and Tikko. And you named us the popes, the popes, the…"

She broke off. Everyone was so intent on her rant that they didn't realize that the new pope had arrived.

"You." Chioma Melky pointed at him. "Why are you dressed like furniture?"

Surprise flickered across Innocent's face. If anything he looked even more impressive than the first time Tikko had met him. His vestments were white trimmed with gold brocade. A golden cross hung on a chain around his neck. "I beg your pardon?" he said.

"Humans," said Tikko, "this is Innocent, whom I've been telling you about. What he's wearing is called a cassock, Chioma."

"It's summer," Chioma Melky said. "Aren't you hot, Your Holiness?"

"Actually, Tikko, it's called a simar, and no, I am perfectly comfortable, thank you." Innocent composed himself. "I'm sorry if my vestments seem strange to you…" He bowed to Chioma Melky. "I'm afraid I don't know your name, ma'am."

She had no chance to introduce herself because the others were already pressing around the newcomer.

"Prince Ferd of Morocco." The prince grasped the pope by the shoulders and gave him a double kiss.

Henrik Diesen shook Innocent's hand and also patted his back. "Welcome, Your Holiness."

"Ben Brown, Prime Minister of the Union. I knew your predecessor, Holiness."

"You mean Pope Robert?" Innocent touched his arm. "Unfortunately, I never had that privilege. You must share your impressions of him with me."

"Later." Ben Brown preened. "I look forward to it."

"I'm Bruce," called a voice from behind the crowd. The popes parted so that Innocent could see Saint Bruce, still cross-legged on the floor. "I had a vision of your coming."

"He's a saint, don't you know?" said Uma Bhattacharjee. "He does miracles."

"Really?" Innocent kept his expression neutral, but Tikko thought that he must realize by now that he was among the truly delusional. As she glanced around the room, she noticed Helen Calabrese leaning back in her chair, watching the commotion around Innocent with a puzzled expression.

"Friends," Innocent raised his hands to quiet the group. "I am honored to meet you, one and all. But I am astonished to find myself in such distinguished company. Tikko, my child, I wish you had given me some warning."

"You didn't know?" said Henrik Diesen. "They didn't tell you about us?"

"Tell me what?"

"We're the popes," grumbled Chioma Melky.

"I don't understand," said Innocent. "The popes?"

Chioma Melky began to clap.

"It's the name the chimps have given us." Uma Bhattacharjee struggled to her feet beside Saint Bruce. "Because of who we were."

"Are." Ben Brown's voice crackled. "Who we *are*."

Innocent glanced at Tikko. She gave him nothing.

"Ah," he said, "I see." Then he chuckled. The sound slipped from him as if he were telling a secret. "If you are popes, then I must be in the right place." The chuckle took on a sardonic music that swelled into an open-mouthed laugh. Tikko could see crinkles at the corners of his eyes. The new pope's face went red as he fell back into one of the chairs. His laughter was infectious. Some of the others joined in. The chimps glanced at one another nervously.

*Humans.* Tikko bit at the air in disbelief. Now all of them were laughing, even Chioma Melky. No, that wasn't right. Helen Calabrese was frozen as if she were sitting for one of the humans' foolish paintings.

———

"Let us pray," said Innocent. "In the name of the Lord, His Shepherd and Their Blessed Thought, lift your hearts to God." He bowed his head.

Tikko's popes knelt in a circle around Innocent on the deck of the base lodge. They were joined for the noon worship by most of Pacito's popes. The three holdouts loitered nearby; two sat at picnic tables finishing their lunches, the last was pinned in the shadows cast by the overhang of the lodge's roof. All watched the prayer group, as did the minders from Tikko's and Pacito's teams. The deck baked under the August sun and Tikko could see a glisten of sweat at Innocent's skullcap.

Pacito leaned close and spoke into her ear. "What do you suppose they are thinking?"

The humans prayed in silence for the most part, although Saint Bruce, Uma Bhattacharjee and Pacito's Lawrence Ketchem hummed *aum* and Chioma Melky emitted a breathy whistle from time to time.

"Prayer isn't thinking." Tikko picked a peach from her lunch basket and rubbed her thumb across the fuzz. "At least, that's what they claim."

"If it's in their heads, it's thought." He waited for Tikko to agree; when she was silent his lips curled. "What else could it be?"

"Maybe someone is thinking for them." She bit into the peach. "Like when we open our minds."

"Who's thinking for them? Your pope of popes?" He reached with his foot and picked up a discarded snack box with his toes. "The bots?"

"You know humans can't open their minds."

"Do I?"

Tikko licked juice off her chin. "The bots say so."

"Because the gathered told them to." He crushed the box into his lunch basket, saving Moss's team some cleanup. "Doesn't mean it's true, dear."

"You sound like my daughter."

Pacito laughed. "Ever since that one arrived—" he cut his eyes toward Innocent "—I've been having strange thoughts."

"Maybe crazy is catching." Tikko sidearmed the peach pit and watched it skitter across the deck. "Look at them," she said. "They just kneel there." She dropped to all fours and began to pace. "At peace."

"That's good, no?"

"I've been minding Chioma Melky eight years. No, nine." She sauntered all the way to the end of the deck, pinched Clin who was snoozing in the swelter and then came back to Pacito. "They never sat still for me. Never once."

"You're saying they're not as crazy as they were?"

"Last week he got a stiff to talk."

Pacito scratched his belly. "Moss says Ed Gluck wasn't all that stiff."

"And look at yours." She rested her hand on his chin and turned him toward his charges in the circle. "They're different after they pray. Maybe even happy."

"They're humans." He yawned. "Humans are never happy."

She rocked back and forth, thoughts tumbling over one another.

"Where's Helen Calabrese?" asked Pacito. "I never see *her* on her knees."

"She's been hiding from him, won't say why."

Pacito threw his arm around her shoulder. "Well dear, if you're worried then I'm worried." He dragged her to him and kissed the side of her face three times. "We're worried, they're happy. The world is turning inside out."

Innocent was standing now; prayers were over. He preached to the assembled popes and even those who had not prayed with him seemed to devour his words. He spoke briefly of hope and going forward. He said humans must rise to a new challenge. God wanted them to spread the Blessed Thought to all.

"Even to our minders." He wasn't large for a human but at that moment his voice made him seem huge. He caught Tikko's eye with his usual rudeness and nodded. "For although they may not yet know it, they are as much God's children as are we."

*God's children.* One of the popes at the picnic table got up and knelt with the rest of Innocent's congregation. Those on either side held out their hands to receive him. One was Saint Bruce. Tikko shivered. There was a shadow passing over their community. She reminded herself that these popes were not the ones who had reinvented chimps and given them the world. Those humans were gone, gathered into the cognisphere. So Innocent was wrong, had to be.

If the gathered had wanted chimps to know God, they would have taught them to pray.

———

Tikko lunged off her high swing toward the perch three meters above her desk. She grabbed the edge, polished from a thousand such catches, and let her momentum carry her toward the wall from which she bounced upwards. Twisting in midair, she landed on the perch's deck on all fours, coiled and sprang for the rope sleeping nest. She scuttled hand over hand across its length and then along the rigging to the iron bar attached to the wall of her room. Hanging from the bar with one hand, breathtaken from her scramble, she could hear her heart drum, feel the blood sing in her veins. It was a relief to fly about her room and not fret about Innocent or the other popes. She dropped to the floor and threw a couple of backwards somersaults just to make the world spin.

"Tikko?"

She bounded onto her desk and saw Helen Calabrese in the doorway. "What?" The lightness of the moment before left her. "Is something wrong?"

"No." She held the door open, hesitating. "Yes." She cleared her throat. "May I speak with you?"

"Yes, yes, come. Sit."

She was surprised when Helen Calabrese closed the door behind her. Tikko knew that she should have opened her mind then. The bots would want to monitor such an unusual conversation. Instead she turned around once on the desktop and squatted, facing the human. "So?"

Helen Calabrese dragged a chair from its place along the wall to face the desk. "I've always wondered," she said, "whether you chimps ever sit in chairs yourselves. You know, when we're not around."

"They're not very comfortable." Tikko's lips thinned enough to show pink gums. "For us at least."

She settled herself. "Right." Helen Calabrese seemed in no hurry to continue the conversation, so Tikko waited. This was the human way; they were creatures of false starts and long pauses. At last Helen slapped both hands to her thighs and seemed to come to a decision. "I want to make the pilgrimage."

Tikko yipped in astonishment. "To Argonne?"

Helen Calabrese nodded.

There was no stilling the buzz in Tikko's head. *A breakthrough.* A few popes had left them for the human reservation in Alabama, but only Lauren Colotta had asked to join the gathered. "You're sure? I know you've been seeing things more clearly, but I never expected anything like..." She could hear herself babbling and didn't care. "I mean, that's wonderful. Amazing."

Helen Calabrese stared at her hands as if she were surprised to find them on her lap. "I understand that I can choose a witness to go with me." She looked directly at Tikko then, a breach of manners that she had never committed before. "A chimp. Would you do me the honor?"

*The honor.* "Yes, yes, of course." Tikko realized that she was nervously pulling the hair on her wrist. With a word—pilgrimage—this human had transformed herself. She had no need of minders; she was one of the gathered, or soon would be. Tikko's mother Bixa would have been awestruck. And submissive. And scared enough to hide under the desk. Bixa used to spin incredible tales of the humans who had given up their bodies, even though she herself had never even seen one. Tikko shivered at the memory but then quickly sought her center. She was not some fearful elder... .

"Tikko, are you all right?"

"Fine." She leaned forward onto all fours; that steadied her. "When do you want this? Can you wait until the move to winter quarters?"

"Sooner would be better. I don't feel as if I belong here anymore."

"So something *is* wrong?" Tikko had been minding Helen Calabrese for six years and could still read her, even if she was soon to be gathered. "Something about Innocent?"

She pushed out of the chair.

"Is he harassing you?"

"He wants to save me, Tikko." Now that she was standing up, she seemed at a loss. "He's got most of the popes now but that's not enough. Before long, he'll have everyone here but the stiffs." Her smile twisted. "Maybe even them."

"You could go to another minder community. Or Alabama—the reservation."

"Why?" Helen Calabrese combed fingers through her hair in frustration. "You don't understand, Tikko. This is God's plan, according to him. Next will be missionaries—to the minder communities, Alabama, wherever there are humans. He's thinks he's been chosen to rally us. Believe me, I've seen what religion can do. I know his kind." She raised both hands to her shoulders as if to surrender. "I knew *him*, sort of."

"What?" Tikko felt a prickle of heat on back of her neck.

Helen Calabrese explained that she had thought all along that Innocent looked familiar, but hadn't been able to place him. Now she remembered. His last name was Velasco; she wasn't sure about his first name. Julio, or maybe Javier. Before the gathering, he had produced a series of feeds which argued that scientists were acting in accordance with God's will when they had grown the cognisphere. He declared that they had created the Biblical heaven promised from the time of the Old Testament. When the newsfeeds started to notice him, the team at Argonne had delegated her to quash his extravagant claims. Velasco had asked for a face-to-face debate, but she had finessed him into a written Q and A format that stretched over several weeks. "So we never actually met. He was just a graduate student at some divinity school and…well…I suppose I embarrassed him. I think he ended up dropping out of his program." She snickered. "And then, apparently, getting elected Pope."

"He isn't the Pope," said Tikko.

"No? If he isn't *the* Pope, he's still their Pope."

"You're not doing this just to get away from him?"

She picked up her chair as if it were made of glass and set it back against the wall. "You chimps have this myth that the gathered were all wise and pure and rational." Her crooked smile scared him. "Six billion people stepped into the cognisphere and they had six billion reasons. Not all of them were good reasons."

After Helen Calabrese closed the door behind her, Tikko slumped onto her back and gazed up at the ceiling of her room. She thought about climbing to her nest but was too exhausted. Being astonished was hard work. Then she remembered that she needed to open her mind and give the bots access to her interview. She rolled off her desk, drooped across the floor to the bot.

It had been years since she consciously opened her mind. She had mastered the technique when she was five—and in just two weeks. Bixa had told her that meant she would probably lead a team when she grew up. Since then Tikko needed only to see her hand on the dome of a bot and her mind opened immediately. She no more noticed the bots' presence in her head than she would notice the whirr of air conditioning in Maple Suite or the chirp of crickets when she was riding a chairlift.

This time, however, she went deliberately through the routine that her mother had taught her. She began by picturing a tree and then climbed it, leaving her thoughts on the ground below her. The higher she climbed the further away they were. At last she stopped and covered her ears with her hands, closed the eyes of her imagination, held her breath. When she was utterly empty she experienced the familiar whispering wind that was not thought, not sensation. She had forgotten that this wind was not one thing but many and that the whispers came from all directions at once. For a dizzying instant she knew everything that anyone had ever known, then the moment passed and she was grounded again and knew only what she did know.

And one thing more. Innocent was a threat.

———

"No, he is *not* coming with us," said Tikko. "He stays right here."

The other elders were startled by her outburst. Their silence was as cold as the concrete walls of the basement meeting room.

"That's all?" Lola spoke at last. "Can you give us a reason?"

"Yes, because we decided this already. Now things change because popes are upset? Who's in charge here?"

"We're considering what's best for this community."

"Helen Calabrese doesn't want him to come."

Lola's lower lip went all floppy. Tikko hated it when her sister made a show of being patient with her. "And her reason is?"

"Because he wants to convert her to some foolish church that doesn't exist. Because he'll try to keep her to from joining the gathered."

"We don't know that."

"That's what she thinks, Pacito. It's her pilgrimage, not Julio Velasco's."

"He changed his name. It's Innocent now."

"He's a crazy pope." Tikko heard herself snarl. "Next he'll have us calling him Your Holiness."

"Be calm, Tikko."

Both Gamba and Moss sidled across the meeting rug to her. Moss began grooming her back. Gamba picked both of her hands up in hers. "Easy dear," she said.

When Pacito spoke again, he used his gentlest voice. "It's happening very fast, I know. So many new things to understand. Innocent. Helen Calabrese. The way the popes are changing. But the humans want this, Tikko. They have never wanted anything before."

"Only because he's stirring them up."

Gamba squeezed her hands, panting in sympathy.

"Whatever their reason, wanting is good," said Lola. "Wanting is healthy."

Tikko knew she had lost. The other elders were scared of what Innocent might do if he didn't get his way. "Do I have a choice?"

Silence was their answer.

"Let him come then." The words were ashes in her mouth. "But only him."

Moss said, "But he's asking to bring…"

Tikko screamed and shot her arms into the air into full aggression posture. "*No.*" Shocked, the other chimps tumbled into submission crouches. They probably thought she was out of control. Maybe she was.

"I'm leaving tomorrow." Tikko bared her teeth and pointed at her sister. "And I'm taking Kulki with me. She's on my team from now on, sister dear. You can have your idiot son Clin back."

———

The entire chimp community turned out to see them off, as well as all the popes and even some stiffs. Innocent had gotten three more of them walking in the last week, although they still needed helping hands.

Tikko, Helen Calabrese, Kulki and Ash passed a crowd of humans on their knees as they climbed the steps to the station. Innocent lingered to bless them. "They're praying for us," he called to Tikko. She ignored him.

The transbot was divided into thirty sleeper compartments; it could accommodate one hundred and eighty chimps or one hundred and twenty humans. Tikko put Innocent, Ash and Kulki in the rearmost two compartments and showed Helen Calabrese to the front, determined to keep the humans separated. When everyone was settled, Tikko opened her mind: her only instruction was to ride. At nine-thirty the transbot floated off its dock and eased into the flux of the Northeast Main.

They hurtled through the Great Northern Forest. Tikko stayed with Helen Calabrese. Had she wanted to talk, Tikko was ready to listen. But she was subdued and seemed content to look out the window at the vast sameness of trees and hills and streams which now stretched south. Eventually Helen Calabrese dozed off and Tikko decided to check on her other charge.

Innocent had crossed over from his compartment to chat with his minders. Ash did not seem pleased with the company but Kulki was indulging the pope. She had been thrilled to be rescued from tending stiffs and was busy trying to impress with her team spirit.

"Ash, why don't you go up front?" said Tikko. "Helen Calabrese is asleep; keep watch on her. We should be eating before too much longer."

He slid off the bench where he had been squatting and hugged Tikko. "Pray for lunch," he whispered. "It's the only way he'll shut up." He let his hand slide down her arm.

She gave a barking laugh, then prodded her daughter's shoulder. "You, go stretch. I'll watch this one."

"I'll stay, maa." Kulki blew a burst of air between her lips. "I'm fine."

"Fine indeed," said Innocent. He was wearing the purple chasuble and plain white cassock she'd seen when she first met him. "You have one smart pup here, Tikko. I look forward to having her on the team."

*Pup.* She settled on the bench opposite Innocent. Kulki was bristling and Tikko rested a hand on her knee to center her. She was grateful that Ash had left the slider into the compartment open. In close quarters the meaty smell of human skin was a little sickening.

"We've slowed down," said Innocent.

"We're coming to the York yards." Tikko tapped a knuckle against the window. A cargo chain had pulled over next to them: container bots, hopper bots, tank bots, and flat bots bobbed in their wake as they passed. "We switch soon to the Lakes Main and then head for Chicago, wherever that is. On a lake, I guess."

"You've never been?"

"The middle of the country is nothing but botscape. When we go to winter quarters we stay on the Northeast Main all the way to Chesapeake and then switch to the Dixie Loop."

Ash slapped the doorsill. "The bot must have heard you. Lunch is ready."

They stretched a table between the benches and trooped out to the galley to pick up the lunch baskets. Gamba's team had packed more than enough provisions for the trip. Tikko got an apricot, a slice of melon, a bunch of cherry tomatoes still on the vine and half a head of cabbage. Innocent lifted the lid of his basket, sniffed at the steaming tureen and frowned. "Another lentil stew." He picked a strawberry from the basket and popped it into his mouth. "You know why our tribes are so listless?" he said. "It's because you're making vegetarians of them. Humans need meat." He pounded a fist against his chest in what he probably thought was a clever imitation of chimp belligerence.

Kulki shook her snack box at him. "Termite?" she said with a deadpan expression.

"No, thank you." He scowled. "I was saying to your daughter earlier how much this part of the country has changed. All the new forests."

Tikko folded a cabbage leaf into her mouth. "It wasn't like this when you were frozen?"

He shook his head.

"And when was that, exactly?"

"Ah, that would be telling." He spooned up some stew.

"Julio Velasco was born on January 30, 2202 in Cartagena, Colombia," said Kulki. "You are Julio Velasco?"

Innocent waved a finger at her. "Was."

"Robert III died on September 22, 2257. He was the last known Pope."

"You get that from the bots?" He seemed amused. "They're so good at dates."

"They estimate that the gathering was completed sometime between March and April of 2294. After that there would have been nobody to elect you Pope."

"Why Kulki, you're trying to trap me. She's just like you, Tikko." He leaned across the table and spoke in a low voice. "Of course, the bots are wrong about the end of the gathering."

"Really?" Kulki said. "How do you know?"

"Because there is one still to join!" His booming laugh shook the compartment.

"Maybe you'd rather Helen Calabrese change her mind."

"Oh, no. I insist that she go through with it."

Kulki considered. "Then why are you here?"

"I need to witness an execution before I can preach against the death penalty."

"This isn't an execution."

"Ah." He gave her a sly smile. "I must be mistaken then."

"There was a time when you claimed that the cognisphere was heaven," said Tikko.

Innocent's cheeks colored. "Did Helen tell you that?"

"She says she knew you when your name was Velasco."

Kulki gave a yip of surprise.

"Knew me?" He stirred the stew with his spoon—once, twice—then pushed the bowl away abruptly. "Odd, since we never met in person." He touched a napkin to his lips as he collected himself. "In any event, my thinking on the cognisphere has changed." He stuffed the napkin into the bowl, set the bowl into the basket and closed the lid.

Tikko knew he wanted them to ask him to explain, but she wasn't going to give him the satisfaction. Kulki, however, couldn't resist. "Do tell."

He rubbed his hands together, as if to warm them. "If the cognisphere is as promised, my child, then it might be very much like heaven. But everyone knows that, in order to get to heaven, you have to die. Now the question is, how do we know that the gathered were actually uploaded? Their bodies are certainly dead. What if their information got erased as well? What if the cognisphere is a lie?"

"Six billion humans believed in it."

"Yes they did. And how many of them have come back from the cognisphere to tell us just how heavenly it is?"

Kulki looked confused. "But why would they?"

"Ah, Kulki, I think your mother sees my point. To those of us left behind, joining the gathered and dying are the same thing."

"But even so…"

"The humans who are still alive, the dissenters, have fallen into error. They've made gods of the gathered. They're convinced that the age of humanity has passed. And that's what you chimps think too, isn't it? That we humans need to be minded. Or else kept on a reservation. You believe that this is your world now. But what if it was the gathered who were deluded? You've been following their plan." He leaned back and steepled his hands. "I believe that God has a different plan. For humans, and for chimps."

— — —

Tikko had heard stories about the botscape, but they did not prepare her for its terrible geometries. Two hours out of Chicago, the dawn revealed a world turned all the colors of gray. The bots had waged war with nature, and in this conquered territory, had brutally exterminated their enemy. There were scattered patches of weed and scrub and some dusty fields but otherwise the land was everywhere paved and built over. It looked as if the innumerable batch plants had flooded concrete in every direction, channelizing rivers and streams, transforming lakes into sludgy clarifiers and settling basins. Skeletal transmission towers disappeared to the horizon, pipelines wound beneath them like steel snakes. Their transbot skirted an endless airport, its asphalt runways shimmering in the morning sun. The Chicago Yards were choked with kilometer long cargo chains. Flat bots passed under huge container cranes, hopper bots waited patiently to receive their burdens from storage elevators.

The transbot switched yet again for the Prairie Main, and then the siding which would take them to the Argonne Science Shrine.

Tikko kept checking but Helen Calabrese's resolve did not falter. She acknowledged her minder's attempts at conversation but did not encourage them. She drank from a water bottle, ate an apple and stared at the world the bots were making, often with her forehead pressed against the window. Innocent on the other hand was manic, bouncing back and forth between compartments, exclaiming and pointing and annoying Ash beyond all reason.

Tikko was pleased that her team seemed to be bearing up, considering how intimidated *she* felt by the botscape. The transbot kept popping words into her head that she had neither heard before nor cared to remember. There were foundries and mills and smelters and blast furnaces and kilns with smokestacks like black fingers ripping the sky. Radomes like giant white wasp galls scanned for storms, a coldbox tower mined the air for nitrogen and oxygen—how was that possible? There were farms where no plants grew, tank farms, data farms, wind farms. In the distance she saw the skyline of a refinery, a vast city for hydrocarbons. Bot excavators tore wounds in the concrete to recycle treasures lost in landfills, to quarry limestone and to dig gravel. Tikko tried closing her eyes but the naming of the bots' countless works continued unabated.

As the transbot settled into its cradle at Argonne Station, Helen Calabrese emerged from her compartment. She had changed into a dress that was pale as the summer sky; a sash of darker blue bound her waist. Her shoes were blue too, with bizarre pointed heels. Tikko had never seen anything like this. Maybe it was some ceremonial outfit, like Innocent's vestments. Helen Calabrese strode down the aisle, holding out an arm out as if to catch herself against a stumble but never quite touching the wall. Innocent, Ash and Kulki watched her approach. She did not break stride and might have run into Innocent had not the chimps dragged him out of her way. Tikko had forbidden the pope to speak to Helen Calabrese unless she spoke first. As she passed, Innocent reached as if to take her hand. She ignored him.

Tikko's dread of traversing the forbidding botscape vanished as she stepped onto the platform. The grounds of the Argonne Science Shrine had lawns and trees and shrubs pruned with machine precision. Flowers nodded in trim gardens around low buildings, most of which appeared to be mothballed. There was still too much brick, concrete and glass for Tikko, but the scale of the place was comforting after the nightmare of Chicago and its environs. The campus was surrounded by a ring road swarming with bots of every description—more than she had ever seen. Come to witness a gathering?

Tikko started toward the nearest bot for instruction but before she took two steps the entire assembly seemed to pry her mind wide open and point her down a path. A five minute stroll brought them to a shell that sat on its foundation like a quarter of a melon. The entrance was on the rounded side; the flat façade faced away from them. Clad in black marble, the building was about six meters tall and six meters wide at its base.

It was not what Tikko had expected.

The floor of the shell was a black and white checkerboard of squares of marble. The half dome of the ceiling was composed of square black coffers: five rows of fourteen. The shell opened onto a garden filled with sedum and butterfly bush. There were white begonias bedded around stands of burgundy calla lilies.

It was empty.

Tikko waited for instruction but the now bots were silent. Kulki gave an uncertain *hoo*. Ash dropped onto all fours.

"Except a man be born again," murmured Innocent, "he cannot see the kingdom of God."

Tikko hissed at him to be quiet.

"It's all right, he doesn't understand." She pushed past him toward the garden. "He never did."

They fell into step behind her. When they were about five meters from the far edge of the shell, its opening filled with a wash of pale light. They stopped, transfixed. The bright colors of the garden were now shimmery pastels. The light seemed so liquid that Tikko thought that she might be able to catch it in her cupped hands.

When Helen Calabrese went rigid, Tikko was certain that she had lost her nerve.

"Do you want to go back?"

The human put a hand on Tikko's shoulder and tried to pet her. "No." Her fingers were stiff and awkward. Or maybe she was just leaning one last time on her minder for support. "Don't let him win. I'll be watching from the other side." Tikko thought she should reply, but what could a chimp say to one of the gathered?

Then Helen Calabrese started toward the light.

Innocent called, "Any last words, Helen?"

"You're wrong, Velasco," she said, without turning back.

Tikko chopped a hand toward Ash and Kulki and they caught the pope by the shoulders. "Don't say another word." Tikko snarled.

The metal on Helen's heels clicked against the marble floor. That's what Tikko remembered afterwards. Helen Calabrese called out a name. It sounded like Cass or Cassy. Then she started to run. *Click, click, click.* When she passed into the light, the clicking stopped. Helen Calabrese pitched forward, only it wasn't her anymore. Her body sprawled in the garden behind the glimmering at the edge of the shell.

Tikko was still holding her breath when Innocent spoke.

"Awful." His voice filled with pity. "A terrible, terrible waste."

"Quiet!"

"Don't you see? She's gone. You can't possibly scan a human mind in an instant."

She felt a rage come over her. It had something to do with the light. She thought it ought to stop now, but it didn't.

Instead it continued to pour down, no longer a wash but a flood. She tried to open her mind for instruction but instead she seemed to hear Helen Calabrese screaming *don't let him win* so she screamed back. Kulki and Ash answered, their mouths wide and their fangs glistening in the murderous light.

"What are you doing?" Innocent said. He began to struggle.

The screams of the chimps echoed off the half dome, echoed in Tikko's head as she circled behind the pope. She charged on toes and knuckles, hurling herself into his back. The frantic human, still in the grasp of Kulki and Ash, lurched toward the light.

"No. *Stop.*"

They brought him stumbling, flailing, right to the edge. Tikko didn't know if this was what the bots wanted but it was what *she* wanted most in all the world. Innocent was screaming louder than any human she had ever heard as Ash and Kulki—her daughter, her *angry* daughter—shoved him hard. As he staggered into the light, he tried to spin but his feet went out from under him and his body slumped through and onto the grass. Only his red slippers still remained in the shell.

There was no sound but their breathing. Tikko's mind closed. The light at the opening of the shell faded.

Overwhelmed, she sat backwards on the cold marble. "What have we done?"

"S-Sent him to heaven." Kulki turned around twice, and squatted facing away from the bodies.

Sin. For the first time in her life, Tikko understood why the word had plagued the humans so. She felt sick with shame, a stranger in her own mind. "But we have to go back now," she said. "Home. How do we explain?"

"Explain?" Ash leaned over and took her hands in his. "Do *you* know what happened." His hands shook as he pulled her to her feet. "We have to go, Tikko."

Four bots entered the garden, walking on spider legs. When two of them rolled Innocent's body over, Ash shrieked and Kulki spun around to watch. The bots rocked backwards, slipped their front legs under the body and picked it up. Like a fallen branch. Tikko put a hand on Kulki's shoulder as the two other two lifted Helen Calabrese. Like a dead rabbit.

Ash screamed again and they ran.

Galloping on all fours, the chimps burst out of the shell and down the path toward the station. Tikko fell behind the younger chimps and was the last one to reach the transbot, still floating in its cradle. The rear door had opened to let them in. She found Ash scrabbling frantically up the center aisle, Kulki huddled under a table in one of the compartments. Tikko tried again to open her mind, but she was alone with her guilt. It was as if the bots had forsaken her.

The door slid shut and the transbot floated onto the fluxway.

———

The chimps hid in different compartments and did not come out until they were well out of the botscape. Tikko spent the time trying to understand what had happened in the shell, thinking what she hoped were her own thoughts about humans and chimps. Bots and the gathered.

In her moment of rage in the shell, she had wanted to kill Innocent, *yes*. But thrusting him into the cognisphere wasn't murder, *no*. Helping humans join the gathered was the duty of all chimps. Tikko knew that she had teetered on the edge of sin, but she had not fallen. Eventually that realization lifted her out of her dread.

Ash and Kulki had brought lunch baskets into their compartment at the rear of the transbot. They also seemed recovered—at least enough to eat. Tikko sat on the bench next to her daughter and picked a pear from her basket.

"We have to get our stories straight," Tikko said.

Kulki gave a *hoo* of approval. "We've just been talking about that."

"He died," said Ash. "He lost track of himself and had an accident and he died." He thrust his arms above his head, as if challenging her to contradict him. "That's all that happened."

Tikko bit into the pear. It was past the season for pears and the white flesh was mealy. "That's good enough for the others," she said. "But what do we tell ourselves?"

Ash let his arms fall and stared at the table.

"Maa, I don't know," said Kulki.

"So, this is what I think happened. We opened our minds to one of the gathered." She took another bite of the pear. "We did what she asked."

"That makes no sense," said Ash, his thick brow furrowed. "We take instruction from bots. The gathered left. They're gone."

"The bots *are* the gathered." Tikko paused, reading her daughter's expression. "Some of them, anyway." She saw the idea taking hold and continued. "I think some of the gathered still watch us. That's what Helen Calabrese was saying."

"Yes." Kulki wrapped her arms around Tikko and pulled her close. "And they can't leave us alone."

"Maybe," said Tikko, "we should make them."

*hhe* Kulki was laughing in Tikko's ear. *hhe hhe*

Tikko thought it was funny too. *hhe hhe* Ash's lips curled away from his teeth and his mouth fell open and then, as the transbot flew up the fluxway toward home, all three chimps were laughing, falling over, rolling on their backs. *hhee hhee hhee hheep.*

It was a sound no human would ever hear.

# Ambassador to
# the Dinosaurs

Tobias S. Buckell

---

Tobias S. Buckell is a Caribbean-born author who sold his first short story in 2000. Nominated for the Campbell Award for Best New Science Fiction Writer shortly after, he's seen over 50 short stories appear in various magazines and anthologies and been translated into 17 different languages. His first novel, in 2006, was *Crystal Rain*. His latest novel, *Hurricane Fever*, will be out soon. He lives in Ohio.

Tobias S. Buckell says: "Growing up in the Caribbean in the 90s I accidentally stumbled across a collection of Silverberg's short stories (*The Collected Stories of Robert Silverberg, Volume I: The Secret Sharers*) at a dive-shop in a take-a-book leave-a-book exchange library for sailors. The variety of stories, the range, had a tremendous impact on me (I remember many of the stories to this day). Silverberg's notes on each story, how he came to write them, and the sharing of his struggles to edit one in particular, were the first glimpses I had into how a writer worked. Getting a chance to write in the world of one of those favorite stories, by an author that helped give me the first tools to write with: how could I say no? I would have let down fourteen-year-old me! And the story "Our Lady of the Sauropods" was always one of those Silverberg stories that left me wondering 'but what happened next?'"

# 1.

The T-Rex giving me the eyeball has the look of a zealot. Give him half a chance, he'll die for the cause. He's sunk deep into a mindset I can barely comprehend, but certainly one I know to give a wide, wide berth.

He's slavering, those fore-arm sized teeth dripping with eagerness to slice through me. But as commanded, he's holding himself back.

That doesn't keep that massive head from tracking me as he awkwardly backs down the dirt path, giving each foot to me with a rumble of innate discontent.

"Fuck you," I tell him. "That's right, you stay in reverse." The dirt path under me shakes with each fumbling step backward he takes.

I keep the abuse up all the way down the path as more dinosaurs melt out of the bushes around us. A linebacker of a stegosaur crushes greenery that looks somewhat tropical, somewhat marshy. Tiny struthiomimus trot along behind me, weaving in and out of the stegosaur's destruction.

The air is rich with carbon dioxide, and it's leaving me slightly dizzy. Certainly over tired.

As pissed as I am about the dinosaur thing, I also want to track down whoever thought creating an entire space station full of them was a good idea. That person needed a good smack upside the head.

With a baseball bat.

Repeatedly.

But I sighed a bit. Because I knew that same person would be the person who created me.

I stopped near the river's edge, and the giant exodus of dinosaur bodies pause with me. The giant brachiasaur in the water shifts it's bridge-like long neck to regard me. As it moves closer and closer, that lean, alien face swinging my way, I raise the metallic egg-shaped device in my right hand high up into the air for all the dinosaurs to see.

Then I yank my coat open to reveal the anti-matter explosive strapped to my chest. Just to remind them what they're dealing with: enough explosive to take us all out.

"That's close enough, lizards! *This*," I wave my hand to draw their attention, "is my dead man's switch."

They all unblinkingly regard me, waiting.

———

Rewind.

Whiskey number ten against the pair of Slovaks did me in.

I'm half convinced *homo sapiens* has been brewing alcohol for so long that you're all highly adapted to the stuff. I'm pretty sure I even read it somewhere. And what is it about Eastern Europeans and hard liquor?

My genes hark back a couple hundred thousand years or so before people probably started fermenting things. I plead guilty, your honor...guilty of not having any ability to handle spirits.

Hand to God, though: most awesome thing *homo sapiens* ever did.

When I stood up from the faux-wooden table the world around me wobbled slightly. Habitat Erekun was tiny enough that you could sometimes feel corolios forces from changing your elevation suddenly, but it was more due to going up a flight of stairs. The whole thing was a tiny tin drum in space, and they were just getting soil properly wormed and microbe-rich so that the next stage could start: parks and farms.

Eventually a hundred or so thousand people would live here. Another human settlement in outer space. Another glinting metal biome in orbit around old mother Earth.

My kind of human adapted itself to the environment. *Sapiens* bends the environs to it.

Neat trick.

I bore no bitterness about it. I was happy to have found work in heavy construction. My natural strength and 'robust' frame meant I handled heavy equipment easily. The money was good, building humanity's future homes.

I did find the fact that Slovak number one had his tongue down my date's throat to be annoying.

"Havel!" I slurred, grabbing the edge of the table.

Havel looked at me with bloodshot eyes. "This one is far to pretty for a neanderthal," he said.

"Havel…" I started looking for the right words, and decided nothing quite expressed my feelings verbally. I picked the table up and used it to club him.

His brother objected.

Everything got shouty and blurry after that.

———

"Johanna Karl?"

I lay on a cloud of cotton mouth and hurt. And some regret.

"Johanna Karl!"

I'd been in the drunk tank before, but from what I remembered I had a feeling I didn't want to open my eyes this time.

"Johanna Karl."

The voice calling my name was right next to my ear. I sat up with a groan. I opened my eyes, and raised my eyebrows. "Guess I've really gotten into some trouble now, eh?"

The lawyer squatting next to my cot is short and power-fully built. Like me. His bright red hair and pale skin make him look clammy in the shitty light. That's something that surprised many when they snagged neanderthal DNA and brought us back out of extinction: we looked like Vikings. But then, Vikings had been living in cold climes for a long time. Most pale humans come from colder climes, was it any surprise that a neanderthal would be pale?

Apparently to some humans it was confusing.

Usually worked to our advantage.

But the sloped back forehead and large skull was hard to hide. The uncanny valley is this thing where human faces that look close to the standard, but aren't quite there, freak people out. Robots and neanderthals. Not quite 'human.'

Like the lawyer in the suit in front of me. Even though I saw a similar face in the mirror, spending all day around homo sapiens for the last few months meant that even I struggled for a second. That shit got laced in deep by culture around you, what was normal, what wasn't.

"You beat your foreman almost to death, Johanna," the lawyer said. "His brother is also in intensive care."

I shrugged. "Been putting up with all their shit for three months. Kept my head down all that time. Got tired of it."

"You were heavily intoxicated."

"Yes. But he still had it coming. Racist asshat. Kept saying we'd gone extinct, and should stay that way. Said we were evolutionary affirmative action. Who are you, company law-yer? Should I be shutting up here and asking for my own?"

My be-suited neanderthal cousin shook his head. "Jakob Engis."

He held out a hand, and I ignored it. "And?"

"I'm a representative of the Distributed Organization for Neanderthal Advancement."

"Shit." I blew my lips out. "If DONA's sending reps out to talk to me, I've done something to 'embarrass the race,' is that it?"

"There is a danger that this could become a political incident. At the very least, DONA is worried that your actions will affect the ability of others to be able to gain employment."

I stood up and looked around the drunk tank. It wasn't an old school jail. It was a small dorm with reinforced doors and fifteen bunk beds, bad LED light strips, and a single bathroom. I was the only one in it.

"I did the fucked up thing, Engis. Just me. They can put me in jail, or wherever they need to. I am responsible for what I did. So is Havel and his brother, though. They've been harassing me for three months."

"There are formal methods for writing them up, channels to go through," Engis said.

"This is a construction crew, Engis. They don't respect paperwork. You and the other eggheads think this is an 'incident,' but the grunts will think twice the next time they insult one of us."

Engis looked a little sad. "Or they'll attack in larger numbers next time."

"So I should have suffered along quietly?"

"No, you should have filed a complaint."

"Engis, what makes you think I've never tried that before?"

That shut him up for a second. Then he rallied himself. "I have an offer for you. DONA would like to hire you to accompany me on a Habitat tour."

I looked at him suspiciously. "As what?"

He blushed, unpacking the meaning in my tone. "Security. Bodyguard. Assistant." He shrugged. "We've already seen what you can do drunk and angry. What can you do with some training and focus?"

I wanted to tell him it was bullshit and move him on. DONA was keeping my close and keeping me busy so I wouldn't embarrass their efforts.

But I was stuck behind a reinforced door. I doubted I'd get back on the construction crew.

I could hitchhike to an interesting habitat and then ditch him.

# 2.

Fast forward.

The tyrannosaur is still giving me the evil eye, the scar over his right eye crinkling a bit as he regards me, head cocked; sort of a like a giant, brightly colored dog with a too-large head. With pointy teeth.

"I'll call you Norm," I say, and look back at the giant brachiosaur. "And you...well, you're the heart of it all, aren't you?"

The head on the long neck regards me blankly.

But that's just what things look like on the outside.

Underneath it all the world is pulsing with a calming flow of energy from the brachiosaur. I'm mellowing out. I've been feeling waves of that superior chill rolling off the big dinosaur since arrival.

Used to be we thought dinosaurs were cold-blooded. Slow. With grayish or green skin.

Lizards.

And then we pieced together more. Feathers. Warm blooded. Ancestors of birds. Fast.

Then the Olsen-process reconstructed them.

Now I'm standing in front of the brachiosaur, and she's the center node of a giant, distributed network. The others all plug into her to create some sort of hive mind.

The dinosaurs didn't create tools, or build great edifices. But who is to say that they didn't have some kind of great civilization? We don't know, but the ones humans made and put in a habitat created a world of their own. They adopted a human researcher, broke out of the habitat they were locked up in.

It was simply a desire to understand where they were.

A desire to get back home.

I know now. The brachiosaur is dropping wisdom on me, pulling me into the fold. I'm in the warm embrace of her stolid mental orbit, like all the other dinosaurs surrounding the river calmly.

It isn't mind control, I'm not under anything like that. But I am plugging into something larger than myself. Big Bertha, I thought. That's what the human researcher called the brachiosaur. Such a shame she disappeared during the assault on Habitat Vronsky.

"Stop it!" I shout, pressing the dead man's switch ever so slightly. To the point where I'm afraid.

That fear causes a ripple of movement around me. The multicolored bodies move back worriedly. A tide of dinosaur flesh shifts to safety.

"It's not going to be *that* easy," I tell Big Bertha. "It never is, with me."

———

Rewind.

Descending orbit. In the posh, executive rotunda arm of a spinning general transport vehicle shuttling some three hundred people from one tin can in space to another.

In the common room and galley, at a fake-oak table surrounded by overstuffed purple chairs, I looked down at the medical patch Engis tossed my way. "Really?"

"I can't have you pale and shaking due to withdrawal," Engis said.

"I'm not some addict. I'm, at best, a functional alcoholic. I keep a job down. I can keep this."

"You kept the job down during light hours, drank during dark, on a regular schedule. The work we're doing is high profile, and always-on. You need to detox." He gestured at the patch. "We're not asking a lot of you, Johanna."

Engis and I both knew I was being given make-work. If he was annoyed he masked it clearly. Service to a higher calling. I resented that about him. Engis knew where his place in the universe was, and he knew what his path was as well. Everything locked in. No qualms. No doubt. He served the cause. The cause was good.

I took the patch, ripped it out of the foil packet, and put on my upper shoulder where it was hidden by my sleeves. "Where are we going?" And where would I be ditching?

"We're headed to Habitat Anagupta," he explained. "I'm scheduled to give a speech there trying to calm habitat fears about neanderthals being able to travel and work in orbit. "

My job, it seemed, was to not get drunk and stay close by to him. To stay out of trouble.

"Don't look threatening," Engis said.

"I thought bodyguards were supposed to look threatening."

Engis sighed. "I'm trying to convince millions of people, hard working people, Johanna, that people like us are normal, hard-working citizens. That we are not a threat. We are not like the dinosaurs."

"I would have thought," I said drily, "that a quick glance would make that obvious."

"You know what I mean. Habitat Vronsky."

Three hundred dinosaurs spilling out of a transfer vehicle, led by a zealous, naked researcher who claimed to be able to commune with their minds slaughtering thousands of bewildered people before some smart admin type started locking down bulkheads. Yeah, I knew what he meant. People regretted bringing things back from the past.

I grunted. "You know I was part of a traveling circus act before that happened. That in your file?"

Engis looked up from his notes, the screen lighting his receding chin and making him look even less human, and a little bit monstrous. He didn't say anything, just waited for me to go on.

"I had a hard time after I left the institute. They offered job placement, but I knew I just wanted away from assholes in lab coats, pricking me, asking me questions, the interviews. The whole edifice. All the bullshit. I joined a circus, did the strong woman routine. I liked the weight lifting, really got into it. A place to put my anger. And it was good, for a while. I fit in there, with all the others. Then Vronsky happened. And things changed."

Engis knew what was happening, and for the first time, the calm neutral expression faded to sadness.

I continued. "There were epithets, and shouts. But it was when they started throwing bottles at me that it got bad." I tapped the scar on my neck. "And even then, I would have kept on going, in a mesh cage for protection. It wasn't worse than the others risking their lives on a high wire. I was tough. But it was when they called me in, one night, all serious and solemn. Explained that booking was down. Ticket sales faltering. And they cut me loose."

"I'm sorry," Engis said softly.

"Even the freaks wouldn't have me," I laughed.

"So you went into construction."

"Yeah. It paid bills. I'm good at it." I looked over across the ship's galley. "Fuck dinosaurs, man."

———

"Have you ever thought about going back down to Earth?" Engis asked at breakfast, a few days in. "DONA could get you a job at the institute."

"Do you ever worry that isn't what they want?" I asked.

"They?"

"The humans. If we keep to ourselves, no one has to do any accommodating or learning. It's the easy way out."

"What's the real reason. Something happen? Something worse than the circus?"

I suddenly realized he was running through prompts from some psychologist's script. The temporary thaw between us frosted. "It's their's," I told him. "They changed it for themselves, they own it. For better or worse. Jesus, Engis: even the Antarctic is getting warm enough they're moving into it. Meanwhile, our blood sings for the cold and sparse."

"Romantic pastoral bullshit," Engis said, showing his true colors for the first time.

"It's not their's yet, is it? And it's cold."

"And they're huddled and cramped."

"Just like the small bands and days of yore, out in the wilderness," I smiled.

Engis grunted. "It'll change here to. They'll get bigger, More people. Less sparse. What then?"

"Then I'll move along," I told him.

# 3.

The metallic thunk of a rapid docking woke me up. I looked around the small, but luxurious, cabin. I'd dozed, listening to the sound of adjustment rockets firing.

And the main drive had been on. Thundering away. That was what had woken me up a few moments before the clang and shiver.

I opened the door and looked out the hallway. A few other passengers were peeking out, blinking their eyes. "What's going on?" Engis asked. His bright hair a crazy mess.

"Feels like a bad docking, but we're not due to arrive for another few days."

These transfer vehicles were slow. Large, comfortable, they traded speed for those luxuries and slow changes in orbit to move their passengers from habitat to habitat. The fact that they'd been wasting a lot of fuel, even turning on the main drive, was odd.

Another loud bang made us all jump. And a mournful screeching sound began to make the hairs on my neck stand up. I felt my weight lessening.

"They hit the brakes," I said to Engis. "The passenger section's gravity is getting turned off." The giant drum was coming to scraping stop.

"Why?" Engis frowned.

"Get dressed," I told him. "Now. Your pressure suit, in the emergency locker in your cabin."

———

Once we were both suited Engis struggled to follow me through the corridors. I'd had plenty of zero-gravity experience, so was able to fingertip my way along. Halfway up towards the cockpit the lighting flickered off, and emergency reds flicked on. The high pitched wail of emergency sirens kicked in, silently pulsing away to the same rhythm as the flashing emergency lighting.

It was the acceleration warning. Everyone in their rooms, strap in, shut up and wait for more information. But we were docked. I wasn't buying it.

I found what I was looking for: an alarmed looking crew-member with a thumb up to his ear, concentrating to hear orders in an earpiece over the alarm.

He screamed when I spun him around to face me in the air, raising his hands defensively.

"Easy!" I shouted. "I'm not going to hurt you. Easy. I just want to know: what the hell is going on?"

The man looked pasty and spooked. Sweat beaded off him to hang in the air. "Fucking dinosaurs, man! Get in your rooms and lock the doors!"

———

"I don't understand," Engis muttered as we spun and flew back down the corridor. "We're nowhere near the dinosaur habitat or Vronsky. They're...on the other side of the planet right now."

I twisted like a cat in the air to look behind me, keeping a hand up in the air in front of me just in case. I gave Engis a withering 'you idiot' glare. "A very low-fuel Hohman transfer puts them right back here, but at a different time. It's for exactly this reason that transport ships are *not* supposed to get near any part of their habitat's orbit. They were trying to save themselves fuel by swinging right through the edge of the dinosaur no-fly zone."

Corporate bottom-line obsessed asshats. They'd saved money on the fuel for the trip. By putting us right in the bulls eye.

We weren't entirely sure what the dinosaurs knew and didn't know. After the crazy researcher died, or disappeared, we had no way to know what the dinosaurs wanted. Vronsky was abandoned after the bloody section-to-section fighting. Vronsky and the dinosaur habitat were quarantined.

For a while there'd been talk of classifying the dinosaurs as terrorists and mounting retaliatory actions. Some spare rocks nudged in the right orbit…but then, who wanted to throw that first stone?

And politicians hated the optics on it. The second mass extinction?

And eggheads pointed out that the orbital debris from such an action would likely kill just as many other humans as it hit other habitats in other habitats.

In the end, a few heavily armed drones took out the transports and any orbital transfer ability. The two habitats were left quarantined.

And for their part, they'd remained quiet. Debates raged about how intelligent they had been. Whether the naked researcher who'd been their prophet, or mouthpiece, had really been part of a larger group mind or just out of her mind.

"Hey," Engis said, startled and looking around. "This isn't the way back to our cabin."

"No," I said. "Good of you to notice. It most certainly isn't."

# 4.

Fast forward.

As noted previously, the great big telepathic dinosaur mind orgy isn't fully coercive so much as something you gently slip into and find comfortable. So I'm not surprised when Norm makes his move, as the big guy has free will.

Being a giant tyrannosaur means it's hard for me to miss the oncoming attack. His head snaps down, tail extends out, and his giant clawed feet thunder as they shift. I'm wearing a suicide vest made of anti-matter, but the threat isn't so much that I'm going to blow myself up. It's that if the dinosaurs kill me *they* will be the ones committing suicide.

Norm doesn't seem to give a shit.

His teeth are all that fills my vision as he opens those jaws wide and tries to grab a mouthful of me and antimatter bomb vest.

Maybe he's thinking that if he bites down hard enough it'll break the equipment and me and they'll make it.

I stare into the abyss. It is hot, fetid, and has little pieces of decaying animal in the crevices.

Smack. The wet sound of something massive cracking bones the size of me and armor-hard flesh fills my world. The jaws strike the dirt just to my right and Norm wobbles.

Smack. Norm staggers back. I can't see shit, his face is hard up in the dirt. I'm looking at the tyrannosaurus rex's eye. Just right at it. And the rest of my sight is filled with giant tyrannosaur.

Smack. The beast is rolled onto his back and away from me. Five triceratops ram into his side, veering across the mud from back in the trees where they'd been waiting.

There's an ankylosaurus, I can see now. It's just whacking the shit out of Norm, who's side is punctured by triceratops horns now. He's roaring, but it's fear.

Big Bertha is laying down the smack. Norm's swarmed by a dinosaurs of all shapes and sizes and dragged, shoved, stabbed, back away from me. The king of the dinosaurs my ass. He's a confused, roided-out thug who thought he had the answers and stepped out of line.

My adrenaline is up so high I'm shaking. There's Norm slobber on my face, and I wipe it away slowly and deliberately, just to convince myself I can move again.

Because I'm rattled.

I can't lie. That was some close shit, and my thumb is trembling on the dead man's switch.

Big Bertha's soothing me. We can work together. There is a path out of this.

"Okay, you big bitch," I say, trying to keep her from mellowing me out more than a bag of good habitat grass. "Let's talk win-win."

———

Rewind.

"You asked me to be your bodyguard," I said to Engis. "So let me try to save both our asses here."

"Where are we?"

"Usually this is the maintenance hold," I muttered. "Yep, there we go. Welders, saws, bottles of compressed gases that explode. EVA packs. Not exactly traditional weapons, but stuff we can use." I was opening strap-down cupboards and looking inside, my heart lifting with each discovery of the tools of my trade.

The beginnings of a plan were setting up in my head.

"I can't hold a weapon," Engis said softly.

"I've never carried one either, which is why your whole bullshit thing about making me a bodyguard was silly. But there's always a first time, and these tools in here can do major damage to a human...or a dinosaur. Plus, this is the first I've ever been on a transport invaded by dinosaurs, so this is all new to me too."

"No," Engis said. "You're not understanding me. I can't. Hold. A. Weapon."

We stare at each other.

"You do realize they're going to *eat* you, right?" I said.

Engis looked down at his hands. "When the debate over what to do about dinosaurs in orbit happened, I was frequently called on to represent the DONA position. Which was that, as a resurrected species ourself, we could not in good conscience call for the second extinction of the dinosaurs."

"Engis, you fucker, they eat each other all the time. And you won't be killing all of them. Just the ones that come through that door."

"What difference will it make?" Engis asked.

There was a bang and a scream in the distance. Englis flinched. I looked back from the airlock I'd dogged shut to him, awkwardly floating in front of me. "Are you fucking kidding me?"

"There are probably too many dinosaurs. We can prolong the inevitable, but eventually..."

"Then we go out fighting. We make a statement!"

"That says what?" Engis asked.

"That we went out fighting!" I said, as if talking to a four year old.

"That's a tautological loop," he said. "And no one will ever know we did it, so what does it matter. It's a statement in a closed room."

"The dinosaurs will know," I raised a hull cutter in the air. The three feet long metal device looked weapon-like, with capacitor vents bristling from it and claw-like plasma arcpoints on the end. "The statement will be impactful."

"And then we die," Engis said. "What's the bigger picture? You want to die screaming and taking a dinosaur with you. I just want to get it over with. Because either way, we're both dead. It won't make a difference to Earth, our kind, dino-kind, or the situation. Therefore, either choice is valid. And I choose to die with my principles intact."

"Well, you don't speak for all our kind, so you can't talk me into not fighting back," I said.

"I've never pretended to speak for our kind. That's impossible. I only represent DONA to the best of my abilities and try to make lives easier. I'm not perfect at it, I've made my mistakes..."

"With neanderthals like you, it's small wonder we went extinct," I muttered angrily.

Engis crumpled a bit in the mid-air. I didn't know you could sag your shoulders in zero gravity, but his did. He said something softly that I couldn't hear, but I got the gist of it.

"I'm sorry," I said. "That was low, even for me."

"Wouldn't even be on this ship if I hadn't had to come out here for you," he said bitterly.

"I didn't ask for your help," I said, rooting around for more weapons and giving him my back. And then I saw the universal symbol for anti-matter storage behind a lock-up. "And I may just save your ass yet."

I fired up the hull cutter and bounced over the thick steel of the lock-up. I didn't have the ship's combination, or the right thumbprint. But the hull cutter could melt right through all that faster than I could call to beg for a way in and be told 'no.' Over the spit and sizzle Engis yelled, "That's antimatter. Isn't that dangerous?"

"Well yeah," I said cheerfully. "But if it doesn't matter how we go out, might as well *really* go out."

I jabbed the cutter's sun-bright claw into the steel.

By the time the velociraptors figured out how to get in I was standing there with a plasma torch, an antimatter bomb vest I'd cobbled together myself, and a big fuck-you grin on my face as I held the dead man's switch in the air in front of me like some talisman.

"Take me to your leader!" I said. "Or I'll blow everyone the fuck up."

# 5.

Fast Forward. Pause. Whatever. It's all caught up and we're all on the same wavelength.

Norm is bleeding out in the bushes somewhere, bellowing sadly and snuffling. I'm still standing, though smelling a bit worse for the wear.

"Do we have an understanding?" I ask the massive brachiasaur. And Big Bertha gives me a nod, a startlingly human gesture on the edge of that long-ass neck. I think I've rubbed off a bit on them while we were all in happy mind-meld mode.

"Fuck yeah," I say, and turn my back to the dinosaur assembly at the river's edge.

I'm unmolested on the way back to the airlock. Just a few tiny ones skitter around in the bush, keeping an eye on me. The thundering types are all well clear.

Detente, motherfuckers. Detente.

I find Engis exactly where I left him. Strapped with duct tape to the side of the mechanic's room and surrounded with anti-matter detonation pellets. The ones the ships use to change orbit *really fast*.

He's sallow, and dripping with sweat. Shivering. To be fair, after a whole forty eight hours of being held hostage by dinosaurs while the ship was maneuvered by a terrified captain all the way to match the dinosaur habitat, then getting duct taped to antimatter bombs while I wandered off to go 'have a chat,' Engis doesn't know up from down or left from right.

Sometimes waiting is the hardest thing.

"Don't say anything," I tell him. "The jury-rigged booby traps are going to be a pain to dismantle, and I'm going to need to focus a bit. Electronics were never my strong suite."

There isn't a peep as I get down to business.

When I free him and help him stand, his legs are all wobbly. He looks at me with hopeful eyes. "Are we free?"

"Well...yes and no," I explain.

"What do you mean?" Engis stares at me from within hollow, tired eyes.

I guide him through the ship by the elbow, this way and that. He's too out of it to really complain and just lets me. "Their group mind, everyone in it influences it. Their last human, she was obsessed with revenge. Some colleague of hers tried to kill her, or at least she thought that, and she became a bit deranged while trapped in the habitat. That colored their impressions and what they learned. They came out the first time jumpy and aggressive."

Engis blinks as we break out from the emergency lighting into the harsh light of a fully light docking bay.

On the other side, an honor guard of velociraptors waits patiently. They've all left the ship, ceding it back to me.

"All they really want is to go home. To be under a natural sky, and forage. But if that is impossible, what they'd like are some accommodations. They've had to eat each other, up to now, which has meant making some hard choices. They'd really like to stop doing that. They want trade, and freedom to move, and education. That sort of stuff. They're not *that* different from most thinking creatures, even if independently they're not all that bright but depend on this group mind. So what Big Bertha, she's not a leader but the center of the group, what she wants is a human mind in the mix. So they can talk to outsiders, learn, strategize. She offered me the gig."

"You?" Engis looks stunned.

"Yeah, I know, I thought it was a horrible idea as well. The last thing I want to be is middle management to the dinosaurs. So I suggested you."

"Me?" Engis looks more stunned.

"Ambassador to the dinosaurs. It fits with what you've been doing. You have the toolset. Not sure if you have to resign from DONA, but Engis, they could really use you."

He looks back from me to the velociraptors. "I don't…"

"I showed them how to fix their comms equipment, you can call out when you need. Leave when you find a *suitable* replacement. Come on, Engis, find your place in history: advocate for the formally extinct."

Engis straightens at that. It's sinking in. He's buying in. He pats his clothes a bit, and nervously looks over at the dinosaurs waiting for him.

"What about you?" he asks.

I step back from him. "I'm sure I'll figure something out," I say. "I didn't really want to be a bodyguard, I was just waiting for the right place to ditch you. It'll feel less messy now." I begin to walk him forward.

He nods. Takes a deep breath. "Okay." He falls into stride, and I stop. He keeps going. The velociraptors fall in around him. "Okay, we're doing this. For the good of all." He's mentally rehearsing speeches already. For posterity. For bringing the species together.

The bay door shuts behind him and I'm alone.

I turn back to the transport. I figure the crew will owe me one and let me off wherever I want.

Or maybe I'll stay aboard and pick up some new skills. The maintenance bay had some very interesting toys, and the chief engineer had been disemboweled by a utahraptor he'd gone mano-a-dinosaur with in the galley.

The job was open.

Applying while there was some good will in the air toward me by humans was a smart move.

# Individual Story Copyrights